Waffle House
on the
Pier

BOOKS BY TILLY TENNANT

TILLY TENNANT

The Waffle House on the Pier

Bookouture

Published by Bookouture in 2020

An imprint of Storyfire Ltd.
Carmelite House
50 Victoria Embankment
London EC4Y 0DZ

www.bookouture.com

ISBN: 978-1-83888-818-3
eBook ISBN: 978-1-83888-817-6

For our real-life Luke, who is a little bit brilliant!

Chapter One

It was on days like this that Sadie wondered what the hell she was doing with her life.

Why was she training to be a teacher and not working out on the glorious bay, as her parents did and as her brother, Ewan, and his wife, Kat, did? Sadie had always told them that a life on the sea wasn't for her, that she didn't want to be reliant on the fickle whims of tourism for her livelihood, which in turn relied on the fickle whims of the weather, or the strength of the pound, or the rating that the little town of Sea Salt Bay – the place she called home – had been given on TripAdvisor that year. She'd wanted certainty, a guaranteed income, a career that she could – more or less – predict.

She'd tried for a while to follow the employment route that almost everyone else in Sea Salt Bay took, which mostly involved looking after tourists in some capacity, but the only work available had bored her and she'd quickly tired of doing the same thing every day. She wanted more; she wanted to explore her academic side, to satisfy the part of her with a thirst to learn and a curiosity about the world to match. And so she'd bucked the family trend and gone back into education – a little later than her classmates at the ripe old age of twenty-two – sat a degree in modern history, and then enrolled on a teacher training course. It meant leaving Sea Salt Bay and its charms behind every day to commute to the nearest big town to study, but that was OK.

Except on days like this, when the sand of the bay was as warm and soft as demerara sugar and the gulls sang their songs of the sea and the waves rolled onto the shore in a hypnotic rhythm, crystal clear and iced with foam, and the sun was like an old friend, warming her freckled skin while the breeze whispered words of love as it gently lifted the auburn hair from her neck. On days like this she wondered why she'd taken the decision to sit in a gloomy classroom when the bay was at its best and brightest, when children were squealing and splashing in the rolling waves, when couples were walking the spray-capped line of the shore hand in hand, eating chips from paper or ice creams from sugar cones, or simply walking and saying or doing nothing else at all because they didn't need to.

She wondered why she spent her days listening to a lecturer who didn't care if she was there or not when she could have been sitting outside her parents' boatshed. On a day like today, the radio would be murmuring in the background while the sun shone down and excited tourists waited to board their boat, hoping to see dolphins or seals or puffins out on the grey rocks that stood proud of the sea – the same grey rocks that looked like tiny teeth from the shore, but mighty and mysterious up close. As a child, Sadie had loved to sail round them with her parents, happy enough just to be on the waves but always excited to see some wildlife when luck was on their side.

But now, while her parents spent their days at sea, smiling at marvelling visitors as they pointed out porpoises or sea birds, or the way the light played on the ancient chalky cliffs, or while her brother took the same tourists beneath the waves to swim through magical forests of silky green seaweed as the sun sent white daggers of light slicing through the cerulean depths, Sadie studied in a dark room. She learnt about how children learnt, how to keep them safe, how to measure their progress and intelligence, how to check charts and fill in forms, how to keep control, how to instil discipline, how to turn them into fine, moral, sensible adults. Where was the wonder in that? She'd had a grand vision, once, that she'd be the teacher to inspire, to fire curiosity, to nurture creativity, and she'd thought that was what she'd learn to do on her training course. She'd believed that she was going to make a difference, that her job would be important, that she was going to shape young lives. Maybe the kids she taught would remember her long after they'd left her care, and maybe as adults they'd think of her once in a while and give silent thanks for the wisdom she'd imparted to them.

But that wasn't what it was like at all. She'd tried to explain this to one of her lecturers once, but he hadn't understood. He'd said that she'd be able to run her own class however she wanted once she'd qualified, but she didn't think that was true, even though she couldn't explain to him why she felt that. She couldn't run her class however she wanted because there were all the rules she was learning right now that would make it impossible. She knew the rules had to be there, but sometimes she felt like there were just too many – so many they weighed her down so that she couldn't think about anything else.

Class 3G of Featherbrook School had done little to allay her many doubts about whether this really had been the right career choice after all. Today had to be her worst day of work experience so far and she'd felt nothing but desperation and an overwhelming fatigue as she'd made the journey back to Sea Salt Bay. There had been no one at home when she'd arrived there – her parents were still working, making the most of the lengthening days and a fresh tourist season, and wouldn't be back until the sun had started to sink below the horizon. Rather than sit in an empty house feeling like a wretched failure, Sadie had decided to make the most of a warm afternoon and head to the beach, hopeful that the sounds of the sea and the feeling of the sun on her face would go some way to healing her. If nothing else, she'd top up her vitamin D.

As she sat on the sand now, looking out to sea, she went over the day's events again. She was supposed to get support from a qualified teacher so that she wouldn't be alone with the kids, but that seemed to happen less and less often. In a way, it was easy to see why – the school was so understaffed and underfunded that they probably grabbed the chance of some cheap teaching with both desperate hands, support or not.

Today, one girl had come to her in tears because someone in the class had snuck up behind her and cut a chunk from her hair. When Sadie had quizzed the class nobody would admit to being the perpetrator – and why would they? Sadie was such a useless pushover of a teacher that they weren't a bit scared of her. Not that she'd want anyone to be scared, but an air of authority might be nice. Then she'd had to leave the room for a moment and had come back to a giant chalk penis on the board that someone had kindly left for her. Throughout her lesson the volume of chat and raucous laughter in the class had grown and grown, as had the rowdiness, no matter how many times she'd called for order, until a teacher from a neighbouring classroom had come in to complain that they couldn't hear the play they were trying to listen to. Of course, the kids had clammed up immediately at the sight of the actual scary, qualified and confident teacher, only to begin their verbal assault again as soon as he'd disappeared, but louder this time. Eventually the red-faced headmistress had had to intervene, beckoning Sadie to step outside the classroom and out of earshot of her young charges.

'Miss Schwartz… I suggest you get your class in order!'

Sadie had nodded helplessly but hadn't known what to say in reply, and perhaps the desperation in her expression had reminded the head of her own training, because she seemed to soften at this.

'You know you can always come and see me if there's anything you need help and advice on,' she'd said. 'I realise that some of the children think they can play the trainee teachers but you do have support in this regard. You must come and seek it when you need to.'

Sadie had nodded again, and she'd tried to mean it this time, but the head's words hadn't made her feel any better. While the woman had given the impression of being sympathetic and patient over Sadie's doubts, Sadie knew that she had about a thousand other things that she'd rather be worrying about than the noise volume of a trainee teacher's lesson, or whether she was managing. Sadie didn't want to be that person who constantly sought help or reassurance. She wanted to be the reliable person who coped, the one that the head could leave to it, confident that she'd do a good job, but it certainly wasn't turning out that way.

Thinking back on it all now made Sadie's stomach sink and her face burn. She didn't want to give up her training because – more than anything else – she didn't want to admit she'd failed, but she was beginning to feel that she'd reached some unnamed and as yet unclear crossroads in her life. She was starting to wonder if fate had something different in store for her; if, perhaps, it had never really meant for her to be teaching at all. And if that was the case, was it really failing to let fate tell her what that thing was? Was it really so bad to stop and listen to the tiny voice for a moment while it whispered to her the real destiny, the one it had been trying to tell her about when she'd refused to take any notice? Perhaps she'd been landed with class 3G of Featherbrook School today for a reason that was not yet clear to her. But was that to steel her resolve, to make her a better and stronger teacher, or was it to make her think twice about the future she'd chosen for herself?

She brushed a fly from her leg and looked out on the white cliffs of the headland, tinged now with the rose gold of the sinking sun and gleaming like Greek marble, the glittering water of the bay swelling at their feet, a shell-pink haze scoring the horizon. A sudden cool gust blew up from the sea and she shivered, reaching for her cardigan and pulling it on. She checked the time on her phone, vaguely surprised that she'd been sitting on the sand a lot longer than she'd realised. If she took a slow walk home now she'd probably arrive back around the same time as her parents, and if she got back a little earlier then she'd make a start on dinner and surprise them with something nice.

Mulling over what she might cook, she shook out the towel she'd been sitting on and rolled it into a neat tube before stuffing it into a cloth bag. Then she poked her feet into a pair of denim flip-flops and headed across the beach to the promenade. Lined along it, windows like eyes looking out to sea, was a long row of terraced cottages that served as Sea Salt Bay's main shops and restaurants. They'd once been fishing cottages, back when that had been the main source of income for everyone in the bay – at least, when they weren't trying to sneak barrels of rum past the King's men, which had been the other little sideline, spoken of only in hushed tones.

Sadie had read all the old classics like *Moonfleet* and *Treasure Island* where the smugglers were painted as romantic heroes and loveable rogues, and she liked to imagine that Sea Salt Bay had been filled with men like that once. But the reality, she acknowledged with some disappointment, had probably been a lot less romantic and a lot more dangerous. Her dad had once done some research on the bay's history and had read some of the old records. Times had been brutal and tough in Sea Salt Bay all those hundreds of years ago, and many people got involved in the smuggling only because they'd had no choice – it was either that or starve. She'd sat at her dad's side one Sunday afternoon just as she'd turned nineteen and looked over at what he'd been reading before wishing she hadn't. It had only confirmed Sadie's suspicions of a depressing reality – though, on days like today, she preferred to think about her version of Sea Salt Bay's past. Her version was more fun and far less grim.

Looking at the row of cottages now, each painted a different pastel shade – apple green, cornflower blue, sugar pink, soft peach, primrose yellow, lavender and lilac – gleaming in the light of golden hour, it was easy to believe in Sadie's preferred alternative history. Sea Salt Bay was still a small town – a village really – and still reliant on the sea, but it was a brighter, happier place these days. Every window of every cottage showed a different display: surfing supplies, beach games and toys, postcards and gifts, swimming costumes and wetsuits. One had freezers full of coloured ice cream standing in the shade of an opened-out frontage, one had tables set on the tarmac for fish and chip suppers and one had a little window-cum-counter where you could buy crab sandwiches and cockles and mussels caught out in the bay. As she passed this house, Reginald, who made the crab sandwiches, was outside rubbing something off the chalkboard menu that he must have sold out of. He looked across and, noticing Sadie, raised a hand.

'How do, Sadie! How goes it?'

'Good thanks,' Sadie called back. 'Business is good?'

'Could be better but won't complain,' Reginald said, and Sadie smiled knowingly because he always said that even when business was astoundingly good. 'Tell your folks I said hello!' he added.

'I will.'

At the last house the road forked off towards the Victorian pier. The pier was the jewel in the crown of Sea Salt Bay. It wasn't much compared to the piers in other seaside resorts, but it was quaint and pretty and everyone loved it. The wrought iron of its fencing panels was painted a delicate sage green and it had old wooden boards that rattled and creaked as you walked them. If you looked down as you went you could see the waves below showing through the gaps between them. This was home to the amusement arcade and a gathering of tame rides, including the carousel and dodgems. And right at the end of the pier stood Sea Salt Bay Waffle House. It was perfectly square with a pointed roof, the exterior candy-striped pink and white like a stick of rock. The old paintwork was faded a little these days, battered by too many sea storms, and the shutters didn't close properly at night and the posters in the windows had been bleached by the sun, but it still drew in a regular and faithful clientele. The best waffles on the South Coast, the sign outside said, and nobody could deny that they were.

Sea Salt Bay Waffle House made Sadie especially proud, because it was owned by her Gammy and Gampy. They'd be Grandma and Grandpa to anyone else, but as a small child Sadie had never quite got the pronunciation right and the names she'd given them by mistake had stuck. Gammy and Gampy were also known as April and Kenneth Schwartz, who'd moved to England from America before the birth of Sadie's father and had run the waffle house in Sea Salt Bay for most of that time. When they'd first opened up in the sixties, for most of the locals waffles were an exotic treat that they'd never had. Through the sixties and seventies their business had grown, drawing customers from far and wide. People were used to waffles now, but for Gammy and Gampy, reputation had proved a powerful thing and business was still good – at least, good enough to keep them trading, even if the building was long overdue a facelift.

Sadie turned that way now. She'd pop in, say hello, see how things were going. If they needed help to clear up after the end of trading, she could do that too. But before she'd taken half a dozen steps she stopped and frowned at the sound of a siren. It was close, growing rapidly closer and louder. Looking around she saw the ambulance racing down the road that led to the promenade. It stopped at the gates of the pier, where it could go no further. Two paramedics leapt out, lugging black bags, one barking into a radio as they began to run across the old wooden boards.

Sadie watched them for a moment, something like fear building in her gut.

There had been two occasions in her life when Sadie had been struck by a strange, almost psychic feeling about something that was about to happen. One was when her dog, Binky, had been hit by a car. A neighbour had knocked on the door to tell her parents and, somehow, Sadie had known before they did. The second was when a girl at her school had drowned in the bay. Sadie had been about fourteen, and as the head teacher gathered them to announce the sad news, she'd already known that too, the information somehow beamed into her head moments before, yet nobody had told her. The last time had shaken her, and for a couple of years she'd lived in fear of it happening again. She hadn't told a soul, thinking it would make her look strange and mad, and she hadn't wanted the responsibility of that kind of gift or curse or whatever it was. Thankfully, nothing like that had happened in all the years since and Sadie had almost forgotten it had ever happened at all. Until now.

And then the truth crashed over her, the confirmation of the horrible, prescient thought that had only seconds before occurred to her, icy cold and breath-sapping. She watched, numb and stunned as the paramedics went into the waffle house.

Dropping her bag, Sadie broke into a run.

Chapter Two

From the vast windows of Henriette and Graham Schwartz's conservatory, Sadie's gaze wandered to the sea as it churned into little rolls of milky foam that crashed against the distant rocks of the bay. It was easy to take for granted how lucky Sadie and her parents were to live in a house that had such an incredible position on the cliffs with such glorious views. Sadie's mother, Henriette, had said often enough that if it hadn't been for the (grudging) help of her own parents, she and Sadie's dad certainly wouldn't have been able to afford such a spectacular house by themselves. Henriette – Henny, as her friends called her – had turned the conservatory into a casual dining space and, summer or winter, they ate most of their meals in there, the drama of the bay a backdrop most people could only dream of. Henriette didn't allow televisions or phones at the dinner table, but then, they hardly needed those kinds of distractions when the beauty of the Dorset coastline was distraction enough for anyone.

The sun was hidden today, struggling to break through low cloud, though it was still warm. Summer was coming into its height and the busiest time of the tourist season was upon Sea Salt Bay. The full Schwartz family, including Sadie's sister, Lucy – who had only come over briefly for their grandfather's funeral and was due to fly back to New York where she now lived – her brother Ewan, his wife Kat, and their children Freya and Freddie sat around a rare shared lunch. Someone was usually missing – there were extracurricular activities, hobbies, regular meetings, volunteer posts and, of course, as both Henny and Graham and Ewan and his wife Kat ran their own businesses, work rarely stopped. None of them kept the more forgiving office hours that other people did.

That was just another reason that Sadie had decided to train for a job where she could at least get some time off, even if it she might often have to do extra work during it. Ewan and Kat ran a diving school, and would go out with a client whenever it was required of them, no matter what day of the week it was, because business was business and they couldn't afford to turn it away. One of them needed to be there in case they got a booking, and they got plenty. Henny and Graham had to run trips every day during the summer months, especially on Saturdays and Sundays because most people who visited Sea Salt Bay came for the weekend. Today, they'd decided the sea was too rough to go out, and Ewan had come to the same conclusion – if it was too rough to sail on, then it was most certainly too rough to dive beneath. So they were in the fortunate (or unfortunate, depending on how you viewed it) position of having a rare Sunday to get together. Only one member of the family was absent: Sadie's beloved Gampy, Kenneth.

It had been a month since the day Sadie had seen the ambulance on the pier and her grandfather's absence was still a gaping hole in the heart of the family, threatening to stop its beating, just as his had done that day. Her thoughts were carried back now like flotsam on the tide, and she recalled running blindly down the pier, the paramedics trying to stop her from gaining access, April's cries for Kenneth that he couldn't hear. She had finally forced her way in and caught just a glimpse of him as the ambulance crew fought to save his life, then wished she hadn't seen it after all. When she thought of her grandfather now, it was hard to separate that vision from the happier memories of the man she'd grown up with. They felt forever tainted.

Sadie's gaze turned from the sea now, where her thoughts had been vague and distracted as she'd watched the waves, towards her Gammy. Still the head of the family – if only by distinction of age and experience – she was surrounded by the chat and noise of a family who loved her very much, the smells of roasted vegetables and meat on the warm air, a light drizzle kissing the windows that looked out on the bay, and yet Sadie had never seen her look so lonely. Small and inconsequential and sad… so utterly lost. Even though her family were all squashed together around the table, it was like there was a space around her that should have contained Gampy – the man she'd loved so much. Gammy's protection, her buffer, her steadying anchor, all her strength, had gone. Life still had to be lived, of course, even when some were lost to it, but though the Schwartz family were doing their best to soldier on, one member – April – was in serious danger of getting left behind.

'Gammy…' Sadie said gently. April turned to her.

'Yes, darlin'?' she replied, forcing a brave smile.

'Do you want some wine?'

April shook her head. 'Water will be just fine for me.'

'It's nice wine,' Sadie said.

'I'm sure it is. Maybe later.'

Sadie glanced at a side plate that had contained a small starter of melon and Italian ham. Everybody had eaten theirs apart from April.

'Didn't you like the melon?'

'Oh yes, I liked it just fine,' her grandmother said. 'I just wasn't so hungry.'

Sadie looked again. It didn't look as if April had touched it at all – not even to taste it – but she let the matter slide. Before she could say anything else, her grandmother had turned to listen to something that Graham was saying.

Sadie had always thought it a little clichéd when people said that when someone died, a little bit of the people who loved them most died too, but she'd been able to see it clearly since they'd lost Gampy. The evidence was there now in the small figure of her grandmother. Once she had been April Schwartz, feisty, outspoken, quick-witted, smart and adventurous, the woman who had forged her own path in life in a foreign country with the man she'd loved by her side. Now she was only a memory of that woman, and even that was fading faster than Sadie could bear to see.

'Sadie…'

Sadie shook her head to clear it. 'Huh?' She turned to see Ewan looking expectantly at her. Clearly he was waiting for an answer to something, though Sadie had no clue what the question had been.

'Salt,' he said, rolling his eyes. 'Could you pass it?'

'Salt?' Sadie repeated.

'Salt…' he said. 'Dopier than usual and that's pretty dopey. Burning the candle at both ends again? Another late night with Whatshisface?'

'No.' Sadie handed her brother the salt cellar. 'Whatshisface is now Gonehisface.'

'Ah,' Lucy said, tossing a dark curl away from her face and picking up her wine glass. 'I didn't dare ask about the love life but as Ewan opened up the discussion anyway…'

Ewan grinned at her and then turned back to Sadie. 'When did this happen?'

'A couple of days ago,' Sadie said with a deliberately airy tone. She knew that she was about to get a serious ribbing from her brother, who seemed to find almost everything she did these days a rich seam of things to rib her over, and she was determined not to give him the satisfaction of thinking she cared.

Ewan looked at Kat with eyes full of mischief. His were a soft brown, just as Lucy's were. Both Ewan and Lucy were blessed with dark, thick curls and dark eyes like their mother's. Only Sadie had inherited the grey-eyed, auburn-haired colouring of their dad's side. It sometimes made her feel like the odd child out, as if she didn't really belong, and growing up that feeling hadn't been helped by the huge age gap between her and her siblings. In his meaner moments, Ewan would tease her that she'd been an afterthought, a baby who had arrived when their parents thought they'd finished, and often Sadie thought that was true, even though Henny and Graham would never have said it to her. But Ewan was thirty-eight and Lucy was thirty-six and Sadie was twenty-six, so the figures spoke for themselves really.

'So,' Kat chipped in as she took the salt from Ewan, 'on a scale of one to ten, how bothered are you?'

Sadie couldn't help a slight smile as she poured herself a glass of water. 'I'd say about five.'

'Oh,' Kat said with a light laugh. 'So you quite liked this one?'

'What was his name again?' Lucy asked.

'Jason?'

'That's it,' Kat said. 'I'm so used to Ewan calling him Whatshisface I forgot!'

Sadie gave a light laugh. 'Jason was bearable, I suppose.' She put the water jug down. 'Better than Ash.'

'Ash is the one before, right?' Lucy asked. 'I lose track these days. How long did he last?'

'I forget,' Sadie said.

'About ten minutes,' Ewan said.

'No,' Kat said. 'At least twenty.'

'Wow,' Lucy exclaimed with an indulgent laugh. Sadie often suspected that her older sister found her a little silly. Perhaps it was the age gap, but it sometimes felt like Lucy thought Sadie immature and misguided. And often, when Sadie reflected on Lucy's success in New York as a theatrical agent, a powerful personality making her way in a difficult, cut-throat industry, Sadie could see why she might view her that way. There was no room for procrastinating in Lucy's world, no time for sentiment or immaturity and definitely no time to waste on unsuitable men.

'So Jason was bearable? That's true love in your world, that is,' Kat said.

'No,' Sadie said, joining in the banter because really she had no choice but to laugh at herself. Even she could see how silly it all looked to everyone else that she couldn't keep a boyfriend. The reason why wasn't so funny, but if she didn't laugh then she'd think about that and cry. 'True love is at least an eight. Seven maybe, but that's pushing it. Jason was definitely not true love.'

'So what went wrong this time?' Lucy asked.

'Nothing really. I just couldn't summon up any enthusiasm at the thought of a date, so what was the point?'

'None,' Kat agreed. 'Is there anyone who does fill you with enthusiasm though? Going by your score chart, I don't think the man exists who would be a seven or eight.'

Sadie shrugged and took a sip from her glass. 'I'd like to think he does,' she said, putting it down again. 'I just don't know if I'll find him in Sea Salt Bay.'

'I don't know if you'd find him in this hemisphere,' Ewan said.

'You could always try New York.' Lucy passed her empty starter plate to Henny, who was collecting them up to make way for their main course. 'Come and stay with me for a few weeks and I'll get you hooked up with some eligible bachelor.'

'New York's alright for a holiday,' Sadie said, 'but I don't think living there would suit me.'

'There's a big world outside the bay,' Lucy said.

'I know,' Sadie replied. 'I went to look for it once – remember?'

Lucy gave that indulgent smile again. 'Yes, I suppose it's not for everyone to leave the bay. Sometimes when I'm back here I do see why you wouldn't want to. I don't miss it when I'm busy day to day back in New York, but when I'm home…' She paused, looking distant for a moment. 'When I'm home I do feel different… sort of calmer. Like I've spent the whole month at a yoga retreat. It makes me remember how lucky I was to grow up here.'

'You could always come back,' Graham said.

Lucy shook her head. 'After I've worked so hard to get where I am in New York? As lovely as the thought is, I'd be mad to do that. For the next few years at least I need to stay put. After that… who knows?'

'I think you *had* found your man once,' April put in, and Sadie turned to her, almost surprised to find that her grandmother had been following the conversation and had managed to muster an opinion on it. Sadie didn't often admit it, because she hated that everyone knew what she wouldn't say out loud, but April was right about that much. Everyone else looked vaguely uncomfortable and probably hoped that April wouldn't say the name of the man she meant.

Sadie gave her a tight smile. The truth was, she'd once imagined she'd found a whole ten, and it had been here in Sea Salt Bay, just as Gammy had said. She'd had him once too, before she'd gone to university and let him slip through her fingers. She'd been fickle, silly and headstrong; she hadn't realised what she'd had until she'd driven it away. And all because she'd been searching for something more, something she hadn't really needed in the end, something she thought was beyond the borders of the town. Now he was with someone else. For the last three years someone else had had the perfect ten, and that girl wasn't about to let go of him. Sadie wouldn't have blamed her either. If she'd had him still, knowing what she knew now, she wouldn't be letting him go either.

However she looked at it though, that door had closed and that life was out of her reach. Though she often saw him around town and they'd always exchange a laugh and a joke for old times' sake, she'd never tell him how she sometimes wondered what might have happened had she never given him up, or that sometimes she fantasised that they'd stayed together and now lived in a little cottage on the cliffs, perfectly comfortable and madly in love. She often thought that the woman he'd settled with was completely wrong for him too and occasionally she daydreamt about telling him so. But to say these things would be unfair to them both, and she couldn't, no matter how she might like to.

'There's no point in going on about that now, is there, April?' Kat said, giving Sadie a sympathetic smile. 'You know what they say: no point in reliving past glories.'

'Who says that?' Ewan asked. 'I've never heard anyone say that.'

'I don't know,' Kat fired back. 'I've heard it so someone does. I'm not exactly going to keep a written record, am I?'

Ewan grinned and Kat's look of irritation instantly melted.

'I'm not going on about it,' April said with a slight look of indignation. 'I'm saying it as I see it. Everybody in town knows they were meant to be and I still say Sadie was crazy to let him go.'

Henny came back in from the kitchen and retook her seat at the table. 'In the end it's Sadie's business. And I for one am glad she's being choosy,' she added, spooning redcurrant jelly onto the side of her plate to go with the lamb Graham had just served up. 'There's no reason for her to rush into anything. You don't settle for second best.'

'Nobody's saying she should,' Ewan said. 'Nobody else around this table has done that.'

'Exactly,' Henny said. 'When you marry, you marry for love.'

Sadie spluttered, choking on her water. 'Nobody said anything about getting married!'

'Apparently everyone is trying to marry you off regardless,' Lucy said.

'Alright then,' Henny said with a slight frown. 'What I mean to say is that nobody should settle down for anything less. Move in together, cohabit... whatever couples do these days.'

'Mum,' Ewan began with a lazy grin, 'you make it sound like you were born when Victoria was on the throne.' He slopped a mound of mashed potatoes onto his plate. 'I'm sure people lived together when you and Dad were young.'

'Shacked up, we used to call it,' Graham said. 'I wouldn't have minded that but your mum wouldn't have had it – too posh. Everything had to be proper.'

'Oh boy, do I remember that,' April said. She looked at Henny. 'I recall the first time Graham brought you home – we thought you'd come direct from Buckingham Palace.'

Henny rolled her eyes. 'For the last time, we were not posh. We were just...'

'Loaded?' Ewan offered.

'Insanely privileged?' Lucy said.

'Descended from actual royalty?' Sadie cut in.

'Terribly distantly,' her mother said, waving the comment away, though if anyone cared to look closely enough they'd see a secret, pleased pride in her expression as she turned her attention to cutting a slice of meat on her plate. Her family was probably as closely linked to royalty as the rest of the world were to Adam and Eve, but Sadie's rather aloof and tedious maternal grandparents loved to tell everyone about the connection anyway.

Sadie was bored of hearing the story. Although the same blood ran in her veins, it didn't really mean anything to her. She often felt that the fact they kept telling everyone was just a bit needy. Those grandparents, living on a remote estate in Scotland with their butler and cook and groundskeeper, couldn't have been more different from the grandparents who lived here in Sea Salt Bay, running the little waffle house with a smile and a kind word for everyone who crossed their paths. They couldn't have been more different from Sadie's mother, Henny, either. It was hard to know whether she had always been that way or if she'd changed after she'd met Sadie's dad and because of him. But somehow, her turning into a normal human being was responsible for the fact that she'd even looked twice at a man whose world was about as far from hers as you could get.

'We had to get married,' Graham continued, looking at his children in turn, 'otherwise your grandparents would never have had me.'

Henny looked up from her lunch. 'I hope you're not insinuating that you wouldn't have married me given the choice. Because if you are it's a bit late to say so, but not too late for me to pack a suitcase for you and send you off to the Sea Salt Guesthouse.'

'Of course not,' Graham said with an indulgent smile at his wife, whose nostrils flared in a way that reminded everyone forcefully that she had once been very posh indeed, and that, in the end, the apple never really fell that far from the tree after all. 'You know I was head over heels with you. Everyone knew it. You were the one making sacrifices, my sweet. You could have been married to some toff now, living on a country estate instead of working the boat with me every day.'

'I happen to like working the boat,' Henny said stiffly, though it was clear that her husband's silky words had worked their magic and the offence she might have taken at his previous statement had well and truly dissipated. 'And I never wanted a *toff*.'

'Well that's alright then,' Graham replied cheerfully. 'Because it won't be changing any time soon, not unless we win the lottery... or your parents decide to help us out a bit.'

'We don't need their help,' Henny said, again with the kind of haughtiness that reminded everyone of the 'good stock' she'd come from. 'I told them the day I left home that we'd stand on our own feet.'

'As I recall,' Graham said with a faint smile, 'what you actually said was that they could stick their inheritance.'

'That was because they were being ghastly to you,' Henny said. 'You know that. We soon made it up when Ewan was born. They travelled down to see him straight away and they've doted on all the children. And they helped us buy this house, don't forget.'

'As if I'd forget that,' Graham said with an unmistakeable wryness in his tone.

Sadie exchanged a look with Ewan but said nothing. *Doted* was perhaps a bit strong a word to describe how Henny's parents felt about Sadie and her siblings. *Tolerated* was more like it. Sadie couldn't recall ever receiving a single hug or compliment or kind word from Henriette's mother and father, not as a child and certainly not as an adult.

'But even after all these years they haven't changed their mind about me,' Graham reminded her.

'Regardless, we've stood on our own feet and we've made a success of it. We don't need their money now and I would never ask.'

Graham smiled at his wife, so obviously full of pride and affection that it warmed Sadie to see it. Her parents were, perhaps, the biggest single reason why she herself couldn't find the right man. Even the one time she'd come perilously close to 'the one', ultimately he just hadn't been able to measure up – or, at least, Sadie hadn't been able to get past the perfect example she was so determined to live up to. Her parents' relationship appeared so faultless, their beginnings so dreamy and romantic, that Sadie had grown up increasingly invested in the notion that all love affairs were the stuff of fairy tales like that. At least, if they were worth having at all. If there were no fireworks, no Romeo and Juliet moments, no all-conquering love against the odds, then it couldn't be right, could it? This conviction hadn't been helped by the fact that Grandma and Grandpa Schwartz had also been completely devoted to each other, not to mention that her brother had been swept off his feet by the beautiful and practically perfect Kat.

Sadie could only thank her stars that good old Lucy who, despite offering to fix Sadie up with an eligible New York bachelor, was herself still happily single. Otherwise she might have started to think that there was something terribly wrong with her for not yet being embroiled in the love affair of the century herself.

'I don't know what on earth started all that anyway,' Henny said. 'If we give another minute's conversation to my silly parents I'm quite sure every bit of food on the table will suddenly go rancid.'

Ewan let out a snort of laughter.

'Steady on, Mum!' Lucy cried, though she was grinning.

Everyone else laughed too. Everyone but April, who apparently hadn't noticed a joke had been made, and Henny, who simply turned a wry smile to her son. She loved her parents, everyone knew that, but she also knew as well as anyone around that table just how difficult, obstructive and constantly disapproving they could be.

'Pass the wine please, Graham,' Henny said. She looked at Ewan and Kat as her husband handed her the bottle. 'It's a lovely vintage. Thank you for bringing it.'

Ewan shrugged. 'It seemed a bit too posh for us to drink at home by ourselves. It's funny what satisfied clients bring in for you. I mean, sometimes I think it's a bit over the top – we've only taken them for a splash-about in the sea, really – but I don't suppose I'm going to sniff at a nice bottle of plonk for doing something I'd love doing anyway.'

'Well I wish I got perks like that from my job,' Sadie said.

'You don't have a job,' Ewan said with a grin for his little sister. 'What you do is just crowd control.'

'She has a vocation,' Lucy said, gallantly riding to her little sister's defence. 'It's better than a job.'

'What she said,' Sadie agreed, wrinkling her nose at Ewan.

'So you fancy swapping with her?' Ewan asked Lucy. 'You can sit with a load of kids every day and Sadie can do the swanky lunches with celebs and Broadway producers?'

Lucy took a sip of her wine. 'God no!' she said, laughing. 'Give me a room full of teenagers for longer than an hour and I'd be reaching for the Valium. The only teenagers I want to be anywhere near are ones I can get cast in the newest production of *Dear Evan Hansen*!'

'Your average teenager gets a bad press,' Sadie said. 'They're challenging – yes – but their views on the world can be fascinating. Teaching *is* a vocation and it's better than any old job. I'm helping to steer future generations; I might be helping a future Nobel Prize winner to realise his or her full potential.'

'I'll ask whether you still feel that way next time you're stuck inside revising and I'm having a lovely swim out in the bay and getting paid for the privilege,' Ewan said.

'Funny!' Sadie said with a pretend grimace. 'At least my job will make a difference… at least, it will when I qualify and finally get one.'

But then she paused, the old misgivings about her career choice resurfacing again, as they had done many times over the previous weeks. She pushed them back down into the depths once more. This was the path she'd chosen and she was going to see it through. What she'd opted to do with her life did matter, didn't it? She was going to make a difference in the world, wasn't she?

'My job makes a difference,' Ewan said. 'I make people happy, don't I? I have a waiting list for new clients.'

'Of course you do,' Sadie said with a theatrical sigh. 'If you were teaching people how to plate up shit you'd have a waiting list because half of Sea Salt Bay is in love with you—'

'Sadie!' Henny exclaimed. 'Firstly – language! And secondly, you can't say things like that in front of Kat!'

'Oh, right,' Sadie said, laughing but still colouring at her mum's chastisement.

'Oh, Mum, please,' Lucy cut in. 'Like Kat doesn't already know that. I mean, it's the only reason most of Ewan's clients book him.'

'Oh, I know that.' Kat gave Ewan a coy smile. 'But business is business, however we come by it. Besides, I've always liked a challenge.'

'Am I a challenge?' Ewan asked her.

'Keeping the marital mystique is definitely a challenge.'

Ewan grinned again. 'Oh, I think you're doing more than OK there…'

'Gravy?' Henny barked, shoving the gravy boat in between Ewan and Kat, just to head off any dinner-table double entendres that might be in the offing.

'I'm OK, thanks,' Ewan said, waving it away.

'I'm OK too,' Kat said. She looked at the children, sitting quietly while the adults chatted. Freya was the oldest, a serious ten-year-old who more often than not had her head in a book rather than a dive helmet. While her parents were outdoor, sporty types, Freya couldn't have been further from that. She'd rather be in a library than on a tennis court. Right now she was reading an old copy of *Malory Towers* that Henny had given to her. Any other child would not have been permitted to read at the table while eating, but Henny doted on Freya and would have allowed her to conduct chemistry experiments at the table if she thought for a moment it would make her granddaughter happy.

Freddie was two years younger and a carbon copy of his dad. Already he was handsome, with soft brown eyes that could melt the hardest heart and a head of dark curls. Although he was good-looking and charming, he was more difficult than Freya, perhaps because he was a bit too boisterous and energetic like his dad – always in trouble, always hurting himself, always intrigued by things that he shouldn't be. If someone put a huge red button in front of him and told him that should he press it the world would end, Freddie simply wouldn't be able to control the urge to slam his hand down on it, just to see what would happen. He loved to go out diving with Ewan, rain or shine, no matter the temperature of the water. He loved swimming in the shallow pools around the rocks, he loved surfing the smaller waves that rolled onto the beach, and he loved running and climbing. He was obsessed with any sport he could get the chance to play, anything that meant he didn't have to sit still for more than five minutes. Right now he was gazing longingly out at the churning sea beyond the windows of the conservatory, perhaps dreaming of a day spent splashing through the waves instead of being cooped up at a sedate family meal.

'You both have enough gravy?' Kat asked them, and both children nodded. Freya's head went immediately back to her book as she absently speared a carrot onto her fork and moved it dextrously to her mouth without even looking; it was clear she'd spent many a mealtime reading. Freddie's gaze returned to the sea where, should anyone have looked closely enough, they might have seen little movies of afternoons spent surfing reflected in the pools of his huge brown eyes.

Henny put the gravy boat down and retrieved her cutlery.

'Meat's lovely, Dad,' Sadie said.

Graham smiled up at her.

'Very tender,' April said, though Sadie glanced at her plate and didn't see how her grandmother could know because her food didn't look touched.

'It is,' Ewan agreed. 'I've always said you do a mean roast.'

'I've definitely missed your cooking,' Lucy said. 'I think I might have put on at least ten pounds since I've been here – it's a good job I'm flying back tomorrow because any more and I'd have to pay for an extra seat on the plane.'

'Oh, darlin',' April said, smiling at Lucy. 'You look just peachy to me. If you've put on a little extra padding it suits you – you were too thin when you arrived back. I think you work too hard.'

'I have nobody feeding me all this lovely home-cooked food either,' Lucy said, and it was telling that she didn't dispute the fact that she did work hard. Perhaps her sister did feel it *was* too hard sometimes, but Sadie knew that even if she did, she thought it was necessary. Lucy had always been ambitious and determined, passionate about the arts and a champion of those involved in them. She'd once wanted to train as an actor herself but had decided very early on that she just wasn't that good; then a chance meeting with a theatrical agent in London who wanted to set up a New York office had set her on her current path – a path Sadie suspected suited her far better and that she loved. It probably made her more money too, though she would never be crass enough to show off about how much she might be making.

'This is all lovely, of course,' Kat said, and suddenly Sadie detected a hint of impatience in her tone. 'But while we're enjoying the chance to catch up, I think perhaps there's something we really need to talk about.'

Henny nodded slowly, her gaze travelling to April momentarily before resting on Kat again. 'I think you might be right.'

'I'm glad we're on the same page,' Kat said.

Ewan looked at her. 'Would someone mind telling me what page that is? Because I'm not sure I'm even in the same book.'

'The waffle house, dear,' Kat said. 'Perhaps we ought to talk about it sooner rather than later.' She looked around the table. Other families might have thought her pointed instruction impertinent – after all, she was only there by virtue of her marriage to Ewan – but the Schwartz family knew that she was probably the only person at the table not so blinkered by emotion that she could be rational about the difficult discussions they faced. Though nobody wanted to address it, Kenneth was gone and they had to acknowledge that the waffle house would be tough for April to run by herself. The place had been closed for a month now, during the height of the tourist season, and money was draining from the business faster than water from a leaky boat. It couldn't continue that way. Something had to be done and today, whether they liked it or not, was one of the rare occasions they'd have to sit together and decide what that ought to be.

'Right,' Graham said. 'And while we have Lucy here, as it concerns her too.'

'I'm not getting involved,' Lucy began, but her father put up a hand to stop her.

'You don't need to get involved but I'd rather not have these discussions behind your back. You're still my daughter and a part of this family even if you've chosen to leave the bay.'

Lucy nodded shortly and turned to her grandmother, and everyone else did too.

'April…' Kat said gently. April suddenly didn't show much sign of wanting to engage, but perhaps that was because she knew that the following conversation might be painful. While everyone tiptoed around, Kat, again, was perhaps the only person detached enough to be a little tougher on her, to make her face what needed facing.

April shook her head.

'April…' Kat repeated. 'We have to talk about this. For a start, do you want to open up again? Do you want to carry on working there or do you think this is a good time to retire? After all—'

'I think it's too much,' Henny cut in briskly. Graham stared at her but she ignored the rebuke. 'There,' she continued. 'I've said it. That's what we've all been thinking after all, isn't it? I know nobody likes the thought of selling up but I don't see what else we can do with Kenneth gone. It's too much for one person to manage on their own, let alone a pensioner.'

'Why does anyone have to manage it alone?' her husband asked.

Henny shot him a withering look. 'Are you going to run it with your mother?'

'Of course not,' he fired back. 'That doesn't mean it has to close.' He turned to April. 'Mama, what do you think? Is it making enough to maybe pay someone to help?'

April shook her head. 'I really couldn't say right now. You know your papa took care of all that – I just cooked.'

'You didn't *just* do anything,' Sadie said. 'You made the magic, Gammy, and that was worth everything.'

'That's sweet of you to say so, darlin'.'

'Yes,' Henny cut in. 'There's no doubting that, but making magic doesn't pay the bills.'

'It does when it brings customers in,' Graham said.

'OK,' Henny said. 'But we still haven't established who's going to run the place.'

'Well you know it can't be us,' Graham replied, looking both flustered and increasingly irritated at the same time. Clearly he wanted to give an answer that served his emotions, they all did, but he didn't have one and Sadie could see it frustrated and saddened him.

Henny turned to Ewan.

'I don't have time,' he said, his argument perfectly valid though he looked guilty about it all the same.

'I know you don't,' his mother said. 'That's my point – none of us has time. Your father and I have the boat – and let's face it, we'd be mad to spoil the income from that for the sake of a little business that struggles to make half what we do.' She held up a hand to stave off objections from her husband and continued talking to Ewan. 'You and Kat have the dive business and the children. Sadie has her studies and we can hardly ask Lucy to come home from New York to do it. I know it's hard to say so, but what choice does all that leave us with? Not much, really, does it?'

The table was silent for a moment. 'We definitely can't hire an assistant or something?' Sadie asked finally.

Henny frowned. 'I hardly think that's financially viable.'

'Perhaps we need to look into that a little more before we say so for certain,' Graham offered. 'Maybe there would be room to take someone on.'

'Graham…' Henny said. 'I thought we'd agreed when we looked at the books…'

She stopped short of completing her sentence and Sadie wondered just what her parents had discovered in them. She had to guess that perhaps the waffle house hadn't been making as much money as she'd imagined it was. She had never really thought about it, because it had always just been there, part of the landscape of the bay and of her life there, and she had never really equated that with the making of an actual profit.

'I fear Henny may be right,' April said sadly, and Sadie stared at her grandmother. Maybe she'd been forced to agree because she knew deep down that the waffle house wasn't making all that much, but it wasn't like her to give up so easily.

'I have to agree with Mum too,' Ewan said. 'I hate to say it—'

'You mean you hate to agree with me?' Henny asked with a faint smile.

'That,' Ewan said with a small smile of his own. But it faded into something more pained as his gaze travelled to April. 'And the fact that none of us has time on our hands to help; we can barely keep on top of our own affairs without running a waffle house as well.'

Sadie looked at her grandmother, waiting for a response, but nothing came. It was like she'd already chosen to retreat, the woman she'd once been choosing to follow her husband into the void and leaving behind someone who simply looked like April Schwartz. It pained Sadie to admit, even privately, that they'd already half lost her. It couldn't be that simple, surely? There had to be a way to get her back, and surely that's what they all wanted? Certainly the one thing they shouldn't be doing was taking from April the only thing that might bring her back to life. If they took the waffle house from her, persuaded her to give it up, what would she have left? Surely it would be better to give her something to focus on, to keep something of what she'd shared with Gampy, even if it was more of a keepsake than a viable business?

But then, Sadie also had to admit that her mother and brother were right. Who could spare the time to help run the waffle house? If it didn't make enough money these days to employ staff, then that was out of the question. If April was going to have help it had to be one of them, but none of them could do it.

'Gammy…' Sadie said. 'Never mind what can be done… What do you want? You must have some idea.'

April looked at her. 'Is there any point in saying what I want?'

'Of course there is,' Lucy said.

'But you're all telling me that it's not possible.'

'That's not what we're saying.'

'But nobody wants to work with me?' April asked. She shook her head sadly. 'I can't say I blame any of you. Ain't enough excitement in an old place like that, and you've all got bigger plans.'

'But if you could,' Sadie asked, 'you'd want to keep the waffle house on?'

'It's not possible,' April repeated.

'So what do you want us to do?' Graham cut in.

April shook her head slightly but she didn't offer a reply.

'We're surely not just going to wrap it up like that?' Sadie asked, her gaze settling on every adult at the table in turn. 'If Gammy wants to keep it on there must be a way around it. If we put our heads together surely we can come up with some kind of solution?'

'Like what?' Ewan asked.

'I didn't say that inspiration would strike instantly,' Sadie replied tartly. 'But you're writing the waffle house off with no discussion.'

'Isn't that what's happening here?' Henny asked. 'I thought this was a discussion.'

'OK, without an informed discussion,' Sadie replied. 'We haven't gone over all the options.'

'That's because there aren't any,' her mother said.

'I'm with Sadie,' Lucy said. 'There must be a way to make things work.'

'I agree,' Graham said. 'I'll admit it's going to be hard to part with that old place – we all have a lot of good memories there. I certainly don't want to see it go.'

'And can you imagine it being sold off to someone who might turn it into something tacky or horrible?' Sadie said.

'Or even knock it down,' Graham added.

'Isn't it protected or anything?' Kat asked.

'Protected?' Ewan glanced at her. 'In what way?'

'It's old, isn't it? A pretty unusual example?' She turned to April. 'Isn't it a listed building or something?'

'I hardly think so,' April replied slowly. 'I wouldn't exactly know.'

Graham shook his head. 'I don't think so – we would know if it was, although I often thought it ought to be. I doubt it's historically significant enough for that kind of protection.'

'So someone could knock it down?' Sadie asked. 'If they decided they just wanted the spot on the pier, and not the business or the building, they could just bulldoze it?'

Graham shrugged, though he looked as unhappy at the idea as his youngest daughter did.

Sadie looked at her mother. 'We can't let that happen.'

'What can I do?' Henny asked. 'I'm not a fan of the idea either. We can all sit here and complain, but unless someone comes up with a solution then we can't change it.'

'The ultimate decision has to lie with Grandma,' Ewan said, and for once Sadie was in full agreement with her brother.

All eyes went to April. She gave a half shrug and a long sigh that Sadie was convinced would end in a heart-wrenching sob. But it didn't – she only spoke quietly.

'I'll do whatever you think is best,' she said, and that statement alone told Sadie all she needed to know about her grandmother's mental state. She'd never have said something like that in the past. Before Kenneth died April would have fought to keep their business; she'd have worked day and night and sunk every last copper into it; she'd have kept it open even if that meant only one customer a day coming through the doors, because while there was a customer, she'd have thought it was worth it. But then, Sadie had to consider that maybe even her grandma had had to see the bigger picture, that some battles just couldn't be won no matter how hard you fought, and that all things eventually came to an end. Perhaps that was all it was; perhaps that era had simply come to its natural end.

'That settles it then,' Sadie's mother said, addressing the table at large as she shook out a napkin and placed it on her lap. 'I know we don't like it but the waffle house will have to be sold.'

Chapter Three

For the rest of lunch, conversation turned to the practicalities of the sale of Sea Salt Bay Waffle House. While there had still been some opposition to it, eventually the family had all agreed there was no other way that they could see. April contributed very little to the discussion, other than to agree to almost everything without question. Every time Sadie looked at her she wished she could look inside her head to see what she was really thinking and feeling about it. No matter what had happened, what had been lost, Sadie didn't believe that what they were planning round the dinner table was truly what her grandmother wanted.

But despite feeling that, and wanting to do something about it, Sadie was stumped every time she tried to come up with a workable solution to the problem. Whichever way she looked at it, she had to admit that her mother was right – nobody was in a position to take on the running of the waffle house. More to the point, it would inevitably mean supporting April too – and Sadie suspected that nobody really wanted that responsibility. And with that realisation she had to admit that some problems, no matter how sad the facts made you, however much you wished they could be otherwise, couldn't be fixed. All things had to end eventually and perhaps – whether they were ready for it or not – the waffle house on the pier had served its last customer. Perhaps it really was time to let it go.

Sadie volunteered to go and check the waffle house over after lunch. Her grandmother was staying with her, Henny and Graham for the time being until they felt comfortable letting her live alone again. Whether that would be back in April's flat above the waffle house had been a cause for some debate during the month since Kenneth had died, but it seemed that today's lunch had settled that too. If the waffle house was to be sold it was unlikely that April could go back there. The family weren't exactly sure where she was going to live instead – whether it would be in some kind of sheltered accommodation in a retirement village, in a new home by herself or perhaps even continuing to stay with Henny and Graham – but it was something they were going to have to iron out over the coming days and weeks.

In the meantime, with April still staying in their spare room and the waffle house empty, the family had been taking it in turns to see that all was well and that the place was still secure. Not so much from a crime point of view – usually the worst Sea Salt Bay had to offer was the odd bit of littering on the promenade – but more to guard against damage caused by something unexpected, such as an undiscovered burst pipe or a gas leak.

So Sadie took her turn now as the afternoon light mellowed. The earlier rain had stopped, but the breeze was still brisk enough to whip the sea into dancing peaks and slap her hair around her face. She tucked the lengths into the collar of her old blue raincoat and plunged her hands into its deep pockets. The temperature wasn't exactly freezing but the wind set goosebumps spreading over her skin anyway.

The waffle house was in darkness. Not that she'd expected anything else, of course, but somehow the fact still jarred. It didn't look right without the welcoming lights in the window that Sadie had always taken for granted until now, the interior a swirl of candy colours and sweet smells. The keys rattled in the lock as Sadie opened up and even that was a strangely mournful sound. The lock tended to stick – there was a knack to it that Sadie was only just mastering – and it took her a minute to get it right before it popped open with a dull clunk.

Letters that had collected on the threshold scattered as the door swept over them and Sadie bent to gather them up. Most of April's suppliers had been told that the waffle house would be closed for the foreseeable future – if only to prevent endless deliveries that they didn't need from sitting and spoiling. But there were still old accounts to settle, the bills for those steadily trickling in. There was personal mail amongst the post too, all the more painful when it was addressed to Gampy. The ones in Sadie's hand weren't the first. She'd add these to the pile at home later; the family were choosing to open them up and deal with them rather than subject April to the distress of seeing his name on correspondence, though there was a lot of it that they just didn't know what to do with and would be forced to consult her on at some point.

Though they were all making regular checks on the building, and Sadie's mother came in every once in a while to clean and air as best she could, despite their best efforts the smell of damp and neglect was beginning to characterise each visit now. It was practically on top of the sea and it was inevitable that a building so close to the water, with no heat or life in it, would soon be affected. Sadie glanced around the dimly lit main room. The sugar-pink chairs were upturned on top of the baby-blue tables and, despite the fact that Henny had only been in a few days before to clean, they were once again powdered in a fine coat of dust. The chrome counter was covered too, and Sadie trailed a finger along it to see a stark track left behind.

Seeing nothing untoward here, she continued through to the kitchen. It was just as silent and depressing as the dining room. Not so long before it would have been the joyous hub of the café, with her grandmother dancing to old tunes on the radio as she mixed her delicious batter while her grandfather took orders out front.

Sadie smiled sadly at the thought. She'd spent many weekend afternoons as a teenager helping out here for extra pocket money, though the truth was her grandparents would have given her the money anyway and they paid her far more than her work was worth. She'd spent even more hours sitting at one of their tables being fed with free waffles with strawberries and cream, or pancakes stuffed with banana and drizzled in maple syrup or crammed with raspberries and melted chocolate and dusted with icing sugar. It was the only way to get some fruit into her, Gammy would say when Henny complained that April was ruining Sadie's evening meals, but she'd fire a conspiratorial wink at Sadie as she did to say that she was only joking. The fruit was just there to make the sugar taste better, and who cared about silly old evening meals anyway. Not jolly, kind, fun old Gammy, that was for sure.

As she'd grown older, Sadie had no longer wanted to sit at the baby-blue tables of her grandparents' waffle house with her grandmother fussing over her, ruffling her hair as she ate, singing old songs in the kitchen so loudly that everyone in the dining room could hear. She'd wanted to head out with her friends to the nearest big towns to eat in trendy new places. But when Sadie remembered those awkward years now she felt deeply guilty and sorry that she'd thought that way. Today she'd give anything to have those years back.

Even though she didn't want to, Sadie flicked the switch to illuminate the kitchen so she could check round properly. Apart from the same fine layer of inevitable dust that covered the dining room, it was spotless. Despite the suddenness with which Gammy been forced to abandon it the day the ambulance had come for Gampy, Sadie and her parents had been in to clean it from top to bottom, throw all the perishable unused food away and switch off the gas. As a result it now looked clinical, unloved, as if no life had ever been lived there. With a deep sigh, Sadie turned off the light again. She couldn't bear to look any longer than she had to because it made her feel more miserable than anything else had for a long time.

As she went back through to the dining room, her gaze was drawn to the figure of a man looking in through the window. Broad shoulders that she knew well, a slight irreverent wave in his hair and eyes the colour of sage leaves, eyes that she'd gazed into so many times over the years they'd been together, eyes that she sometimes still gazed into as she dreamt at night. On any other day she'd want to smile at the sight of him, even knowing she shouldn't, but that smile didn't come so easily today. She'd seen him around town many times in the checked shirt he wore now and had remarked to herself every time, with a pang of longing, that he'd looked good in it. She'd always had to chase the feeling away as he'd stopped to say hello, handsome and relaxed and unaware of the turmoil he caused in her heart when he did, but today, perhaps because of her heightened emotional state, she was finding it harder. There was no coat over his shirt, because he'd always been far too hardy to worry about a spot of rain.

Sadie went to open the door, doing her best to shake feelings that she'd given up the right to long ago.

'Hi,' he said. 'I saw the light on and I thought I'd better check who was in here. I mean, you never know...'

'It's just me. But thanks. It's good of you.'

'It's alright. I was on my way back from seeing Melissa anyway. It's only neighbourly after all, isn't it?'

'Well thanks anyway, Dec. I appreciate it.'

Declan shoved his hands into the pockets of his jeans and blew out a breath.

'So…' he began, the merest hint of awkwardness in his voice. 'How is your grandma? I didn't like to come to yours and ask because… well, I thought it might not be welcome just yet.'

'Oh, I think she would have liked to have seen you. She's bearing up. Sort of. She's very… introverted right now. I don't know, maybe seeing you might cheer her up a bit.'

Declan raised disbelieving eyebrows and Sadie had to give a small smile.

'OK, so maybe not,' she admitted. 'She's pretty terrible if the truth be told. She just seems like… like she's gone out. Like she's a house and the person who lives there went out but forgot to turn out the lights. But not in a crazy way, just a really lost, absent sort of way.'

Declan nodded. 'I was sorry to hear about your grandpa – we all were. He was a lovely guy, and everyone around here was very fond of him.'

'Thanks,' Sadie said, doing her best to hold back the tears suddenly pooling in her eyes. She sniffed hard and pulled herself back from the brink.

'If you need anything… I mean, if April needs anything, just ask. I can't promise I'll be able to help all that much but I'll do whatever I can.'

'I'll tell her that – it'll mean a lot to her.'

'Well…' He shrugged. 'That's what we do, isn't it? In Sea Salt Bay, I mean.'

Sadie gave a stiff nod. 'How's your mum and dad, by the way?'

'Oh, the same as ever,' he said, his tone more cheerful now, more certain.

'And Melissa?'

'She's good too. We're looking for a house, actually.'

'A house…' Sadie hesitated. What was she supposed to say to that? She was supposed to be pleased for him, she decided quickly, and she would be. 'Wow… so things are going well.'

'Yeah. She says it's about time we thought about living together and I suppose she might have a point. I mean, it's been three years now.'

'It's not all that long – not for a huge decision like moving in together.'

'Try telling that to Melissa.'

'Will you stay in the bay? There aren't so many places around here for sale and they're certainly not cheap.'

'Don't I know it. We're looking here first though. I'd like to stay, and I don't mind if it takes us a little longer to find the right place if it means we can do that.'

'And Melissa?' Sadie asked, sensing a caveat to his statement.

'She says she'd leave given half a chance. But then she doesn't have the same ties here, does she? She wasn't born and raised here like me so I can hardly blame her for being less attached to the place. I think we'll work it out in the end – she knows that I love it here so even if we had to leave we wouldn't go far.'

Sadie nodded. 'Well, I'm pleased for you if that's what you want. I know you have to find the right place for both of you but I hope you don't move too far away; I'd miss you.'

'Nah, you wouldn't,' he said with a warm smile. 'You'd soon forget about me. Anyway, won't you be on your way out of the bay when you qualify? Wasn't that what you always said? That there was nothing in Sea Salt Bay – no jobs, no prospects, no excitement? Once upon a time you were desperate to get out.'

What he didn't add, but what they both knew, was those exact reasons were the ones Sadie had given him the day they'd split up. He'd wanted to settle, but she'd been restless, and after a long and tiring argument they'd decided that the two simply couldn't be reconciled and that had been that. Looking back, Sadie had had plenty of time to regret her decision, but that regret hadn't come until much later – too late to put it right and too late to take her place in Declan's life again.

Sadie shrugged. 'I know. But all this with Gampy has changed things somehow. I don't know what I want these days. My family are here and at times like this that seems more important than anything else.'

'But not Lucy. Unless she's moving back to England… to the bay?'

Lucy. The prime culprit in Declan's eyes – at least she had been that fateful day when she and Declan had split. Sadie had looked up to her big sister, had watched her leave the bay and achieve amazing things, and she'd wanted to do that too. In reality, with the age gap, Declan hardly knew Lucy, and yet Sadie knew he disliked her sister for something that Lucy didn't even know she'd done; an innocent and unintended consequence of the life she'd chosen to live. She'd set an example that Sadie had been desperate to follow and, eventually, it had led to the end of Sadie and Declan. The irony was that things hadn't worked out like that at all in the end – Sadie was back where she'd started, the big ambitions silenced, while Declan, the one who hadn't wanted to, had moved on.

'No chance,' Sadie said. 'She's got some big deal going down – her biggest yet, she says. She's always got some big deal going down to be honest. This is something as glamorous and showbizzy as ever but these days even I've started to glaze over when she tells me about it. I mean, we're all incredibly proud of her and everything, but it all seems so far away from our lives here that it's hard to get your head around it, you know? I can't help feeling like she's… well, it doesn't matter.'

Declan gave his head a tiny shake as he regarded Sadie with a look of such compassion and affection that it made her want to cry again. 'You always did try to live up to Lucy's impossible example. Not that I ever thought you weren't capable of amazing things, but there's only so much room in the world for people like Lucy. The rest of us just live ordinary lives, but there's nothing wrong in that. We can be just as happy… happier sometimes.'

'Yeah.' Sadie took the keys from her pocket. 'I suppose so.'

'I'm sorry,' he said, glancing at the keys. 'You need to get back and here's me keeping you talking.' He stepped back, out of the doorway and onto the boards of the pier.

'No, it's not that. I mean, I do have to get back but you're not in the way at all. It's nice to catch up; I don't see you all that often these days…'

Without Melissa, she wanted to say but stopped herself. Would that have sounded bitter or childish or resentful? Sadie certainly had no right to be any of those things.

'Are you heading home now?' he asked. 'I could walk some of the way with you.'

'I am,' Sadie said. 'That'd be nice.'

As they started to walk the length of the pier, chatting easily about nothing and yet everything, it was almost like old times. Almost, but never quite, because Sadie could add those times to a rapidly growing list of ones that she wished she'd treasured a bit more when she'd had them.

Chapter Four

The Listing Ship was Sadie's favourite pub, which was lucky, because it was the only pub in Sea Salt Bay. Overlooking the far side of the bay and the wall of the grey cliffs, it was small and cosy, with orange lamps embedded in the teak walls and canopies of fishing nets hanging from the ceiling, and when the narrow windows were open and the breeze rolled through the snug, the air smelt of salt. It had a history that went right back to King James and had once been stocked entirely by the illegal rum that came into the bay when the moon was high and the army was looking the other way, the landlord always serving it with one eye on the door should the revenue man come calling. These days patrons were more likely to find guest ales and craft gins behind the bar, but Sadie loved the sense of romance about the place, the idea that it had always belonged to the bay and that its history was inextricably bound up with that of the sea that rolled onto the nearby sands.

Sadie wasn't inside today; the weather was far too glorious to be indoors. Today she and best friends Natalie and Georgia were in the sunniest nook of the Listing Ship's beer garden. It was early in the evening and so they had the garden almost to themselves. She'd said goodbye to Lucy earlier that day, leaving her at the airport to board her flight back to New York, and already Sadie missed her. It wasn't even that they were close – not as close as she'd always been to Ewan anyway – but blood was still blood, and despite the miles between them the bond of blood was stronger than any distance. Close or not, her sister was still her sister and Sadie loved her. She'd needed to get out of the house soon after they'd got back from the airport because everyone in the Schwartz household was missing Lucy too and the atmosphere had been tetchy and miserable. She needed the brand of cheering entertainment that only her old school friends could provide to give her at least a few hours' respite. By tomorrow morning her family would be back to normal, she hoped, used once again to Lucy's absence.

Natalie shifted on the bench, straightening her skirt over tanned, generous thighs. She plucked a lip salve from her handbag and applied a little, regarding Sadie keenly from a face framed by a dark, glossy bob.

'I'm sure even your grandma didn't think that place was going to stay open forever,' she said. 'She might be sad to see it go – we all will – but she'll get used to it and she'll probably be glad of the chance to finally slow down. I mean, how old is she now?'

'Seventy-eight,' Sadie replied. 'But age has always been just a number to her and it's the slowing down that actually worries me. I'm not sure it won't just mean sending her down the slippery slope.'

Natalie dropped the little pot back into her handbag. 'The slippery slope to what?'

'Like, running on adrenaline for years and years and then suddenly stopping to find that you've been completely exhausted the whole time but you were so busy you didn't notice. Once you stop and you see it, you just can't rev up again.'

Natalie glanced at Georgia, who was looking at her phone. She turned back to Sadie. 'What does she need to rev up for? Isn't she a bit past revving up these days? When I'm seventy-eight – if I make it that far – I want to have some strapping male care worker in a tight shirt wheeling me around in my bath chair all day; I don't want to be rushing around.'

Sadie smiled slightly but shook her head. Natalie joked like that all the time but everyone knew that wasn't really what she wanted for her future; she wanted to grow old with the man of her dreams... she was just having trouble finding him right now.

'The waffle house... I don't know. Without Gampy she doesn't seem to have anything to keep going for. I'm scared that if we take the waffle house away as well then she *definitely* won't have anything to keep going for.'

Georgia raised her head. 'I see where you're coming from,' she said, locking her phone and shaking her freshly dyed violet hair free from her collar. 'And I understand why you want to help your grandma keep the place but I don't see how you can do that and continue your teacher training.'

Sadie chewed vaguely on her bottom lip for a moment. 'I'd have to get help,' she conceded finally.

'Good luck finding someone you can trust,' Natalie said.

Sadie raised her eyebrows. 'There are plenty of people I can trust.'

'Yes, but they're not all available or willing. When you say you'll get help I assume you mean free, voluntary help?'

'I could pay someone, I suppose. Not a lot, but maybe if we started to make enough money...'

'And I'm sure you'll be able to offer a huge wage,' Natalie replied with not a little sarcasm in her tone. 'Along with pension contributions, holiday pay, sick pay... It's not as simple as bunging someone a few quid every now and again, and I'm assuming you've considered all that?'

'Yes, yes...' Sadie shot back. She hadn't considered any of that but she wasn't about to admit it to Natalie, who could be so irritatingly shrewd about things that Sadie hadn't even thought of. 'But I sort of hoped that my friends and family might be able to lend a hand every now and again.'

'You know we would if we could,' Georgia said.

'Oh I know that,' Sadie replied quickly. 'It's not what I'm asking you.'

'Yes, but you know we'd do almost anything for you because we absolutely love you and your grandma to pieces. If anything, it's more of a case of how much use we'd be if we did have time to pitch in. You might find you'd be better off without our so-called help.'

'You'd be great,' Sadie said, though even she struggled to show any kind of conviction in her tone.

'We'd be terrible and you know it,' Natalie said. 'I don't know the first thing about cooking for a start. And don't forget we both have full-time jobs of our own – there wouldn't be as many hours to spare as you might imagine.'

'Anything at all would be a help,' Sadie said lamely, though she already knew her friend was absolutely right.

Natalie shook her head. 'It's not a practical solution at all, is it? Even if we could help you'd end up coming to rely on us and if something happened one day and we couldn't come you'd feel let down and resentful. It might cause bad feeling between us. And if we let you down, we'd feel guilty too and a little resentful that we were being made to feel guilty, even if you were as nice as pie about it and didn't intend that at all.'

Georgia fished a strawberry from her glass of Pimm's and popped it into her mouth. 'What's the fam said about it?'

'Nothing.'

Georgia frowned.

'I mean, I haven't exactly discussed it with them yet,' Sadie added. 'Obviously, we've discussed the future of the waffle house but I haven't exactly told them I was thinking of taking it on. I mean, I hadn't really decided if it was a good idea. In fact, I still don't know if it's a good idea, I just feel that it's the *right* idea… you know?'

'Oh,' Georgia replied, chewing. 'Don't you think you ought to before you make all these plans? What if they're not happy about any of it?'

'They probably won't be,' Sadie said. She had a fairly good idea what her family's reaction would be and that was partly why she hadn't broached the subject with them yet.

Her mobile phone pinged the arrival of a message. She looked briefly to see that it had come from Lucy, who was letting her know that she'd arrived in New York and was on her way back to her apartment, and that even though it had been in sad circumstances, it had been lovely to see her. Sadie smiled slightly and locked her phone again. She'd reply when she had more time to write something meaningful.

'If you think that,' Natalie put in, 'what does that tell you?'

'That it's probably a terrible idea – I know,' Sadie said as she pocketed her phone and rejoined the conversation, irritated again at being called out a second time. Of course Natalie and Georgia were both right but knowing it didn't help. Sadie couldn't shake the notion that no matter what she thought about it all personally, no matter what misgivings she might have about reopening the waffle house, she couldn't let it go. For all the reasons she'd stated, and for many more that even she couldn't convey or understand, she was gripped by this unshakeable conviction that reopening was the right thing to do, no matter how hard it might prove to be. If nothing else it would be something for Gammy to focus on so that she wouldn't be overwhelmed by her grief for Gampy.

'You need to discuss it with your family before you do anything else,' Natalie said.

'I will,' Sadie replied shortly. 'I wouldn't be so silly as to do anything without discussing it with them first. I just wanted to see what you both thought before I did. I mean, it's not even a firm idea yet… it's more of a daydream.'

'So, is what we both think what you expected?'

'Pretty much.' Sadie swished her lager around in the glass before taking a sip. It was cold and bitter and crisp, just the thing for a warm evening in the sunniest nook of the beer garden of the Listing Ship. Sadie didn't know what magic happened in the cellars of that pub, only that she'd never had better lager, no matter where else she went. Once she'd dreamt of running away from Sea Salt Bay as her sister Lucy had done, but more and more these days she was finding reasons to be glad she'd never had the courage to leave. Or at least the courage to leave for good, because her brief few years at university – though they'd felt like an adventure to the other side of the world – hardly counted at all when you got down to it.

'So,' Georgia said. 'Changing the subject for a minute, what's happened to Whatshisface? Why did you get rid of this one?'

Sadie couldn't help but smile. '*Jason*. Why can't anyone remember his name?'

'Because,' Natalie cut in, 'he was such a boring nonentity that we've all had to block it out of our conscious minds for fear of falling into a coma should we utter it.'

'He wasn't *that* bad.'

'He made me want to go and watch concrete set,' Natalie said.

'I'm sorry but he was pretty boring,' Georgia agreed.

'Really?' Sadie blew out a breath and glanced at each of her friends in turn.

'You must know,' Natalie said. 'You dumped him after all.'

'I didn't dump… Oh, alright; I suppose dump is as good a word as any for it, though I can't help feeling it sounds a little mean to put it that way. Anyway, it was more of a mutual separation really…'

'Instigated by you?' Natalie asked carelessly.

'Well,' Sadie replied. 'Yes. I suppose…'

'Then you dumped him. Face it, Sadie, no one is ever going to live up to—'

'Don't!' Sadie thumped her glass down, lager sloshing over the rim. 'I know what you're going to say and it doesn't help.'

'If you know what I was going to say then you'll also know that my opinion hasn't changed on the matter,' Natalie said. 'I don't know why the hell you let Declan go in the first place—'

'Nat!' Sadie cut in, a real note of warning in her voice now.

Natalie shrugged. 'Whatever. You know I'm right even though I'm not allowed to say it. The only bloke hotter than him in Sea Salt Bay is Ewan and—'

Sadie grimaced, holding up a hand to stop Natalie's flow. 'I don't want to hear that either. No girl wants to hear all the dirty thoughts their best friend might be having about their older brother.'

'Make that two best friends,' Georgia said, fishing another strawberry from her drink. 'In fact, I'm having one right now, and you *do not* want to know the details.'

'Ugh!' Sadie cried. 'You're disgusting!'

'I can't help it,' Georgia said with a wicked grin. 'I'm only human. If he wasn't your brother you'd see exactly what I mean…'

'But he is!' Sadie said, shuddering.

'Georgia's got a point,' Natalie said. 'I think I might have a filthy daydream coming on too…'

'You're both disgusting,' Sadie said, folding her arms, though she had to laugh despite herself. She pointed an accusing finger at Natalie. 'And you're a married woman!'

'Not for long,' Natalie said. 'Just as soon as my useless solicitor gets her finger out and dishes up those documents I'll be as free as the wind.'

'Well Ewan won't be so you can have your pervy thoughts about someone else,' Sadie said, trying to sound serious but not doing a very good job. She knew half the women of Sea Salt Bay would throw a party if Ewan and Kat ever split up – a few men too – but everyone also knew that it was as unlikely to happen as actual Martians landing on earth. Ewan had met Kat at a lido up the coast and, as she was about as close to a mermaid as you could get, he'd been instantly smitten. He was obsessed with the water and so was she – a match made in heaven if ever there was one. It seemed inevitable that they'd end up together and that they'd make a living from the sea they both loved so much. Sadie knew, too, that this conversation was just the usual harmless banter from her two best friends, even if sometimes they had a tendency to take it just that little bit too far for her liking.

Natalie let out a theatrical sigh. 'His endearing loyalty to Kat only makes him more attractive – you do realise that, don't you?'

Georgia nodded. 'Yes, it's absolutely no use pointing that out because it doesn't put anyone off. If I were a girl with looser morals it would make me try harder if anything.'

'Well, anyone with looser morals can forget it.' Sadie knocked back a mouthful of lager. 'Ewan and Kat are made for each other and I'd have serious issues with anyone trying to split them up – we all would.'

'Don't worry; your brother is safe,' Natalie said, grinning at Georgia. 'Just let us carry on looking and we promise not to touch.'

'I think you ought to wait until you've got rid of the current one before chasing a new one anyway, Nat,' Georgia said. 'There's only so many hours in the day after all.'

'True.' Natalie gave a solemn nod. From anyone else the comment might have been overstepping the mark, but even Natalie had to take on board the slightly critical observation with good grace. Going through her second divorce in five years hardly looked good to her, let alone anyone else. Her friends all told her she fell in love too quickly and too deeply to make sensible decisions but she'd never really taken the advice seriously until her second marriage had begun to break down after only six months. Once she'd seen it was headed, irretrievably, in only one direction, she'd been forced to take stock of her life and the way she loved and admit that they'd only been speaking a truth she'd been too close to recognise. Though she joked about it for the most part, in darker, lower moments she had admitted to Georgia and Sadie that she was determined to show more caution the next time love came knocking.

Natalie's head went up and her gaze to the gates of the beer garden. 'Aye, aye…'

Sadie turned to look. A couple were carrying a drink each and looking for a seat, the man holding a wooden spoon bearing a number for a food order. Natalie lowered her voice.

'Speak of the devil and he will appear… And he's got your nemesis with him.'

'I wish you'd stop with that,' Sadie said, her head snapping back round to face Natalie and her voice dropping. 'It really doesn't bother me as much as you seem to enjoy thinking it does. He's with Melissa now – they're together and he's happy. End of.'

'Happy?' Georgia leaned in to join Sadie and Natalie. 'That's not what we've been hearing.'

'Well—' Sadie began, but was interrupted by the man hailing them. 'How's it going?'

All three women set their faces in bright, innocent smiles as the couple walked over to their table.

'Hey, Dec,' Natalie said. 'How are you?' She looked at the woman, her blithe smile growing even wider. 'Melissa… have you lost weight? You look amazing!'

'About half a stone, that's all,' Melissa replied, beaming.

Sadie offered her most encouraging, open smile. Not because she liked Melissa – she didn't, despite the fact that Melissa had really done nothing to deserve her dislike except date Declan after Sadie had finished with him – but for Declan's sake, because she still considered him a dear friend and he seemed genuinely happy with Melissa. If she made him happy, then she couldn't be all that bad, could she? Even if Natalie and Georgia, and to some extent Sadie herself, said that there was something off about her that none of them could quite put their fingers on.

Natalie was right about the weight. Sadie couldn't deny that Melissa looked great this evening too – her dark shoulder-length hair was glossy like Natalie's but much finer and poker-straight. The weight she'd lost sharpened her already quite spectacular cheekbones, and though she favoured heavier make-up and tighter clothes than Sadie would ever dare wear, they suited her. This evening she was in a short white jersey dress that possibly nobody else in the world could pull off. Declan was his usual relaxed self, giving all three women at the table an easy smile as he rested his beer on a nearby table for a moment so he could roll up the sleeves of his denim shirt.

'I think Sea Salt Bay's amateur dramatics society are missing the three witches from their production of *Macbeth*,' he said, his smile turning into a broad and cheeky grin. 'What are you three cooking up? You look shifty as hell sitting huddled in this corner.'

'Hubble, bubble, toil and trouble,' Georgia said.

'We're actually making a voodoo doll of you and deciding what to do with it,' Natalie added sweetly.

Declan's grin spread further still. 'Make it something nice, won't you?'

'I can't think of anything nice that you might deserve,' Natalie replied airily.

'Aww, come on, there must be something.'

'Hang on… Nope.' Natalie laughed. 'Nothing.'

Declan chuckled. Then he looked at Sadie and the merriment disappeared. Sadie hated when that happened, but it happened a lot. He laughed all the time at Natalie and Georgia, but always, when it came to her, though they were friends and things were good-natured, he was more serious. He didn't use to be serious, once upon a time. Things had changed and he had become this different man with her. There was no way back and the thought made Sadie sad.

'How's your gran today?' he asked. 'I saw earlier that the waffle house is still closed. Is that it now? Have you all made up your minds?'

'It's locked up,' Sadie replied, a little confused.

'I know, but he was hoping it would be open so he could eat,' Melissa said. 'I don't know what I would have eaten if it had been open – everything your grandma serves is covered in sugar.'

'A hollow banana?' Georgia offered, and if Melissa noticed the sarcasm she didn't show it.

'Probably. I'd have had to watch Dec stuff something nice into his face while I drank water. It's hardly fair, is it?'

'Well, beauty is pain,' Natalie said, with almost the same degree of subtle mockery as Georgia. Melissa didn't appear to be concerned by this either, though to Sadie there was no mistaking it was there, and she had to stop herself from frowning at Natalie in disapproval. Natalie and Georgia were doing their friend thing, backing Sadie because they thought that Dec and Sadie ought to be together. They'd never really understood or believed that Sadie had accepted her fate and were essentially siding with Sadie in an argument that didn't really exist.

'I can't help that my job burns lots of calories,' Dec said cheerfully. 'And I keep telling you that you don't need to diet; you're perfect as you are.'

Melissa threw him a flirtatious look. 'No, I'm not,' she said, though clearly she wanted to hear more about how perfect he thought she was.

'So have you decided?' Declan asked, turning to Sadie again.

'It's not really up to me,' Sadie said.

'But what about your family? What have they said?'

'Mum thinks it ought to be sold. Ewan agrees but I don't think Dad is convinced.'

'And what about you?' he asked, and Sadie saw that serious man again, the one reserved only for her these days, the one that made her feel as if the ground was giving way beneath her. She gave her head a slight shake.

'Doesn't matter what I want.'

'Doesn't it?'

'It ought to be about what Gammy wants, if anything.'

'Hmm, you said that the other night but—'

'The other night?' Melissa cut in.

'Oh,' Declan said, seemingly oblivious to the sharpness of her tone, 'we bumped into each other when Sadie was checking up on the waffle house.'

Melissa said no more, but she suddenly looked as if someone had shoved half a lemon into her mouth.

'You've always been very fond of Sadie's grandparents, haven't you, Dec?' Natalie said with the utmost innocence, chancing a keen glance at Melissa. She seemed to be enjoying a new sport she'd just invented on the spot: Melissa-baiting. 'You were very close when you and Sadie were going out, weren't you? Like an extra grandson... They spoilt you rotten...'

'I was there often enough, that's for sure,' Declan said, continuing to be blissfully unaware of the dark shadow crossing Melissa's features. She still looked gorgeous, but more sort of evil gorgeous now. And she also looked like a woman determined to put an end to the current conversation.

'We'd better find a table,' she said, nudging him hard. 'Our food will be out in a minute and the waiter won't be able to find us.'

'I'm sure Josiah can shout up,' Declan replied. 'And he's hardly going to miss us – it's not like the place is packed.'

Nobody could deny that he had a point. Apart from the five of them, there was only one other occupied table in the garden. They looked like a family of tourists – it was usually easy enough to spot them.

'Still...' Melissa said lamely.

Georgia had run out of strawberries in her drink and had now started on the slices of cucumber. 'We were just about to drink up and leave anyway,' she said.

'I might get another actually,' Natalie decided. Sadie stared at her. They had agreed to leave after a quick round because they all had things to do. What was Natalie up to? Sadie had a feeling that she might be in the mood to cause mischief with Melissa – she was often in the mood to cause mischief with anyone unfortunate enough to be in the vicinity.

And maybe Natalie thought she was doing Sadie a favour, giving her more time to sit with Declan, but she wasn't – far from it. However, once Declan spoke again it was clear that Sadie was stuck with Natalie's unasked-for favour.

'In that case maybe we can sit with you for a while,' Declan said.

Natalie looked at Georgia. 'Shove up,' she said, before patting the bench next to her for Declan to sit.

Declan took the offered space, leaving Melissa to take the only other available one, next to Sadie at the other side of the table. While there had never been any observable animosity between the women – despite Melissa being fully aware of Sadie's past with Declan – the situation they found themselves in now was still one neither would have chosen.

'It seems like ages since I've seen the gang together,' Declan said.

'Well, we've been out and about,' Natalie said. 'So I don't know where you've been.'

'Clearly not in the Listing Ship,' Georgia said.

Declan grinned. He turned to Melissa. 'When I was at school with these three they were inseparable, always up to some mischief, but they were jammy; the teachers never managed to catch them, even though they knew.'

Melissa tried to smile and Sadie had to feel a little sorry for her. Sea Salt Bay could sometimes be the sort of place where it was hard to fit in if you hadn't been born there. It wasn't that it was unfriendly or unaccepting, but everyone who grew up there together also grew close. It was almost like the town was one big, extended family and there was a shared history so entwined that it was often hard for a newcomer to insert themselves into the fabric of it.

It had to be doubly hard for Melissa. Not only had she not grown up in the bay, but she was now dating Declan. He was a popular member of the community, as Sadie and her family were, and when Sadie and

Declan had been dating, many people in the community had openly expressed hopes that they would marry one day. They still said this, even after Sadie had broken his heart and left for university. It was no wonder really that Melissa looked so sour when Sadie was around. But then, it worked both ways because nobody wanted to see that the ex they regretted giving up every day had gone on to someone better than them. Melissa was prettier, sexier, better dressed and arguably more worldly-wise than Sadie, and nobody felt that comparison more keenly than Sadie herself. Melissa was almost thirty too, compared to Sadie's twenty-six, and so she had experience and maturity on her side to go with everything else. She was at an age when she was probably ready to settle down – which Sadie hadn't been when she and Declan were together. But it had been something he'd always talked of because he'd known from a much younger age than Sadie that family and stability were the things he craved and needed more than anything else. He'd always appreciated how good that kind of life could be, whereas Sadie, who'd already had it, had wanted nothing more than to turn her back on it and find adventure.

In fact, the one puzzling thing about Melissa and Declan was that after three years together they still weren't engaged. What were they waiting for? Who was holding who back? Nor were they living together – though, according to Declan the last time he'd chatted to Sadie, that would soon change.

'I think we've all been sort of busy,' Georgia said.

'I know how that feels,' Declan said.

'Still apologising to the trees before you chop them down?' Natalie asked.

Declan grinned again. 'You have to have a quiet word to explain yourself before you tackle the job,' he said. 'I think they understand it's for the greater good.'

'I still don't see how cutting anything down helps the forest,' Georgia said. 'I'd feel so guilty if I had to do it.'

'I don't actually cut that many down,' Declan said. 'I suppose some of the things I do for the commission do seem a bit counter-intuitive to anyone who doesn't know all the ins and outs of forest management.'

'Don't get him talking about his job,' Melissa said, 'not unless you have a month to spare so he can talk to you about what a crime it is that half of the bugs that ought to live there are becoming extinct.'

Sadie gave a small smile. When she and Declan had been together he'd been volunteering as a ranger and studying long-distance for the necessary qualifications to work in conservation. He'd often come to her house so full of excitement and passion for the subject, and for what his training would enable him to do, and she wished now that she'd taken more notice back then, offered more encouragement and praise. Instead, she'd been too wrapped up in her own plans to escape the bay and that had really been the beginning of the end for their relationship.

She tried to convince herself that this was how the universe had meant things to be, but sometimes it was hard. Like now, to see him so happy, so relaxed and content, handsome and mature. She'd had plenty of time to reflect, since her decision to come home to the bay, that she'd left a boy when she'd gone, but she'd returned to find him a man. A man, she'd been stunned to find, that she was still very much in love with. But by then it had been too late, even if she could have swallowed her pride for long enough to admit she'd been wrong to let him go – and that was one thing she'd been unable to do.

'Sorry,' he said, looking adorably sheepish. 'Melissa might have a point there; I know I must bore her to tears most nights going on about work.'

'It's nice to do something you feel passionate about,' Sadie said tightly, suddenly feeling the overwhelming urge to defend him.

'Like you?' he asked.

'Well, yes…' Sadie replied, though instantly she found herself on uncertain ground again. Hadn't she just been mooting the possibility of giving up teaching? The profession she'd been training so hard for and given up so much to pursue didn't seem so appealing these days and it made her feel sad to acknowledge it.

'I wouldn't know,' Georgia said. 'The discount store wasn't exactly where I saw myself when I left school full of bright hopes.'

'At least you had the bright hopes,' Natalie said. 'And you worked your way up to manager so it's not all bad. I just wanted to earn money as soon as I could and I didn't care how – well, within reason, of course.'

'But you did alright in the end too,' Declan said.

'I suppose, if it's your sort of thing,' Natalie said.

Melissa looked at her. 'What do you do?'

'Housing officer. It could be worse; at least the area I work in is nice. I'd hate to do it in a big city. It still means commuting out from the bay every day and I wish I didn't have to do that.'

'That's the thing about the bay,' Sadie said. 'There's not a lot work-wise here if you don't want to sell buckets and spades or work in the chip shop.' She looked at Declan with an apologetic grimace. 'No offence,' she said.

He smiled. 'Don't worry; I know you didn't mean anything by it. My dad loves the chip shop but it wasn't for me either, even though he was disappointed when he realised that I had no intention of taking over when he retires.'

'I'm glad you won't be taking it over,' Melissa said. 'I don't think I could cope with you smelling of fish and chip fat all the time.'

'All I meant was,' Sadie said, not dignifying Melissa's comment with a response and preventing anyone else from doing so either, 'it was inevitable that most of us would end up working away from the bay.'

'Your family does alright.' Natalie turned to Sadie. 'I guess it shows that if you use your imagination the work is there. Perhaps we're all just not very imaginative.'

'They do more than alright,' Declan agreed.

'It *is* hard to find work here,' Melissa said. 'When my parents bought the amusement arcade on the pier and moved here I thought it would be fun to move here too and live by the sea in a lovely little town. If I'd known I'd end up having to work for them dishing out bowls of coins all day I might have thought twice about it.'

'But then you wouldn't have met me,' Declan said, turning to her with a soppy grin.

Sadie studied them as they looked at each other. Much as Sadie liked Melissa's parents, and as kind and neighbourly as they'd been to Kenneth and April since they'd taken over the amusement arcade not far from the waffle house, Sadie couldn't help but share at least that wish with Melissa. If Melissa had never moved to Sea Salt Bay with her parents, what would that have meant for her and Declan? And why was Sadie even thinking about any of this at all? More to the point, why did it sting so much more today, at this moment, than it usually did? Was it because the rest of Sadie's life seemed so uncertain right now? Was it because she was beginning to wonder if she'd thrown what she'd had with Declan away for nothing if she gave up her teaching course and came back to work in Sea Salt Bay? It certainly felt like that, and yet, she was still torn over the decision.

'Anyway, Sadie might yet end up taking over at the waffle house,' Georgia said airily.

Sadie stared at her, but Georgia didn't seem to realise she was being stared at. That hadn't been a discussion for sharing and Sadie had by no means decided. She looked to see both Melissa and Declan regarding her keenly, though she suspected that they both had very different reasons for that.

Declan nodded slowly. 'I think it's a brilliant idea. Everyone in the bay would miss that old place if it closed down.'

'You have the ice-cream parlour,' Melissa said. 'And what about your dad's restaurant?'

Declan turned to her. 'It's hardly the same. The waffle house has been there forever. I just can't imagine this town without it. Anyway, I don't think fish and chips are any substitute for pancakes and waffles.'

'I certainly put most of my puppy fat on in there,' Natalie said.

'It was lovely,' Georgia agreed. 'Your grandma loved to spoil us rotten, didn't she? Every day after school we'd call in – remember, Sadie? I used to go home full of whatever yummy thing April had cooked for us and not wanting what my mum had cooked. I didn't dare tell her why I couldn't eat her food and in the end she was convinced I had an eating disorder. When she found out what was really going on, that was the first time I saw someone in the bay get angry with April, but even my mum couldn't stay angry for long because who can? April is just so lovely and sweet it'd be like shouting at a puppy.'

Declan and Natalie laughed, but Melissa simply aimed an uncertain smile at Sadie. Georgia's recollection of their schooldays was probably just the sort of shared childhood memory, growing up as they all did in the bay, that she must have felt put her at a disadvantage. She must have felt there was a part of Declan's life that she could never know. It happened to many couples, of course, but in this case, the only woman that she might perceive to be a threat – Sadie – did know that. In fact, she'd been a huge part of it. Once again, Sadie found herself feeling a bit sorry for Melissa, though it did nothing to allay the weird, intensified sense of rivalry she was suddenly gripped by.

'Well…' Sadie looked at everyone in turn, 'as I've said about twenty times now, I haven't made up my mind what I'm going to do.'

Her gaze flicked back to Declan, though she dared not let it rest there too long. She might say she hadn't made up her mind, but maybe, at some point during the last ten minutes, she had after all.

Chapter Five

Sadie adjusted her face mask. If there was one person whose opinion she trusted more than her friends', even more than that of her parents or Ewan, it was Kat's. Technically, of course, Kat was family, but it wasn't quite the same. In fact, it was strange how her sister-in-law had very quickly become a confidante to a younger Sadie when she'd first started seeing Ewan, and these days, with Sadie's sister Lucy mostly absent, Kat had taken the role of honorary sister/auntie/best friend. She was level-headed and saw emotionally charged situations with more clarity than other family members, and thus was able to offer thoughts (especially on family situations) that were much more balanced and trustworthy. Perhaps because she had a different relationship with them all, or perhaps just because that was the sort of person she was, Sadie didn't know; she was only glad that she had someone like that in her life.

They were perched on the rocks now like black-clad mermaids, the afternoon sun mid-sky and warming their shoulders as they prepared to snorkel together. Sadie could scuba, as Kat could, but she preferred the freedom of snorkelling as opposed to dealing with the weight of extra equipment and – frankly – the stress of diving with air tanks. Snorkelling was their bonding thing; it had been from very early on. Kat had taught Sadie how to do it – Sadie's parents weren't interested in diving, preferring to see the sea from the surface, and Ewan was so critical of Sadie's technique that they'd always end up bickering. But with Kat, Sadie could just relax and enjoy it, and it gave her space to open up because them diving together was often an excuse for an hour alone to catch up.

This afternoon, Freddie and Freya were with Ewan, further up the beach looking for sea life in rock pools, which had allowed Sadie and Kat to steal away for a little privacy.

'It seems like ages since we've done this.' Sadie's wetsuit-clad legs dangled into the sea. She kicked out, sending a spray of water up from the surface that glowed like crystals in the sun. The weather had been calm over the last couple of days and so the sediment that sometimes got stirred up from the sea bed to dirty the colour was firmly settled where it belonged, making the depths a glorious turquoise. On a day like today, if you squinted and looked around – ignoring the very British pier and shops lining the shore – you could almost imagine you were on some Greek island. Today would be a very good day to see so many things below the waves, and no matter how often Sadie saw swooshing rays or forests of vibrant blue snakelocks anemone and seaweed in dazzling shades of green, darting fish or tiny crabs scurrying along the ocean bed – even the odd sea horse – she never tired of it. Every dive was a new adventure as thrilling as the one before, and even on those occasions when she saw hardly a single creature, just the act of swimming in the sea itself left her feeling as relaxed and content as any bottle of wine or yoga session.

'It has been,' Kat said. 'I don't think we've been out together since last year.'

Sadie raised her eyebrows. 'It's been that long?'

'Honestly,' Kat said. 'Think about it – we haven't been out yet this summer and you won't go in the winter.'

'Nobody in their right mind would come out to snorkel in the winter,' Sadie said.

Kat laughed. 'No, but I do, so what does that say about me? Besides, get the equipment right and it's fine.'

'That's because you're a diving addict.'

'That's what comes of marrying your brother. You know what they say – if you can't beat them join them. I have missed swimming with you though,' Kat added, winding her hair into a neat coil which she fastened with a ponytail band.

Kat was almost forty, just like Ewan, but she could have passed for something much closer to Sadie's age. She was trim and petite, her arms and legs toned and smooth from the amount of swimming she did, and despite her tiny frame, she was incredibly strong. She lowered herself into the sea now with barely a ripple to trouble the surface, cutting through like a dart as she pushed herself away from the rocks.

'Oh, it's not cold at all, is it?' Sadie called, half laughing, half gasping as she followed Kat into the sea. The sun might have been shining, but the water temperature was still a little on the cool side as the waves lapped at the exposed skin of her face.

'See, you've gone soft,' Kat shouted back. 'That's what comes of being lazy.'

'I'm not lazy – I've just had a lot of other things on my mind.'

'I bet they weren't as much fun as this, though.'

Sadie struck out to catch up with Kat, who was now bobbing in the water, waiting for her, savouring the taste of salt on her lips. She'd missed days like this – she just hadn't realised how much until now.

'Ready?' Kat asked.

Sadie nodded, and as one they dipped their faces into the water. Sadie let herself become weightless and felt her body rise to float on the surface. With her hands tight over her chest, she began to kick and move through the water. The sun had been playing peek-a-boo with the clouds all morning, so although Sadie and Kat were swimming in fairly shallow water and the sediment was nicely settled, it was still a little murky when the sun dulled. Aside from the relaxation of the swim, there might not be anything really to see. But as they continued to move along a path that Kat knew well, one safe from currents and riptides, they were rewarded with bars of rippling light, illuminating the sea bed as the sun broke through the clouds again. Sadie glanced to her right to see Kat gliding beside her, and an old peace and contentment she hadn't felt in a long time stole over her. She'd come today mainly to seek Kat's counsel, but this wonderful peace wasn't a bad bonus.

They swam for a while, eyes picking out crabs and anemones and brilliant slivers of darting silver and blue fish, mounds of purple algae caressing the rocks. Sadie lost herself in the tranquillity of a world so different from her own, marvelling – as she always did – at every little sight. She forgot that she could feel the chill of the water even through her wetsuit, and that her hands were wrinkling, and that her leg muscles were beginning to tire. She could have stayed here in this magical watery kingdom until the sun went down.

But then she felt something prod her and looked to see that Kat was gesturing to the surface. Kat's head went up, so that Sadie could see only her legs kicking out as she trod water.

Fired by a sudden rush of mischief, Sadie submerged herself fully and tugged at Kat's legs playfully, as if to pull her under again. Then she saw Kat come back down below and they began a silly tug of war with each other, trying to pull each other further down. After a few seconds, Sadie let go so they could go up for air. She watched Kat shoot up and quickly followed herself, grinning, happier than she'd been in months as her head broke through and she filled her lungs again. She turned to Kat, but the grin died as she focused on her sister-in-law's face and saw only shock and panic.

'Sadie – look out!'

Sadie whipped around, but everything happened swiftly while she could only react slowly – far too slowly. The bow of the boat loomed, not speeding towards her but moving with an inevitable steadiness. There was no way she could escape the collision that she realised – with horror – would come. It wasn't huge, she thought quickly – it was more of a rowing boat really. Perhaps it would be OK.

But even as those vague, half-formed observations raced through her mind, it struck her a glancing blow to the side of her head, enough to send her beneath the waves, lights popping and vision failing. Sadie's limbs were suddenly heavy, uncontrollable; her lungs empty of precious air as she drifted downwards into the depths.

Chapter Six

Sadie opened her eyes to the worst headache she'd ever had and a circle of faces framed by the sky above her.

'Ow,' she said, and never had an exclamation felt less appropriate for the gravity of the situation. She could see by the faces surrounding her that something very bad had just happened, even if it had all taken place so fast that she couldn't remember much of it.

'You always did have a way with words,' Ewan said, the sharp edges of his frown softening a little.

Sadie tried to acknowledge him with a smile but it wouldn't come.

'Jesus, Sadie, you nearly frightened me to death. I thought…'

Kat's sentence tailed off. Sadie didn't know how it would have ended and perhaps it was better that way. Next to Ewan, Freddie and Freya looked down at her too, something more like awe on their young faces.

Sadie tried to engage her trembling limbs and pushed herself to sit, sand gathering under her nails as she dug for traction. It was a shock to feel so weak, and for the world to start spinning as it did.

'Steady,' her brother said. 'Take it easy. How do you feel?'

'Like I've been hit by a boat,' Sadie said.

'All those clients for all those years,' Kat said. 'And I've never had to save a single one of them from drowning, not ever. An afternoon out with my sister-in-law and… honestly… You're just lucky I could remember my training.'

'I am,' Sadie said, though she realised that it was Kat's shock talking. She updated her training on a regular basis and she and Ewan ran practice lifesaving drills all the time – there was no way she wouldn't have been able to rescue Sadie despite what she'd said. 'I'd like to say I'll return the favour one day but I don't expect I'd be able to.'

Ewan turned to his wife, dreamy and lustful for a moment. 'You're brilliant,' he said in a husky voice. 'Just bloody amazing.'

Sadie felt queasy, and this time it wasn't from the bump on her head, or the amount of saltwater she'd swallowed.

'Get a room, would you?'

Ewan turned to her now and started to laugh, while Kat blushed. At least their kids seemed oblivious to the whole thing, still fixated on Sadie's situation.

'I think that tells us everything we need to know,' Ewan said. 'She's alright – no serious damage. And if there was it might be an improvement anyway. At least she might not be such a sarcastic little mare.'

'Watch it,' Sadie fired back. 'I may be incapacitated now but I'm sure I'll recover enough to kick your backside later.'

With Ewan still chuckling, a note of huge relief in it, Sadie looked down the beach. A small, shallow-bottomed boat rested on the shingle at the water's edge. Close by she saw Andy Travers – one of Sea Salt Bay's volunteer lifeguards – talking earnestly to a man she'd never seen before. She'd have put him in his early to mid-thirties. He was dark-haired, tall, toned and tanned. It was hard, even in her current state, to ignore that there was a certain pleasing symmetry in his looks.

'There's the dickhead who nearly killed you.'

Sadie turned back to Ewan. His tone was far more serious and menacing now than the one he'd just been teasing Sadie with. He glared in the direction of the man, jaw twitching. If Sadie hadn't known him better she would have sworn he was about to run over with his fists flying – he looked as if he was desperate for a good punch-up.

'Mummy... did Daddy just say—'

'Yes, Freddie,' Kat said, frowning at Ewan, who continued to glare at the man. 'But he didn't mean to; he's just very upset.'

'Sometimes I feel upset—' Freddie continued, but Kat cut him off.

'I expect you do,' she said. 'But you still shouldn't say it. If someone almost dies, right in front of you, that's the only time I'll allow you to say it. Got it?'

Freddie looked disappointed but he didn't argue. Instead he glanced at Sadie with that strangely inappropriate look of awe again. She supposed what had happened probably seemed rather dramatic and adventurous to him. He watched movies all the time, tales of derring-do and heroism where the protagonists had regular brushes with death, and it always looked glamorous and cool. She could have set him straight – that being hit by a boat and almost drowning left you feeling sick and a little bit stupid, rather than heroic – but she didn't have the heart (or the stomach or concentration span) right now.

Sadie's gaze went back to the man talking to Andy. Or rather, being given a firm telling-off by Andy.

'I don't think he's a local, is he?'

'Probably not,' Kat agreed. 'I certainly haven't seen him around here before.'

'When Andy's finished I'm going to have a word myself,' Ewan growled.

'Don't,' Kat said. 'If it's anyone's, this whole thing is my fault. I didn't leave a marker buoy to warn people where we were—'

'You've never had to in that stretch of the sea before,' Ewan began to argue, but Kat put up a hand to stop him.

'And I should have kept my wits about me. If I'd been out with paying customers I would have, but because it was Sadie I relaxed my guard and I shouldn't have. By the time I realised he was there and which direction he was heading in it was too late.' She shook her head. 'Poor fella. He was properly shaken up – very upset about what had happened.' She looked at Sadie. 'He said he hadn't seen either of us.'

'Should have been looking then, shouldn't he?' Ewan said through gritted teeth.

'Good thing it was a tiny boat,' Sadie said.

'It was still big enough to cause damage, and he has a responsibility to keep not only himself safe but others. He's probably one of these idiots who's never taken a boat out in his life and thinks all you do is hop in and float away.'

'And he couldn't have hit me head-on,' Sadie continued, ignoring her brother's tirade. 'It would have done a lot more damage if he had.'

'I think he did enough,' Ewan said.

Sadie looked along the beach again. 'What's he doing with Andy – they've been ages.'

'If I know Andy, he's giving him a good ticking-off and a few pointers about safety at sea.'

'Hmm. I feel kind of bad for him now.'

Kat looked at Sadie with a vague frown. 'Why should you feel bad?'

'Like you said, he couldn't help that we just popped up out of nowhere. And Andy's safety lectures…' She gave a theatrical shudder that made Kat laugh lightly, despite the gravity of the situation. 'I wouldn't wish one of those on anyone.'

'Perhaps he might know what he's doing for next time,' Ewan cut in. 'People ought to get proper training; not just go on holiday and suddenly decide they're expert mariners and take to the sea. I'd like to know where the boat came from – whether it's his or he hired it. If he hired it I might well have to have a word with the company that let him take it out.'

'I'm alright though, Ewan – no harm done.'

Ewan turned a critical eye on his sister. 'Hardly,' he said. 'You wouldn't say that if you could see you from where I'm standing.'

Sadie raised her eyebrows. 'That bad?'

'You've looked better,' Kat agreed. 'Sorry, but there it is.'

'Well…' Sadie shrugged. 'I did say I fancied a dip. This isn't quite what I had in mind though. And ow again!' she added as an extra-large throb reminded her of the sizeable bruise on her head. Her headache wasn't helped by the sudden wail of a siren, distant at first, but rapidly getting louder as it drew closer. Sadie looked at Ewan and Kat in turn. 'Please tell me that's not for me.'

'Of course it is,' Ewan said testily. 'What else were we meant to do?'

'You could have waited!'

'For what? For you to die? "Oh, Kat, she's dead now, do you think we ought to call the ambulance after all?"'

'Just until you'd checked if I was really injured.'

'You *are* really injured!'

'A lot.'

'You don't call being unconscious when you're hauled out of the sea injured? Sadie, we had to do CPR on you. If you don't think that's serious enough to call for an ambulance then please, whatever you do, never volunteer your services to Andy because you won't save many people like that.'

Sadie let out a sigh. She had to concede that Ewan might have a point, though she just couldn't see why he was so angry and upset. Perhaps it was a case of delayed shock, but she felt curiously unconcerned by what he'd told her. Maybe it would sink in later but, right now, she just felt her brother was overreacting. Then again, she had to admit that her head hurt a lot. If nothing else, she supposed she ought to get some advice about concussion. And who knew, maybe one of the ambulance crew would be an attractive man she could flirt with?

But then even those hopes were dashed when she looked at where the vehicle had parked on the promenade and saw two women getting out. Not having noticed Sadie sitting on the sand some feet away, they walked towards Andy and the man who'd caused all this fuss. After a brief exchange, Sadie saw Andy point in her direction and the paramedics strode over, Ewan stepping forward to greet them tersely.

'So, who do we need to look at?' one of the women said, giving Sadie a quick glance. She'd have thought it was self-evident, but apparently they had to ask. She stuck a sheepish hand up.

'I'm the idiot.'

'My sister had an argument with a rowing boat out on the sea,' Ewan said. 'The boat won.'

'It's only a little bump to the head,' Sadie said. 'I'm sure it's nothing,' she added, even as she felt gingerly for the bump on her head and realised that she'd probably eaten smaller boiled eggs.

After a few checks the paramedics gave Sadie a leaflet on what to look for post-head injury and when to go to hospital or call another ambulance and left. By the time they'd packed and gone, quite a little crowd had gathered. They stared at Sadie and she just wished they'd stop because it was starting to freak her out more than the actual accident had. Most were people she didn't recognise, because the beach would have been heaving with tourists and day trippers, and she hadn't really thought about that until they'd closed in on her. Andy the lifeguard had gone back to his station, and the man who'd been piloting the boat was pacing up and down the sand a few yards away, talking on his phone. But when he saw that the ambulance crew was done with Sadie, he quickly ended the call and jogged over.

'God, I can't tell you how sorry I am for all this,' he said earnestly. He bent down to Sadie. 'Are you alright?'

'Apparently I'll survive,' she said.

'No thanks to you,' Ewan cut in. Kat laid a warning hand on his arm but he shook it off.

'I know that,' the man said. 'I can only apologise. I didn't see you, I swear, I couldn't… didn't know how to stop the boat and I couldn't make it turn in time… I feel just terrible.'

'Not as terrible as my sister feels right now.' Ewan seemed to grow taller and broader and more menacing right in front of Sadie's eyes as he faced the stranger. 'You nearly killed her! Do you understand?'

'It's fine,' Sadie insisted. 'Kat was there and I was always going to be in good hands. I don't want a fuss – there's no real harm done.'

'There's plenty of harm done,' Ewan said. 'People like this' – he shoved a finger at the man – 'need to understand that stupid actions have consequences.'

'Please, Ewan,' Kat said gently. 'Sadie has said she doesn't want a fuss and this is hardly helping her.'

The man looked between Ewan and Sadie. 'What can I do to make it up to you?'

'Stay away from boats for a start,' Ewan cut in.

'Ignore him,' Sadie said. 'Accidents happen. I should have had my wits about me too. You couldn't have known I'd pop up there when I did.'

'I have to say, you're taking it better than I would,' the man said with a wan smile.

Sadie tried to offer him one in return but her head hurt too much and the best she could manage was to look vaguely non-threatening. There was the briefest fraction of a second where their eyes met.

You have nice eyes, Sadie found herself thinking. *They sort of crease into little half-moons when you smile. I bet when you smile properly it's gorgeous…*

She pushed away the thought. One thing she'd always vowed was that she'd never get involved with a tourist – which he clearly was. Chances were they'd have their fun and you'd never see them again; and even if you did, long-distance relationships were so much harder to keep alive. And now she had a new rule: don't get involved with tourists who try to run you down in their boat, even if they do have lovely eyes the colour of the sea on a cloudy day that crinkle into little half-moons when they smile.

'Like I said,' she replied, 'no real harm done.'

'I wish I could believe you mean that,' he said.

'I do,' Sadie said with a lot more enthusiasm than she felt. What she really wanted right now was to get away from the scrutiny of a curious crowd and head home, have a shower and a long lie-down and forget all this happened.

The man turned to Ewan. He offered a hand to shake but Ewan simply stared at it, and then up at his face with a look that was so full of aggression that Sadie hardly recognised her usually easy-going and charming brother at all. The man let his hand drop to his side again.

'Look, I really can't express how sorry I am. I feel absolutely terrible about this. If you wanted to take things further then I'd completely understand—'

'We don't,' Sadie said firmly. She looked at Ewan, daring him to argue. He might have looked scary to everyone else right now, but he wasn't intimidating Sadie. 'Do we?'

'If it was left up to me—'

'But it's not,' Sadie cut in. 'It's up to me and I'd rather let it drop. It was an accident and I'm fine; there's no point in ruining' – she glanced at the man – 'this man's holiday over it.'

Sadie glared at her brother but he didn't even flinch. Deciding that she was going to have serious words with him later, she abandoned the argument for now. When Ewan was in this kind of mood – it wasn't often but he did have his moments – there was no point and, at the end of the day, she at least recognised that he was just looking out for his little sister.

Instead, she turned back to the man, about to say something else when she heard her name frantically being called. She glanced around to see her mum and dad racing up the beach towards them and then gave a weary look at Ewan and Kat.

'Who told them?'

'I did,' Kat said. 'Sorry.'

Sadie held in a groan. 'Now they're going to make it all twenty times worse. And I bet they've cancelled a boatload of customers to come.'

'It's not Kat's fault,' Ewan snapped. 'What else was she meant to do? I don't think you're fully appreciating how bad things looked to us. We didn't call the ambulance and Mum and Dad for fun – we actually thought you were seriously injured. Stop complaining and be glad that we care!'

Any further complaint withered on Sadie's lips. She understood all the reasons why they'd done what they'd done and, of course, was grateful that they cared so deeply for her but she hated all the fuss and attention.

'Sorry.'

'I can't help but feel I'm still continuing to cause you all a lot of problems,' the man said. 'I can only say sorry again. I'll go and meet with your parents – explain and apologise to them.'

Sadie was twenty-six years old, and she hardly needed anyone explaining anything to her parents when she could manage the job perfectly well herself. She was just about to say something along those lines to him, only with more tact and politeness, when Ewan cut across her.

'Don't you think you've done enough for one day?' He folded his arms tight across his chest and Sadie noticed Kat stiffen again. Sadie had never seen her brother throw a punch in anger but she wondered whether she was about to because he looked like he really wanted to have a go at this poor guy, who might have messed up in a huge way but was doing his best to make it right.

'Right…' The man took a business card from his wallet and offered it to Ewan. Sadie was pleased to see that although he looked deeply sorry for the accident, he didn't look intimidated by an obviously fuming Ewan. His expression was open and frank as Ewan took the card. 'I can see that my presence is a bit, well… I'm probably not the most popular man in town right now. My number is on there if you need me for anything.' He looked at Sadie again. 'Anything at all; just call me and I'll be glad to do what I can.'

Ewan gave a grim nod, gripping the card so tightly Sadie felt the urge to jump up and take it from him before he creased the information on there out of recognition. She realised she would do well to resist the urge though, because Ewan had gone into overprotective big brother mode and when he was like this it was better to let him get it out of his system in his own time. In a few hours he'd be back to his old amenable, affable self, full of banter and teasing at every opportunity. Although, sometimes Sadie wondered whether that wasn't just as bad...

She found her gaze drawn to the card in her brother's hand again. Everything that she wanted to know about the man she should have hated but instead found herself intrigued by was tantalisingly close. Nothing or nobody was prising it from Ewan's grip right now, but maybe later, when things had calmed down, she might be able to get it from him.

'I'm glad you're OK,' the man said, looking at Sadie again. 'I really am so sorry for everything.'

Sadie didn't get to reply, didn't get to hear any more exchanges between the stranger and her family, and she didn't even get to see him leave, because in the next moment she was smothered by a distraught Henny. Then Graham joined in, and by the time they'd finished fussing and checking her over with more than a little disbelief at her insistence that she was alright the man had gone, and the little boat that had caused so much trouble had gone with him.

Chapter Seven

Monday morning found Sadie back at Featherbrook School. Mondays seemed to come around so quickly – too quickly these days, especially when she was due to be in school. She'd always imagined that the work experience bits of her teacher training would be the best bits, but she was quickly beginning to view each approaching day in the classroom with dread. She'd discovered that she wasn't good at discipline, easily fooled by the kids, not tough enough and that, really, she wanted nothing more than to be a friend to them all. But teachers couldn't be friends as well – that's what her university mentor kept telling her – but Sadie, despite this advice, had been determined to try it her way regardless. It turned out that her mentor had given her sound advice after all, and the lax start Sadie had got off to with the class had done her no favours. What was worse, the kids she'd tried so hard to befriend didn't see her as a friend at all – they saw her as a pushover and once they'd spied the chink in her armour they'd continued to prise it apart, determined to make it crack wide open. Sadie had despaired, tried to backtrack and reintroduce the discipline she should have begun with, but it was too late – the damage had been done.

It wasn't all of the class, of course, but the few more than made up for the diligence of the many. Sadie had known this Monday was going to be the worst one yet when she'd arrived at school to hear that the qualified teacher who was usually in class with her had been involved in a minor car crash and was currently sitting in accident and emergency at the hospital with severe whiplash. So, at the behest of an overworked and desperate head teacher, Sadie found herself, not for the first time, managing the class alone.

The head had promised to try to find someone who could spare time to come and support her, but Sadie had realised that not a lot of effort was being made in this quest. She'd seen three teaching assistants in the staffroom where she'd stored her belongings before school began who'd informed her as they sat and sipped coffee that they were all busy doing other very important things and couldn't come and help her unless the head gave them explicit instructions to drop those other things. When Sadie enquired what other things they were, the list included updating the noticeboard and weighing out cake ingredients for a cookery lesson later in the day. Hardly pressing, Sadie thought, though she knew better than to say so. The last thing she wanted was to turn the teaching assistants against her as well as the kids. As for explicit instructions from the head to help Sadie instead, nobody had been given any yet, and, as the clock counted the minutes towards the start of the first lesson, it looked unlikely that it was ever going to happen.

The noise level was deafening as Sadie walked into the classroom and barely a child was sitting at their own desk ready to start work. As she waited expectantly for them to notice she was there and for the pandemonium to die down, not one person so much as looked her way. She cleared her throat.

Still nothing.

'Good morning!' she called.

The noise levels seemed only to increase, and none of it included a 'Good morning' in return.

'Class!' Sadie yelled.

A few pupils now looked her way. One or two even returned to their own seats voluntarily. But most of them simply went back to what they'd been doing before she'd walked in.

'Seats! Now!' Sadie roared.

She looked around the class, almost surprised herself at the assertiveness that had come from nowhere. Maybe she could do this after all. Maybe it had only taken a crisis to show that she *did* have the mettle to teach. There were many other expressions of genuine surprise in the room too, and perhaps they'd all suddenly realised that they'd got Sadie wrong. The noise stopped dead and everyone took their places to start the lesson.

So, all she'd needed was some backbone and a loud voice. It was just a shame, Sadie reflected ruefully, that it had taken a minor car crash and whiplash to make it happen.

'I think we were looking at Hitler's rise to power last week, weren't we?' she asked the class.

'No!' someone shouted from the back.

'That was a rhetorical question,' Sadie said. 'I know we were looking at Hitler's rise to power last week because I was here teaching it.'

'Why did you ask then?'

Sadie ignored the jibe. They were still trying, but they weren't going to get the better of her, not this time. 'Turn to page eighty-five in your textbooks.'

'We don't have textbooks, Miss,' a girl said. Sadie looked at her.

'Why not? The school provides them. Where are they?'

'In the cupboard, Miss.'

'And you can't go and get them because…?'

Sadie instantly realised her mistake, but it was too late to do anything about it. The room was filled with the sounds of chairs scraping the floor and a stampede to the cupboard, accompanied by jostling, banter, threats and bickering – all interspersed with a healthy serving of swearwords. She should have instructed the girl who'd pointed out their lack of books to go and get them all from the cupboard to hand out but she hadn't been quick enough. Now, she was faced with yet more chaos.

'Quickly now!' she called, feeling the control she'd had only moments ago slipping away again. 'No messing; get your books back to your desk and open to page eighty-five or we won't have time to do anything!'

There was a barely perceptible pause as that statement seemed to collectively sink in, and in that nanosecond Sadie realised she'd made another fatal error. If there was one win-win result for the kids in that room, it was to run out of time to read about Hitler's rise to power. And as she'd feared, her words only meant it now took twice as long for everyone to return to their seats and look remotely ready to learn. If having your head on your desk, or gazing out of the window, or sniggering behind your hands with the occupant of the neighbouring desk counted as being ready to learn, that is.

There was the briefest silence, a lull into false security during which Sadie readied herself to begin the lesson proper, and then a hand shot up.

'Yes?' Sadie looked at the boy.

'Can I go to the toilet, Miss?'

His request was followed by stifled giggles on the row of desks behind him. It was a red flag to Sadie.

'Couldn't you have gone before class began?'

'I did, Miss. I've got a condition.'

More muffled laughter from the desks behind followed, this time a little louder and more brazen.

Sadie shook her head slightly. 'What?'

'A condition, Miss. I can't control it. When I've got to go I've got to go, you know? Otherwise...' He began an elaborate mime that Sadie really didn't want or need to see.

'Yes, yes...' she snapped. She just wanted to get the lesson started. In all honesty, it would have been far easier and more painless to let them all mess around for the next hour, but she would have to evaluate this session later with her mentor and she could hardly do that if she hadn't actually taught anything. Besides, she wouldn't have put it past one of them to tell the proper teacher about it on her return, which wouldn't go down well. Then there was the added disadvantage that if Sadie ever had to take this class alone again they really wouldn't take her seriously. Not that they were doing anything of the sort now.

'If it's really that urgent,' she continued, biting back a reply that also expressed extreme doubt about any 'condition' because then she'd be leaving herself wide open to accusations of bullying and discrimination, 'then you'd better go, but be quick about it.'

The boy slid from his seat and slouched out with a look that Sadie just knew meant she'd been played. But what could she do about it? If she'd lost this one little battle maybe it was better to let it go and focus her energy on winning the war. Or, at least, a few minor skirmishes, which was probably the best she could hope for with class 3G.

Once the door had slammed behind him, she turned to the rest of the class. 'Right,' she said, 'page eighty-five.'

'Aren't we going to wait for him, Miss?' the same girl who'd began the book-cupboard debacle asked. Sadie was beginning to think little-Miss-goody-two-shoes ought to shut her mouth for once.

'I'm sure he'll catch up quickly enough once he's back.'

Another voice piped up. 'Bobby's gone home, Miss.'

Sadie looked sharply at her. 'What?'

'He hasn't gone to the toilet. He's gone home – he said he was going to because he didn't want to read about Hitler.'

'He didn't take his bag.'

'Didn't bring a bag either,' the girl said.

Sadie hesitated. 'He won't be able to get off the grounds without being seen,' she said in a tone full of confidence that she didn't feel. 'Someone will spot him and he'll be marched straight back here with a detention for his trouble.'

At least I hope so, she thought, but either way she was now in the shit too for letting it happen on her watch. The only saving grace in this situation was that things would be a lot worse if Bobby did manage to escape the school grounds, so she had to hope that she was right about his chances.

'He's done it before,' the girl said. 'Nobody sees him go. He does it all the time.'

There was a murmur of agreement.

'What?' Sadie stared at the class. 'Just asks for the toilet and goes off expecting nobody to go looking for him?'

'Oh, no, it's only you he's used the toilet excuse on. Usually he just sneaks out.'

Sadie slammed her own copy of the history textbook closed and slapped it onto the desk. She bolted out of the room and into the corridor. It was deserted, though she'd hardly expected anything else, because the rest of the school were in lessons, where they ought to be. She marched towards the boys' toilets. She hardly expected to find the missing Bobby in there either, given what she'd been told, but she didn't know what else to do. After a brief hesitation, she knocked on the door.

'Bobby!' she called, as loudly as she dared. She needed him to hear her if by some miracle he was in there, but she didn't want to alert the whole school to the situation. 'Bobby… are you in there? Come back to class right now!'

When she was greeted by depressing but fully expected silence, she turned to go back to class, and saw that almost every member of 3G had now gathered round the open door watching her with some amusement. She had to admit ruefully this was probably the best entertainment they were going to get this week – maybe even this year.

'Want me to go in, Miss?' a boy asked.

Sadie was silent for a moment. She didn't want to lose another but if he was only going into the toilets to check them out, what harm could it do?

'Yes, please…'

'Tristan.'

'Yes, thank you Tristan.' Sadie looked at the others. 'The rest of you can go back to your desks.'

Nobody moved but when Sadie marched towards them with her fiercest glare they shuffled as slowly as they could get away with back into the classroom. She couldn't have them all gathered out there, drawing unwanted attention to the situation. She closed the door of the room and went back to her desk.

'Right.' She took up the textbook again and flicked to the right page. 'We're going to talk about Hitler today if it kills me.'

And it probably will…

'Miss!'

Little-Miss-the-books-are-in-the-cupboard had her hand up again. Sadie let out a long sigh. 'Yes?'

'Miss, Tristan's gone home too.'

'What?'

'He said he was going to do it when you went out to look for Bobby.'

'And nobody thought to tell me!' Sadie cried.

At this, some of the class at least had the decency to look a little sheepish.

'This is ridiculous!' By now Sadie's voice was so strangled she was certain it would never go back to normal again. Her first instinct was to go and see if Tristan really had disappeared from the toilets and made a bid for freedom, but she was afraid that she might return to find her entire class had disappeared.

'Want me to go and see if he's in the bogs?' Another boy leapt out of his seat.

'No!' Sadie shouted. 'Don't you dare! Nobody else leaves this room, not even if the four horsemen of the apocalypse come riding through with ice cream for all! Understand?'

'Who?' someone asked.

Sadie shook her head, fighting to regain some semblance of calm. 'Never mind. Turn to page eighty-five and read through the first four paragraphs. When you're done we'll talk about them.'

For the first time that day, the room was silent as heads went down to books. But Sadie didn't see much actual reading going on. There was a lot of doodling, note passing, eraser destroying, boob inspection and gum chewing. By this point she was past caring. They could be constructing a long-range cruise missile and she wouldn't have given a fig. The main thing was it was quiet so that if the head came past on one of her random corridor inspections (and where had she been when two of her pupils had escaped?) she'd at least give the illusion of having everything under control.

Sadie rested her head in her hands and closed her eyes for a moment. Before the accident with the boat out at sea with Kat, Sadie had wanted to discuss the waffle house with her. She'd been so full of uncertainty, so torn, and though she valued the opinions of Georgia and Natalie, she didn't trust that they were necessarily the right people to give her the sound advice she so badly needed. Good solid advice always came from Kat. But the accident had put all of that out of Sadie's mind (not that it would have been possible to talk about it anyway with all the chaos that followed) and there hadn't been another chance to bring it up. Even though Sadie had felt torn over the decision, she'd wondered whether the pull to take over the waffle house was for the wrong (though emotionally right) reasons. It was for Gammy more than anything else, because Sadie hated to think of her as a sad, directionless, useless old lady sitting in a retirement village. Twenty years previously, if anyone had asked April what she feared the most in her future, it would have been that. And because Sadie was certain that Gammy would feel the loss of her livelihood and independence so keenly on top of the loss of Gampy, it might just be the end of her.

On the other hand, it wasn't the future Sadie had mapped out for herself, the one she'd sacrificed so much for. That was here, represented by this classroom, though today, she wasn't sure if that future was the right one either. Had it ever been the right one? But if it wasn't, then what was?

'Miss!'

Sadie was dragged from her musings by a voice from the front row of desks. Little-Miss-the-books-are-in-the-cupboard was off again. Sadie looked up.

'Miss... is it true you nearly drowned?'

'Who told you that?' Sadie asked, her heart thumping in her chest now. The school wasn't in Sea Salt Bay, but in a neighbouring, much bigger town. She would have expected that sort of news to travel round the bay (and it had, at lightning speed) but she wouldn't have expected it to come this far.

'My cousin, Miss.'

'Does your cousin live in Sea Salt Bay?'

'No, Miss. But my uncle's ex-wife does and she knows the lifeguard. Was it you, Miss? Did you nearly die?'

Every head flicked up from their textbooks now and thirty pairs of eyes regarded her with keen interest.

'I don't think this is a conversation we ought to be having now,' she said stiffly. 'This class is not about my private life—'

Sadie stopped dead. She'd never thought about it like that before, but wasn't that exactly what had happened? She'd tried to make light of the incident, for Kat and Ewan's sake and for the sake of her parents and the guy who'd caused the accident and even – to a certain extent – for herself. But if nobody had been there to pull her from the sea as she'd lost consciousness and slipped beneath the waves...

'It was fine,' she said, shaking herself, though it was harder to shake the sudden slap of realisation, the recognition of just how lucky she'd been that day, how fortunate she was to be alive and how easily the story could have had a much darker ending. For the first time she truly recognised how fleeting and precious life was, how easily it was lost, and the epiphany shocked her to the core.

'Page eighty-five please,' she said slowly, like a malfunctioning robot. 'Come on, get on with it.'

For once there was no argument.

Chapter Eight

Sadie's parents had repeatedly told her that to leave her teaching course was folly. She'd discussed it with them at length, because their family always discussed things, though in truth she'd made up her mind even before the conversations had begun. She was making a huge mistake, they'd said, underestimating how difficult running the waffle house would be, how she might regret her decision. Ewan had taken their side, strongly in agreement, while Kat, for once, had been uncharacteristically reserved in airing her opinions.

Gammy, on the other hand, had been the most animated Sadie had seen her since Gampy's death. While she wasn't exactly jumping for joy, she did seem to be filled with new purpose and set about trying to instruct Sadie in order to help her to be ready when the big day came. Most of what she needed to know Sadie had already gleaned from the years she'd spent hanging around the waffle house, and some of it – though she couldn't be certain – sounded a bit mixed up. But Gammy still wasn't really herself and perhaps it would take a while for her to get back into the swing of things. Once she was working again, the tills of the waffle house ringing with the most joyful, satisfying sound, she'd start to come to life again, of that Sadie was sure.

And in the end, no matter what, Sadie was always going to win the battle to get the waffle house reopened. She had her now infamous knock on the bonce to thank for that. Her parents were just so relieved to have her safe and sound they'd have agreed to almost anything she could think to ask for.

The place had been kept relatively clean during its closure, but April and Sadie went in early anyway on reopening day to give it a more thorough going-over. It had been April's suggestion – she'd insisted that it had to be cleaner than clean if it was going to give returning customers confidence that the standards hadn't changed in the time it had been locked up, and that made perfect sense to Sadie.

April's seemingly methodical planning and common-sense ideas gave Sadie hope that she'd be back to normal sooner rather than later. It meant that she didn't see the other, more hidden clues that her hopes might just be dashed. Perhaps she'd simply wanted too badly to believe that her gamble would be a roaring success, to prove all the doubters wrong, to prove to herself that she'd made the right choice when she was still terrified that she hadn't. Whatever the reasons, in the weeks to come she would wish that she'd taken more notice.

As it was, Sadie yawned widely as they walked the silent pier, the dawn light still pink and peach over the grey line of the sea. 'I could do with a coffee before we do anything.'

April gave her a sideways look. 'You could have had one before we left. It wouldn't have mattered if we'd had to leave the house a few minutes later.'

'I did. I'm so tired I need another one! I'm going to need coffee on a drip today. There's some at the waffle house, right? I never thought to check the larder.'

'If nobody threw the tins away then there ought to be.'

'I don't think anyone did. I hope not.'

'Then there'll be some – only enough for a few days if we get busy though. We'll have to get some more.'

'I hope we do get busy – I'll be happy enough to go to the wholesalers for coffee once we've closed up if it means we've sold enough to run out.'

'It might take some time for people to notice we're open again, darlin'. Have patience.'

Sadie smiled. She'd always loved that little lick of an accent that Gammy had never lost, despite all the years she and Gampy had spent living in England.

'The first thing I'll do when we're cleaned a little is call the wholesaler and see if we can get some essentials delivered. I just hope they've kept our account open.'

'Maybe we shouldn't order too much,' Sadie said doubtfully. 'Not yet.'

'Why ever not?'

Sadie didn't want to say 'In case this doesn't work out and in a few days I realise we're in way over our heads and have to abandon thoughts of getting the waffle house running again', because while she'd pushed the idea to everyone, she was by no means confident that they could do it. More to the point, that *she herself* could do it and – in the long run – whether she'd even want to. She only knew in her heart that something in her life had to change, even if she didn't know what yet. The waffle house had seemed as good a place as any to dip her toes in the water and test a new direction.

'We just don't want to spend too much money at first,' she said instead. 'In case business takes a while to pick up. Like you said, people might not realise we're open again straight away. It might take a couple of weeks to be at full capacity again.'

April shook her head. 'It won't take long, darlin'. Once word gets round folks will come back.'

Her voice was filled with such conviction and optimism that it warmed Sadie to hear it. This was the way to bring Gammy back to them, whatever doubts Sadie might have about her own involvement. And when she felt those doubts, she just had to remind herself of all the reasons she was even trying this and she'd find herself on solid ground again.

She had the keys in the pocket of her jeans and as they arrived at the front door of the waffle house, she handed them to April.

'Want to do the honours?'

April didn't miss a beat. She poked one into the lock and twisted to click it open. They stepped inside together. April looked around in silence, and Sadie's optimism evaporated as suddenly and completely as sea spray on a sun-baked rock. Her stomach dropped as she saw her grandma's face.

It was the first time April had been in since Kenneth's death. She'd been unwilling to face it, and nobody had imagined that she'd have to, and so they'd shielded her, taking on the basic maintenance until they could get rid of the place. Nobody had really imagined that this day might come, that April would be setting foot in there again and, in doing so, would have to come to terms with the memories of what had happened on that last fateful shift. While coming in here since her grandfather's death had made Sadie melancholy, she had to imagine what her grandma felt now was more like a breath-stealing smack to the gut in comparison. Looking at her now, she quickly realised that the family's collective decision had been a mistake, and that the biggest portion of the blame for that mistake now lay with Sadie, as the person who had instigated the reopening of the waffle house. Instead of shielding April, she ought to have brought her back in to see the place the moment they'd agreed a day to start working there again.

'Gammy...' she began hesitantly. 'We could just clean today... Open tomorrow? I mean, if this is all a bit too—'

'No, darlin',' April said, forcing a smile for her youngest grand-daughter. 'It's like getting back on that horse after a fall, isn't it? You can just stand there and look at that creature all day and you'd scare yourself half to death, but then you'd never ride again. Best to just climb right back into that saddle and show him who's boss.'

'You will take things steady, won't you?' Sadie asked carefully. April always hated being reminded that she was well past retirement age and that younger women than her had spent many blissful years by now sitting quietly in their gardens or in favourite reading chairs, not working long hours in a busy eating establishment. Sadie would never dare do that now because she knew that April wasn't like those women. She'd always thrived on the work and it had kept her sharp and focused and well for all these years. But that was before she'd lost Gampy. His death was an event that had aged her, right before their eyes. Though this morning she looked more like the April Sadie had grown up being in awe of, Sadie was aware that her rehabilitation was by no means a fait accompli.

'Oh, there's no need to worry.' April took Sadie's hand and gave it a quick squeeze. It felt thinner, more delicate than Sadie remembered, and rather than reassuring her, as her grandmother had meant, it only made Sadie more uneasy.

'Why don't I get us that coffee?' April added. 'If you like, you can make a start by getting the utilities up and running again and then I can fix our drinks.'

Sadie nodded. 'The electricity is already sorted because Dad came in last night to check round and left it on for us. I'll get the other stuff going. I'm guessing we might have to run the taps for a bit, get some water through the system before we drink it?'

'Oh, don't you worry about that – I know what I'm doing.'

'Yeah, I know, I just...'

Sadie didn't finish the sentence, because to do that would mean saying out loud all the doubts that currently plagued her and she wouldn't do that to Gammy, not now. Instead, she pushed a bright smile across her face and went to find the stop tap to get the water supply going again.

It was stiff, and it took two hands to get it moving, but eventually Sadie heard the satisfying whoosh of the water flooding the system. Then she turned her attention to the gas. Even though it was summer, and despite their frequent visits to check round and air the building, the place still felt a little damp and musty. Perhaps an hour of heating would sort that out. Now seemed the best time to do that, while it was still early morning and a little chillier than it would be later on, and so Sadie took it upon herself to fix that too. She listened carefully as the pipes clanked and groaned, but any worries she'd had that they wouldn't run smoothly were soon put to rest as the radiators began to heat up.

With all that done, Sadie went back to the dining room to see that April was standing in the middle of the floor, staring into space.

'Gammy?'

April jumped, and then turned to Sadie, seemingly surprised to see her there.

'Oh my!'

'Gammy... are you OK?'

'Sure, darlin'. But I clean forgot about the coffee, didn't I?'

'It's OK. Want me to make it?'

'No, I said I'd do it so I'll do it. Why don't you go in the office and call Timpson's about the batter mix? The number's in the little claret address book on the shelf. We could do with some batter mix as soon as he can get here. I think there may be some in the larder but probably not much.'

'It's a bit early, isn't it? Will they be open yet?'

'Oh...'

'But I could email them from my phone?'

'Sure...' April said uncertainly. 'I always call them but...'

'Well if you'd rather do it by telephone then we could do it later. As long as we don't forget if we get busy in here.'

April paused for a moment, her gaze going to the windows.

'No,' she said finally. 'You're right. I'm a silly old woman insisting on doing everything the way we've always done it. If you want to email go right ahead.'

Sadie nodded and went through to the tiny office at the back of the restaurant. It was really more of a broom cupboard – narrow, windowless, lined on one wall by shelves. A plank of wood had been attached lower down and fashioned into a sort of desk and on it sat an old telephone, a caddy containing pencils and pens, and a jar of assorted sweets. Sadie looked at the sweets and smiled sadly. Gampy had a sweet tooth that meant he ate sweets in the same way smokers snuck out for crafty cigarettes, and he'd frequently retreat to the office pretending to do admin but really using it as an excuse to sit munching on his candy. Sadie often thought it was a wonder he had any teeth at all, but by some miracle, despite his advanced years and sugar intake, he did have some, though the gaps had been gradually filled by dentures in later years. It wouldn't have mattered if he'd had none though, because he still would have found some way to eat his sugary treats. And if he wasn't eating sweets secretly in the back, when the shop had closed he'd have Gammy cook him a special waffle or pancake.

Shaking herself, she searched for the claret-coloured phone book that Gammy had told her was in there. After a minute of rummaging through out-of-date directories, recipe books, unused stationery and yet more unopened packets of sweets, she found it and flicked to the page she needed. As she'd suspected, there was nothing more than a phone number in there, the name of a contact, and an address. She could do an internet search for the company and there ought to be an email contact on there; she only hoped that they'd modernised a bit more than Gammy and Gampy had and actually had a website.

As she pulled out her phone to search, she could hear the muffled sounds of April in the kitchen. Half paying attention to her task and half listening to the clinks of spoons on china, she hoped and prayed that April's lapses of concentration this morning were only a temporary thing. *They were*, she tried to tell herself, making her inner voice as confident and certain as she could, though that confidence was starting to feel like a desert mirage that might dissipate if Sadie allowed herself to remember for one second that she was still in the desert and that the oasis was still a long way off.

After establishing that Timpson's did have a website and emailing them, Sadie flicked through the rest of the address book to see if there was anyone else she might need to contact. She'd have to check with Gammy, of course, but there might be some names she'd recognise instantly. They'd need to contact anyone they used on a regular basis anyway, just to let them know that the waffle house was now open again and to check what their customer status was in light of its recent period of closure. Was their credit still good? Could they still get the same service and discounts they'd enjoyed in the past? Had stocks or supply chains altered in any way that might affect what the waffle house was able to buy?

There were a few names she recognised, but many she didn't, so she decided to take the book through to the dining room. They had a little time, so it might be a good plan to sit with Gammy and go through it with her.

April was already sitting at a table when Sadie went back into the dining room. The smell of strong, bitter coffee was in the air, just the thing to wake Sadie up. But as she approached the table to sit with her grandma, she felt that cold dread settle in her stomach again. On the table in front of a smiling April sat three mugs.

'Gammy... who's the other one for?'

'Why, you know who it's for, silly...'

But then April paused, her smile dying, suddenly looking confused and distressed. 'Oh... I guess I made too many, didn't I?'

Sadie swallowed the tears that would have fallen if she'd been alone and tried to look calm and unconcerned. 'It's OK. Habit, I expect. And I'm gasping for a drink anyway so I reckon I could drink two cups no problem.'

'Oh, that's alright then,' April said, sounding far from convinced but happy to let it go at that.

Sadie sat at the table and put the address book down to take a sip of her coffee, all the while her eyes never leaving her grandmother.

'What's the book for?' April asked.

'I thought we could go through it. I need to know who these people are so I thought you could give me a bit of background about what they do for us. Then I thought we might contact the ones we use the most or we might need soonest to let them know we've reopened. Is that OK?'

'Sure, darlin'.' April nodded and reached for her mug. Neither of them looked at the spare, as if it was dangerous and they'd turn to salt if they did. Sadie beat down the misgivings that were beginning to scare her. What was going on? Had Gammy made that other drink thinking Gampy was close? Or had she really made one for him simply out of habit?

Whatever the reason, the fact that she had made it did nothing to settle Sadie's nerves. She'd pushed to reopen the waffle house against the advice of everyone else in her family. Had they known something like this would happen? Had they known something about Gammy's state of mind that they hadn't seen fit to share with Sadie? They'd often treated her as the baby of the family and she couldn't argue with that, because she was, but she couldn't believe they'd keep something this important from her, not given the steps she'd taken to be here today. And so she quickly dismissed the notion.

Which left what explanation? Was it simply that they'd all come to the conclusion that Gammy had reached a natural crossroads in her life with the death of Gampy, a sign that it was time to start winding down? Sadie had to admit that the conversations that had taken place were along those lines, but she hadn't been listening. The truth was, she hadn't wanted to listen. Who were they opening this place up for? Was it really for Gammy, or was it for Sadie, who already felt as if she'd lost so much that was precious to her, so much that had given her life meaning and context, that she didn't want to lose the waffle house too?

Or maybe she'd simply been looking for a convenient escape route for the real big mistake she'd made – her teacher training. Because now that she looked at it from the outside, she realised that she'd never really been suited to that profession. She'd said as much when she'd been into the office only a couple of days before to tell her mentor that she was leaving the course, and though she'd felt like an abject failure, she couldn't deny that she also felt a sense of relief that she'd never again have to step into a classroom.

So where did that leave Sadie now? Could she still make this work, regardless of the obstacles that she could now see strewn along the path? What if her family were right? What if she'd messed up again?

It was ten o'clock by the time they were ready to open up, but Sadie wasn't too worried that they'd missed a good chunk of the breakfast rush. They'd been closed for over a month and they hadn't exactly announced their reopening – not least because they hadn't been certain themselves if it was actually going to happen. Besides, Sadie, for one, would be glad of a slow start. She was nervous enough, and a delay of the big moment wasn't entirely unwelcome. In fact, if her grandmother had suddenly announced that she wanted nothing more to do with Sea Salt Bay Waffle House and wanted to close it down for good immediately then Sadie thought she might be just a little relieved to hear it and might not offer all that much in the way of argument. It was one thing to help her grandma and granddad out occasionally on a Saturday afternoon, or to hear them talk about the business over dinner, but another thing entirely to suddenly find yourself running the place. Because, despite Gammy's presence, Sadie was beginning to realise that running the place was exactly what she'd end up doing.

Despite all the doubts and nerves, they did open the doors. The day started quietly, the only real activity neighbouring traders or local residents coming in to express surprise and pleasure that the waffle house was open again and sorrow for Kenneth's passing. Sadie found some of those visits hard and she could only imagine how much harder April found them. She watched each conversation closely for a reaction which would have meant little to anyone else but which would set alarm bells off for her. But Gammy only put on a brave smile and thanked them for their kind thoughts and words of condolence – lovely, warm and dignified, as she'd always been, the woman Sadie had always been proud to call grandmother even when she'd been unable to say so. They didn't sell much apart from the odd hot drink and some crepes to take out for a hungry family with northern accents.

By midday things had started to pick up as day trippers and holidaymakers turned their thoughts to lunch. It wasn't exactly a return to the mad rushes of the waffle house's heyday but it was busier than Sadie would have liked for her first day as a significantly important member of staff. As a teenager, when things got busy, Gammy or Gampy would step in and take the heat off her so she never felt the stress of a full dining room. But that wasn't going to happen today. If they were overwhelmed now, Sadie would have to step in to take the heat off April, just as she would once have done for her granddaughter.

The difference was, Sadie felt as if she didn't have the first clue what she was doing. Back then she'd ably assisted (so she'd thought) but now she was in charge, whether she liked it or not and whether she knew how to do that or not. April was on hand with all her years of knowledge and experience, of course, but while she could tell Sadie how this thing switched on, or how long that dish took to cook, or the codes for the till, or a million other little things, it was clear that she wasn't a hundred per cent present. Often Sadie found her slack-jawed and absent in the kitchen as she went through with a new order, or to find out whether a previous one was ready, and it was abundantly clear that all the real drive and impetus to keep things ticking over would have to come from her. And seeing how her grandmother was operating now, she had to wonder for the first time whether this had been the case for longer than anyone had realised. Had this been happening while Gampy had been alive? Had he been the one keeping things running smoothly? Had he been keeping Gammy on task, allowing her to function, making sure she was safe? Had he been doing all this because he was afraid to share that she might no longer be the vital, fiery, turbo-charged woman she'd once been?

Grief was a funny thing, and there was no doubt that April had been affected deeply by hers. In fact, it was hard to deny that she was still grieving, and probably would be for many months to come. But there seemed to be more than that at play – at least Sadie thought so. She was seventy-eight after all, so she could be forgiven for slowing down a little. Maybe she'd been slowing down for a while now but nobody had noticed. Perhaps they hadn't wanted to notice, or perhaps Gampy had hidden it well. Now that it was there in plain view, impossible to ignore, acceptance of that fact was more problematic, especially where April herself was concerned. Sadie was beginning to see that even though she'd already felt out of her depth simply opening the doors to customers today, things might be about to get a whole lot worse.

It was around twelve thirty. Sadie was chatting to a family with four young children about her brother's dive school while they waited for their banana and hazelnut chocolate waffles and strawberry and cream waffles. They'd been asking for recommendations for fun things to do in the area – they didn't want the usual sitting around on the beach or strolling the pier suggestions (though they had no objections to those things, they said they wanted a little more to make the holiday more memorable). And while they'd asked specifically for ideas a little out of the ordinary, the parents seemed doubtful about the prospect of diving, or of snorkelling. Sadie explained that Ewan always took children out to a little cove where the water was never above three feet deep, where it was clear and warm and there were no currents, a place that was teeming with underwater life and where, if you really wanted to believe you were diving in the Mediterranean, it wouldn't take all that much effort. The longer she spoke about it, the more excited the older children (who looked to be perhaps ten and eight or thereabouts) got, while the younger two (maybe around five or six, who looked like a twin boy and girl to Sadie's untrained eye) simply got swept up in their older siblings' enthusiasm.

When she'd first taken the order, Sadie had worried that it was quite a big one and a lot for Gammy to remember – there were six of them after all – but she reasoned that it was nothing Gammy hadn't done before, and in all honesty, if this business was going to continue trading then she was going to have to cope with this and much bigger orders. Sometimes, you just had to throw someone in and force them to swim, and April wouldn't have appreciated Sadie's doubts about her abilities, even if Sadie had been able or willing to articulate them.

But then one of the older boys at the table wrinkled his nose. He looked at his mother.

'Can you smell something?'

The mother looked at Sadie, and Sadie could see that she'd quickly come to the same conclusion as she had.

'Oh!' Sadie exclaimed without meaning to. Immediately she smoothed the look of panic from her face. 'Please excuse me, I need to…'

Without finishing her sentence she hurried to the kitchen to see her grandmother staring at the waffle iron as smoke poured out of it.

'Gammy!' Sadie cried, rushing to unlock the contraption. Inside was a black mess that had once been pristine batter, and then briefly transformed into a perfect waffle, before it had continued on its journey to complete incineration. It was now something that would even offend the bin.

'Oh…' April said, looking blankly at Sadie. 'That's been in too long. The setting must have been real high. I wonder how that happened…'

'No idea,' Sadie replied briskly, trying to scrape out the mess as quickly as she could and burning her hand in the process. She cried out, the pain all the worse for the fact that it was red-hot sugar sticking to her skin, but there was no time to worry about it now. She had to get this stinking mess out of the restaurant and get some windows open so the smell wouldn't infect the entire building and put everyone off their food. And she had to get a replacement order on the go for the customers who were waiting. The burnt food wasn't coming off the waffle iron though, and it was going to take time to clean – more time than she had. 'Is there another…?'

Sadie's gaze fell on an unused iron on a nearby counter top. She rushed over to get it and turned it on before going to fetch an already prepared jug of batter.

'You'd better throw that mess away,' April said, looking at the burnt offering in the other iron. 'We can't serve that.'

'I'm going to. Gammy… do you think you'll be OK to do some fresh ones? Only I really need to be at the counter…'

'Of course!' her grandmother said, looking a little bemused and a little irritated too. 'Why else do you think I'm standing here? I don't know why you came back here interfering anyway.'

Sadie offered a tight smile. 'Thanks, Gammy. I'll get back to the dining room, then. Call me if you need me.'

'I won't,' April called after her as Sadie left her to it. Sadie's stomach dropped and her hand throbbed where she'd burnt it, but she took a deep breath and started to make her way to the table she'd just left to apologise that their food was going to be delayed. She'd have to give it five minutes, she decided, and then she'd sneak back into the kitchen on pretence of needing something from there to check if everything was under control.

'I'm so sorry…' Sadie began as she got back to the family. 'Your order will be out just as soon as we can get it remade.'

The father smiled and waved away the apology and none of them seemed particularly concerned or upset that they would have to wait for their food. They were obviously nice people, and Sadie felt she and April had got off lightly on this occasion. But next time they might not be so lucky.

Chapter Nine

April and Kenneth had always closed up at 4 p.m. They'd never seen the point in staying open later; they'd always felt it was around the time of day that most people turned their thoughts to the evening meal and didn't want to fill up on sugary snacks. Waffles and pancakes, they'd said, were a sweet treat for the young and young at heart and, as such, reserved for the time of day when youngsters were out and about. There was a logic in this that was hard to argue with, but it also left the waffle house closed for a large chunk of every day. Sadie had always felt sure that there would be trade to be had in the evenings – though it had never been her place to say so.

Certainly, on this, April's first day back at work, Sadie had no desire to address it, and even if she'd wanted to she was too tired. Her grandma didn't look much better and so Sadie was grateful to switch the sign on the door from open to closed and lock up for the night. Not only was she tired, but Sadie had been subjected to more than her fair share of worries and stresses during the day, from the incidents with Gammy that ranged from not knowing what day it was (frequently), to making cups of coffee for a man who'd never drink them, to actually almost setting fire to the restaurant, and a million other little things in between. And those were on top of the stress of trying to do a job that she'd thought she'd known how to do but, once there, realised that she hadn't known all that much about at all. She'd heard of learning on the job, the old saying that there was no substitute for experience, but the people who said that had never had to learn at a million miles an hour with a shop full of hungry people and an unpredictable situation in the kitchen.

Sadie had to believe that things were going to get better than this, otherwise, why was she here? She could easily turn to Gammy now and tell her this wasn't going to work out, that she couldn't do it, and she could make up more than enough compelling reasons why. But she didn't want to, and so that had to mean something. And, despite the exhaustion clear on Gammy's face, despite all the narrow misses and lapses throughout the day, her grandmother had looked happier and more purposeful than Sadie had seen her for a long time. If nothing else positive came from this day there was that.

Sadie could drive, but Sea Salt Bay was so small that she tended to walk when she could and they'd both walked to work that morning. It wasn't exactly a long trek home, but there were steep roads and Sadie really didn't fancy it now that they'd done a full and surprisingly hectic day at the waffle house. Gammy certainly didn't look up to it and so Sadie suggested that they go down to the harbour to see if Ewan or Kat were free to run them home. Sadie's brother and his wife carried so much equipment everywhere and their home was a little further out than Sadie's so they always went to work in their station wagon. It was a safe bet that they'd have it parked up now in the space outside their little harbour headquarters.

Sadie held back an impatient click of her tongue as they drew closer to the harbour and could see straight away that the parking space outside the grey hut that housed the diving school office was empty.

It couldn't be helped and she could hardly be annoyed at Ewan and Kat, who hadn't known they were coming and probably had lessons booked in anyway. Sadie decided to press on regardless – perhaps one of them would be in manning the fort and whoever was out with the station wagon wouldn't be too long. It was getting late in the day for diving after all.

The door was open and Sadie ushered April in, following after.

'Hello, you two.' Kat smiled brightly, looking up from the desk in the welcoming – if extremely compact – waiting room. She had one of her regular, lurid green protein drinks in front of her and a laptop shoved to one side with a diary page open. Sadie glanced with some suspicion at the protein drink. She'd often thought they must work because Kat looked incredible but it was a sacrifice of taste that was just too big for Sadie to make – everlasting youth or not. She'd take an oozing ice-cream shake any time and the consequences for her waistline with it.

'Hey,' Sadie said. 'Are you busy?'

'A little bit,' Kat replied. 'Never too busy for you. What can I do for you?'

'We were hoping for a ride home.' Sadie flopped onto a teal sofa nestled in a nook beneath a panelled window that framed the harbour and the forest of tiny white boat masts bobbing in it. April sat down next to her.

'Tough day?' Kat asked, looking between them both. Sadie could see her calculating, quickly trying to work out what kind of day they'd had.

'Busy,' Sadie said carefully, remembering that even if she'd wanted to confide in Kat – as she often did – her sister-in-law might feel obliged to tell Ewan. And Ewan had been one of the doubters who had warned Sadie against this venture, and Sadie didn't want to give him any reason to say *I told you so* or any other variation of that most irritating of phrases. Maybe, somewhere down the line, she'd have to admit that they'd been right all along, but she wasn't ready to admit it yet.

'I'd drive you, but Ewan's out with a client and I can't lock up here because I'm expecting a party of four in the next half hour. I need to be here, just in case they turn up early and think we've forgotten them. Don't want to be handing out four refunds.'

Sadie glanced up at the clock on the wall behind Kat. 'Isn't it a bit late to be taking people out?'

Kat gave a slight shrug. 'They have a bit of experience so they're not complete novices. Besides, it's not dark for ages yet. If they want to go out then who am I to refuse their money?'

'Right. Where are the kids?'

'On the boat, actually, with your mum and dad. Freddie was desperate to go out because your dad said he'd seen dolphins in the bay this morning. I think Freya was less bothered but she wasn't going to miss out.'

Sadie nodded. She'd been like Freddie once – full of energy and interested in everything. She'd been so lucky to have grown up in a place like Sea Salt Bay where she could indulge her passions and experience a life that many girls her age would have given their right arms for, and to have parents who had the means to enable that indulgence. She'd taken it for granted, of course, as all children do, and she'd been convinced that the adventure she craved lay in the world outside the bay. There had been plenty, naturally, and it wasn't that she hadn't enjoyed life outside the bay. But sometimes, she reflected now more and more often, you simply had to look a little closer to home to find the things that mattered, and it was only by going away that you learnt to appreciate that.

'If you want to wait for Ewan he'll be finished in about ten… fifteen maybe, then he'll be heading back. I'm sure he'd run you home then.'

Sadie was about to say they'd walk it, sure that her brother would be tired and the last thing he'd want to do was be their taxi, until she glanced across at her grandma, whose eyelids were heavy and closing even as she sat in the bright light that flooded the office through the window they sat beneath. Sadie had to admit she sort of felt like falling asleep herself – it had been a long day and the warmth of the sun on her neck as she sat here was lovely and relaxing.

'We'll wait if it's OK with you,' she said.

Kat smiled. 'You want a drink?'

'Have you got tea?' Sadie replied, eyeing Kat's protein drink doubt-fully. Kat gave a light laugh as she noticed the distrustful gaze towards her plastic bottle.

'I'm sure I can find a couple of teabags. Give me a minute.'

She disappeared into a back room while Sadie sank deeper into the sofa and let the sun warm her, allowing her eyes to close for a moment. Before she could do anything about it she'd started to drift, letting the room and her tiredness fall away.

'Um… Hello…'

Sadie opened her eyes. For the briefest moment she was disorientated as she looked to see April was smiling up at a man who'd just come in. Why the hell had she allowed herself to fall asleep knowing that Kat was expecting clients? Although, hadn't she said a party of four was coming? There was only one person here that she could see.

'Kat will be right out, darlin',' April said.

'Right, thank you,' the man replied, jamming his hands into his trouser pockets. But then he turned back to Sadie. He paused, and she could see the same cogs and gears shifting into place in his head as were in her own.

'Haven't we met…?'

With a jolt, Sadie realised that they had met before and where, and she saw that he'd worked it out too. They'd met before alright!

To his credit, he blushed.

'Oh, right…' he said awkwardly. 'Of course… How are you feeling?'

'I'm OK,' Sadie said.

'I'd wanted to check up on you but… well, I wasn't sure where to find you or if I'd even be welcome if I did.'

'To be fair,' Sadie replied with a rueful smile, 'I don't think you would have been welcome. Not that I hold a grudge,' she added hastily. 'I think my parents might though. It's probably a good thing you didn't come looking, especially not at the house.'

'Well.' His hands couldn't have got any deeper in his pockets but he shoved them down anyway with a half shrug, half embarrassed stoop. 'I guess it's just as well I didn't…'

A brief silence followed. April looked up at him with an unconcerned smile. She didn't appear to have worked out that this was the man who'd practically mowed Sadie down in his boat, but he clearly didn't realise this fact because the smile he gave her in return was one that said 'Ground, please swallow me now'. Sadie didn't blame him for feeling awkward, and she even felt a bit sorry for him, because there was no obvious polite or plausible escape from this excruciatingly awkward moment. He could run out, but that might leave Sadie or her grandma offended, and if he'd come into the office for something specific then it would mean running out on that too.

'Oh… this is my grandma,' Sadie said into the silence, desperate to fill it with something and not knowing what else to say.

April nodded. 'Hello. You can call me April.'

'Good to meet you, April,' he said with an awkward smile. 'I'm Luke.' Then he turned back to Sadie. 'When I left my card for you at the beach, I take it you didn't…'

'Oh, Ewan has it,' Sadie said. Her brother hadn't offered to give the card to her at the time and in all the excitement of so much else going on she'd forgotten all about it until now.

'Ewan? That's your…?'

'My brother,' Sadie said. 'And you're Luke? I'm Sadie,' she added, but Luke's attention had gone to the walls, where various photos of Ewan and Kat showed them out on location with clients and friends, some in their swimming gear, more often than not in wetsuits. His face seemed to lose three shades as he recognised the faces as belonging to the people he'd upset on the beach the day he'd rowed right into Sadie's head.

'Your brother owns this place?' he asked as his gaze settled on one photo that had a smiling Sadie in it, a large crab hanging from a careful grip.

'Along with his wife,' Sadie replied. 'Have you booked a lesson with him?'

'Not yet but I was hoping… I probably ought to…'

He began to back away, moving towards the exit, but then Kat returned and he turned to her, looking vaguely mortified that he'd been caught here at all. She was carrying a tray of hot drinks and set it down on the desk as her gaze fell on him. For the shortest second she looked as confused as Sadie had when she'd first woken to find him standing before her, but then it was replaced by illumination.

'Oh,' she said, though not with the anger that the man might have been greeted with had it been Ewan.

'I was just about to…' he began sheepishly, but his sentence faded to nothing.

Kat's manner – though not angry – was immediately stiffer and more formal than normal, though she remained courteous.

'Did you want to book a session or something?'

Luke rubbed a hand over his chin, glancing at Sadie and April in turn before looking at Kat again. 'I had wanted to…'

Kat went to her laptop. The screen had timed out and the screensaver showed a stunning picture of the bay at sunset. She logged back in. 'Have you ever been diving before?' she asked as she looked at the screen.

'A couple of times in Greece. I'm no expert but' – he glanced at Sadie again, his expression looking more sheepish than ever, but this time Sadie was convinced there was a hint of humour there too – 'at least I'm safer in a wetsuit than I am in a boat.'

Kat stared at him, but Sadie found herself giggling. It was hard to stay mad with a guy who had such obvious charm and humour, so much so that it was hard to keep down, even in a situation like this. And now that Sadie could look without a huge bruise and a thumping headache, she could appreciate that he was very attractive too. And, judging by his choice of hobbies, he not only had charm and a sense of humour, but he had an adventurous streak as well. Not that it mattered, of course, because she was quite sure her entire family would think she'd gone mad for so much as airing any of these thoughts to them. And she could hardly blame them – he had almost killed her after all. As introductions went, it was hardly conventional.

April suddenly straightened in her seat. 'Is this the man?' she asked.

'I'm afraid it is,' he said. April opened her mouth to say something but Sadie got in there first.

'Don't get mad,' she said to her grandma. 'The poor guy's already had enough of a roasting from just about everyone else in Sea Salt Bay.'

'Deserved, though,' he said. 'I can't believe what a clumsy idiot I was. I'm not usually like that and I still feel just terrible about it. And, like I said to you that day, if there's anything I can do to make it up to you, just say the word and it's done.'

'Hmm,' Sadie said, giving him a playful grin, 'I don't think you want to go around making promises like that.'

'Within reason,' he added, smiling himself now – a proper, more relaxed smile.

Kat seemed to relax a little too.

'So, about this session,' she said, turning back to the laptop. Business was business, she and Ewan always said, and Sadie was glad to see her sister-in-law had enough sense to view this situation in that same way. The last thing she wanted to do was lose money for Kat and Ewan.

'Oh, I…' Luke began to edge towards the door again. 'Maybe another time…?'

Kat looked up from the screen. 'You don't want to book now?'

'It's not that I don't want to, it's just—'

He stopped dead as he backed into Ewan, who was walking in, hair still wet from his last dive.

'Ewan,' Sadie said firmly, as her brother's face darkened, 'we've already had about a thousand apologies; let's not make it a thousand and one, eh? After all, it was my head and I'm happy to leave it.'

'Even so,' Luke said, 'I'm truly sorry for the whole thing.' He held out a hand for Ewan to shake. 'Could we at least call a truce? I've just moved here and I really don't want to make myself an army of enemies before I manage to make any friends.'

Ewan automatically took it and shook stiffly, though he looked annoyed with himself afterwards.

Sadie sat up straighter. 'You've moved here? You've moved to the bay?'

'Yes,' he said, and despite the confrontational situation there was a sort of boyish glee in his expression. 'I've always dreamt of living somewhere like this and finally, at the grand old age of thirty-five, I've managed it.'

Kat frowned slightly. 'There's only one house I know of for sale around here and that's—'

'Yes,' Luke cut in. 'The Old Chapel.'

It was Sadie's turn to frown. 'But the conversion is only half finished. I didn't think it was ready to sell.'

'I think the last owner had had enough of the job. As far as I know he's gone to a new build somewhere near Poole. I've got time on my hands and no family to worry about so I'm happy to finish converting the chapel. In fact, I'll enjoy it.'

Sadie nodded. Nobody had really known much about the previous owner of the Old Chapel, other than he was another out-of-towner who'd moved to the south coast from London and was planning to turn the disused little church into a second home. It meant the full-time residents of Sea Salt Bay hadn't made much of an attempt to get to know him all that well. It wasn't that they were being deliberately unfriendly, but most of them knew from experience that he probably wouldn't be around that often – if he even kept hold of the chapel at all once it had been converted to a home. It seemed that they'd been right too. But Luke… this might be different, Sadie mused, because he was making Sea Salt Bay his proper home by the sounds of it. It meant there was every chance he was going to stay for good, and so people would want to know more about him. In which case, she had to feel for him, because he hadn't got off to a very good start.

'You're planning to live here full-time?' she asked.

'Oh, yes…' Luke shot a glance at Ewan, whose expression gave nothing away. He began to back towards the exit again. 'Maybe I'll come and book that lesson another time, eh?' And with a last awkward smile, aimed more at Sadie and Kat than at Ewan, who even he could probably see was a lost cause – at least for now – he let himself out.

Kat aimed a withering look at Ewan as the door closed. 'Well done.'

Ewan blinked at her. 'What does that mean?'

'What do you think it means? He was just about to book a lesson.'

'Well I wasn't about to take him out so I don't know what he'd be booking it for.'

'Don't be so childish. Honestly, sometimes I think I get more mature decisions out of Freddie than I do you.'

Ewan's mouth fell open. 'I was perfectly civil to him!'

'But not exactly friendly and welcoming,' Kat said.

'I'd say it's still pretty obvious that you don't like him,' Sadie agreed. 'And there's really no reason to keep holding this ridiculous grudge, because I'm alright now and he's just told us he's going to be a new neighbour. You probably ought to make an effort to be nicer.'

Ewan huffed as he went round to the back of the desk to drop his kitbag down. Kat let out a sigh, and there was a brief silence, in which they all came independently to the same conclusion that there would be no common ground on this matter for the foreseeable future and it was probably better for the sake of some family harmony that they dropped it.

'If you're not too busy, darlin'…' April said into the silence, 'Sadie and I would very much appreciate a ride home.'

Ewan looked at Kat.

'I've got a party of four due – remember?' she said in answer to his silent question. 'Could you give them a lift? I said you'd be able to.'

He paused, and then gave a surly nod.

'Thanks,' Sadie said. 'We're just absolutely exhausted after the day we've had.'

'It's OK,' Ewan said. 'Give me two minutes and I'll be with you.'

Ewan was still sulking as he started the car but it didn't last long. It never did. He didn't know how to stay angry with anyone for long, least of all Sadie or April who, other than Kat and the children, were probably his favourite people in the world. Rose-gold light fell on his face as the station wagon climbed the cliff road to Sadie's parents' house and, after a bit of gentle ribbing, Sadie got him talking again. As the conversation began to flow, she saw him relax back into his usual easy-going self.

'So you two have managed a day working together and you're still on speaking terms,' he said, feeding the steering wheel through his hands as they negotiated a sharp bend in the road.

Sadie pretended to pout. 'Did you think we wouldn't be?'

'Well,' he replied, 'I'd be lying if I said I didn't.' He gave a low chuckle. 'Come on, you must have known we were all wondering it a little bit.'

'I don't know why you would think that,' April replied indignantly. 'Sadie and I are always the best of friends. Now, if it had been your mother or father working alongside me…'

'It's one thing getting along at home, though,' he said. 'It's another to stay on good terms trying to run a business together. Take it from me; I should know.'

'You and Kat get along brilliantly,' Sadie said.

He flicked a sideways glance her way. 'Then we put on a good show for the customers. Kat regularly tears a strip off me when she gets annoyed and we don't always see eye to eye on the best way to run the business.'

'And it's only Kat who gets annoyed?' Sadie asked with a playful grin.

'Oh, I get annoyed,' Ewan said with a laugh, 'but I know my place. I wouldn't dare show it, and it's not often I win an argument with Kat anyway, so why bother?'

Sadie laughed too. 'Point taken.' She twisted round to look at her grandmother. 'But we've got on just fine today, haven't we?'

'Oh yes!' April beamed. 'It's been just lovely having you there today. But when your grandpa gets—'

She stopped mid-sentence, her mouth open, still formed around the words she'd been meaning to say. But she didn't say them, and instead closed her mouth and looked out of the window. Sadie stared at her – she couldn't help it – with a mixture of dread and relief. Dread, because she'd had a horrible idea where her grandmother's statement had been going, and relief that she'd stopped herself before she'd uttered it. If April was getting a little confused from time to time, at least she wasn't so far gone that she no longer had any recognition of reality. At least she was aware that Gampy had passed, even if she allowed herself to occasionally and briefly forget it.

Sadie exchanged a meaningful look with Ewan, but both of them knew now wasn't the time to say out loud what they might be thinking. He'd want to talk to her later though. Could she tell him about the other worrying little slips of the day? Did the fact they'd happened even mean they were something to worry about? Perhaps this was Gammy still adjusting to her new life after all, and nothing of concern.

But she saw in her brother's face that he was already concerned, even without the knowledge of those other things, and that as soon as the opportunity arose he'd want to know more about how their grandma had been that day. At home she'd been quiet and a little withdrawn, and perhaps that had been the reason nobody had seen just what was happening in her head until now, when necessity had persuaded her to function and engage with the world again. Sadie only hoped that Ewan wouldn't bring this conversation up with their parents before she'd had a chance to discuss it fully with him, because Henny and Graham were already strongly in favour of Sadie and April 'giving this madness up' and they didn't need any more reasons to pressure them into thinking again about reopening the waffle house. If she allowed herself to dwell on it, Sadie had enough doubts of her own too, but she was still as determined as ever not to give those doubts room to grow.

'We are opening again tomorrow, aren't we?' April asked uncertainly, as if she'd been able to read Sadie's thoughts, or at least the strange, charged silence that had passed between Sadie and Ewan.

'That's the plan,' Sadie replied, sounding as confident and airy as she could. 'That's if you can stand another day of me getting everything wrong.'

'Oh, you did just fine, darlin',' she said, her features relaxing now.

'That's good to know.'

April nodded. 'A few days and you'll be running the place good enough to make your grandpa proud.'

Sadie welled up as the thought of her recently lost, dearly loved Gampy squeezed her heart in a way she'd been completely unprepared for. If she was honest, there were times when Gammy wasn't the only one who momentarily forgot that he was no longer with them. They were all getting on with their lives and, for the most part, coping – as people did – but his loss had changed them all forever, even if it was hard to admit it. It seemed to Sadie that losing a loved one always did that for everyone, even if the change was so small it was hardly recognisable, because how could a person fail to change when the world around them had changed? Someone who had once occupied a space in the world was no longer there, and the world was forced to bend anew around that space, so that even though they no longer existed they wouldn't be forgotten.

Sadie turned to the window, not wanting April to see her cry. She didn't really want her brother to see it either, but at least it wouldn't set him off if he did, unlike April. Sadie didn't want to be responsible for upsetting her when she'd already cried so hard and so long since Gampy's death.

'Dec asked after you today,' Ewan said. Perhaps he'd wanted to distract Sadie with something innocuous. He couldn't have realised that this was probably the only other subject that would make her feel worse. But she tried to look unconcerned.

'Yeah?'

'He'd wanted to pop by at the waffle house to see how it was going but he didn't get time.'

'Oh,' Sadie said. 'When was this?'

'Oh, it was late. I was on my way back to the office and he was going to meet Melissa from work.'

'That's so nice of him,' April said. 'He's such a thoughtful boy – he always was my favourite.'

'Your favourite what?' Sadie asked, though she knew full well what April meant.

'My favourite of all the boys you brought to meet me. I always thought he was the one you'd settle with.'

'The others never lasted more than five minutes, that's why,' Ewan said, and Sadie stuck her tongue out at him in exactly the same way she would have fifteen years before.

'Just because you married the first girl who would have you,' she said, 'doesn't mean we all have to do that.'

'So you're into girls now?' he fired back. 'I wish you'd told me this before; Kat's got loads of single friends and I think one or two of them might be into girls too.'

Sadie rolled her eyes. 'Hold my sides – I think they're about to split. I don't know why Kat married you – you're such a dick.'

'Sadie!' April chided.

To her credit, Sadie blushed. 'Sorry, Gammy. I meant idiot. Ewan's an idiot. And even you have to admit that he is.'

'I'll admit no such thing,' April said. 'He's a fine boy. You're both wonderful.'

Sadie glanced at Ewan. Banter was an art that had completely passed Gammy by. She either meant something or she didn't – sarcasm, irony and teasing; they were concepts she'd never really understood.

'I *am* a fine boy,' Ewan said with a grin. 'Kat was lucky to get me and she knows it.'

'You were lucky to get her more like,' Sadie shot back. 'You might be good-looking – though that's up for debate as far as I can see, even though everyone else seems to think you are – but you're still as annoying as hell. I can't even imagine how annoying you must be to be married to.'

'Kat says every moment married to me is like heavenly bliss.'

'I'll ask her if that's true when I see her next. I think she might have something different to say about it.'

'Yeah, yeah… you say all this but you'd be devastated if I ever left the bay and you couldn't see me every day.'

Sadie grimaced and pretended it wasn't true at all, but it was. She couldn't imagine life without Ewan on the doorstep. Her sister Lucy was almost a stranger to her these days, but she and Lucy had never been that close anyway, not like her and Ewan. From the moment Sadie had arrived in the world it was Ewan. Lucy hadn't been interested in Sadie as a baby – as it turned out, she wasn't interested in babies at all – but Ewan had loved her. Over the years he'd become her unofficial guardian and protector. Whenever there had been bullying at school he'd been there to sort it out, unsuitable boys had been warned off (though they didn't always heed the warning and Sadie didn't always either), misdemeanours had been covered up and hidden from their parents with his collusion and shoulders had been offered to cry on. By the time Sadie had turned eighteen, it was common knowledge in Sea Salt Bay that if you messed with Sadie Schwartz then you messed with her big brother too.

These thoughts led to others as Ewan turned his attention back to the road, wearing a grin. But then Sadie spoke again and wiped it from his face, even though she hadn't meant to.

'You had Luke's business card, didn't you?'

'Who?'

'You know who I mean – don't pretend that you don't. Luke. Boat man… the man you were so mean and rude to earlier on.'

'Oh, him.'

'So you must have already known he'd moved to the bay.'

Ewan shook his head. 'The card shows an old address. He had absolutely no intention of being available for assistance if we'd needed it – he was trying to stitch us up.'

'I don't see how that makes sense because he must have realised that sooner or later we'd find out he'd moved here.'

'Who knows what he was thinking, but I don't believe for a minute he was accepting any kind of responsibility for what happened.'

'Aww, come on, Ewan… that's ridiculous. You saw him – he couldn't have been more sorry. What did you want from him? And I'm assuming that there would have been a mobile number on the card and there was a good chance that would still be valid.'

'Maybe.'

'So he wasn't trying to stitch us up.'

'Sadie… what does it matter?'

'It doesn't – I'm just curious.'

'Right.'

'So, what did you do with the card then?'

'I don't know,' he said evasively. 'I expect it'll be lying around somewhere.'

'You didn't throw it away?'

'No. You never know when you're going to need to sue someone.'

'But you said it was useless because it had an old address on it.'

'Ah, but you said that there would be a mobile number on it.'

'Hmm. Which means you *do* know where it is…'

She didn't wait for his reply. Diving for the glovebox, she began to root through.

'What are you doing?' Ewan snapped.

'You know what I'm doing.'

'You won't find it in there.'

Sadie continued to search. Then she held up a letter. 'This is your mortgage statement. You're terrible for stashing things in this glovebox – you put anything and everything in here. I'll bet Luke's card is in here… ah!' She pulled out a white square and flicked it with a look of triumph. 'Luke Goldman… this is it, right?'

'I don't remember...' Ewan replied lamely.

Sadie slammed the glovebox shut, pocketed the card and sat back in her seat. 'You won't mind if I take it – after all, it can't be that important to you if you can't remember where it came from.'

Ewan grimaced. 'And what are you going to do with it?'

'I haven't decided yet. I just thought I'd keep hold of it. After all, my head's the one that got damaged.'

'I'm beginning to think it got really damaged,' Ewan muttered, and Sadie had to laugh at the look of sheer bemusement and annoyance on his face.

'Dear God – please tell me you don't fancy this guy,' he added.

'Would it matter if I did?'

'Yes. For a start he's a lot older than you.'

'How do you know?'

'Because he told us he was thirty-five – remember?'

'Oh, right. OK. So what? Next objection please.'

'I'm willing to bet he'll end up another in your long line of rejects.'

'Ouch. Harsh.'

'But true.'

'You do realise you're the only person who could say that to me and not get a smack in the face. Besides, the law of averages says one of them eventually is going to turn out to be right for me.'

'You had the right one,' April said.

While the banter between Sadie and Ewan had been in full swing, they'd almost forgotten she was there until she made herself known again. But at this intervention, Sadie's good humour evaporated. She hardly needed reminding of that fact. Had anyone ever considered that she might know that she'd loved and lost her Mr Right and now the best she could hope for was Mr Almost Right? Did they ever consider that her Mr Almost Right was hard enough to find, but harder still when you were constantly reminded that Mr Right was achingly close but always just out of reach? It was like being in a locked room, starving and being forced to stare at a huge luscious cake through an impenetrable glass screen. There was no way you were ever getting the cake, but you were so hungry that if someone pushed a slice of bread and butter through the door you'd damn well grab it, cake or no. If Sadie was lucky perhaps her slice of bread would be soft and fluffy and the butter would be creamy and she might even get a little jam to go on top. It wouldn't be cake but it would still be nice, and she wouldn't complain about the fact that it wasn't cake because at least she wouldn't be hungry anymore, and anyway, she'd once said she was never going to eat cake again so she couldn't really complain when someone else had decided to eat it.

'Here we are…'

Ewan stopped the car and Sadie looked to see that they were at the gates of her house. She'd never been so pleased to see it.

She unclipped her seatbelt and looked up at Ewan. 'Are you popping in to get Freddie and Freya and say hello to Mum and Dad? I'm sure they'll be back by now.'

'I'd better get back to sort out the office while Kat's out with her last clients. Tell Mum and Dad I'll call later to pick up the kids if that's OK… and I'll talk to you then…' he added in a very deliberate tone, which led Sadie to believe that he'd be grabbing a quiet moment with her specifically to find out more about how Gammy had been that day – if not to tell her again what a bad idea it would be to get involved with Luke Goldman. Sadie needed to have some convincing answers for both scenarios, but at least she'd have time to think about them. That was, unless her mum and dad cottoned on as quickly as Ewan that all had not been plain sailing in the waffle house. If that happened, Sadie would just have to think on her feet.

She hopped out and went to help her grandmother.

April took Sadie's offered hand. 'Thank you darlin'.' She stepped carefully down onto the road and then went round to look in at the open driver's window. 'Thank you for the ride – I don't think I could have walked another step today; I'm worn to the bone.'

Ewan smiled at her, but then looked at Sadie, who gave an inward groan. Statements like that from their grandma, made as lightly as they were, only gave everyone more ammunition in the battle to prove that reopening the waffle house wasn't the best thing for her, even if she wanted it. And again, Sadie couldn't deny that she was still asking herself that question even if she was the person hell-bent on helping April to reopen it.

April leaned in to kiss her grandson lightly on the cheek before making her way up the path to the front door of the house. Ewan and Sadie watched her for a moment as she pushed the door open and went inside. Sadie was about to follow when Ewan called her back.

'Don't,' she said in a low voice. 'Whatever you're going to say, just don't.'

'You have no idea what it is.'

'If it's about Gammy then yes, I do, and it's only what I've been thinking myself all day.'

'So she's struggled? And be honest with me.'

'Not struggled, exactly.'

He raised his eyebrows.

'I *am* being honest,' Sadie said. 'She's enjoyed it. I just noticed… well, one or two moments where she wasn't quite with it.'

Ewan frowned, silent for a moment as his gaze went to the now closed front door of the house.

'I'm sure it'll pass,' Sadie said. 'She just needs time to readjust. She's been sitting around for a month and really she's still in mourning. And before you agree and use that as a reason for her to be rotting at home, I still say the best way to get her through that is to get her occupied again doing something she's always loved.'

'Maybe doing jigsaws or watercolours,' Ewan said quietly. 'Not running a busy café.'

'She'll be fine,' Sadie insisted. 'Give us a few weeks – to the end of the summer at least. I won't hold back on you – you know that. If she's still struggling then I'll say so and we'll do something about it.'

'You said she wasn't struggling.'

'You know what I mean.'

He shook his head. 'The end of the summer is too long. Let's try the end of the month.'

'But, Ewan—'

'That's enough time to see how this is going.'

Sadie pursed her lips. 'It's not your decision. You're not the head of the family, even though you think you are, and it's not for you to tell me what to do.'

'Ordinarily I wouldn't dream of even attempting to tell you what to do. But this is as much about Grandma as it is about you. If anything, it's all about Grandma.'

'So it doesn't matter that I gave up my teacher training to do this?'

'That was your choice and, anyway, we all told you not to do it. Your bed, you go and lie in it.'

'Thanks,' Sadie muttered.

'Believe it or not, I'm actually trying to look out for you here. For both of you. If the worst came to the worst and the waffle house closed down for good you could reapply for teacher training next year.'

'They wouldn't have me back.'

'Of course they would.'

'And what am I supposed to do with myself while I waited for that?'

Ewan started his engine and shrugged before he pulled away, leaving Sadie standing at the roadside.

'Great,' she said, watching as the car got smaller. 'Just great.'

Chapter Ten

Sadie had woken with dread in her heart for what the following day would bring, but she needn't have done. April was more her old self than Sadie had seen her since Gampy's death, and she had the waffle house kitchen running like a well-oiled machine. Could it be that the previous day had simply been a period of readjustment, a bump on the road to Gammy's recovery?

For most of that morning, between serving customers, keeping tabs on the wait times for food and ensuring the dining room was clean and tidy, Sadie flitted in and out of the kitchen where April worked to keep an eye on her. Each time she was fully expecting to find a vacant, slack-jawed stare while smoke billowed from a waffle iron, or salt was poured onto peachy pancakes, or coffee was mixed into a milkshake, but none of these things happened. April was brisk and bright, and by midday Sadie felt able to breathe a relieved (if still a little cautious) sigh.

She was also thrilled when Natalie and Georgia made time to pop in and say hello during their lunch breaks – Natalie mostly to wave around the letter that advised her the decree nisi for her divorce had been filed and now all she had to do was wait for the shortly-to-follow decree absolute and she'd be free. She was so excited that not only did she show it to Sadie, but she also went through to the kitchen to tell April about it.

'People used to marry for life,' Gammy said in response, giving a dismissive shrug and wiping a hand down her apron before bustling off to prepare Natalie's order. But, just as Sadie came in to see what was happening, Natalie grabbed a shocked April and gave her a big hug.

'But you know me better than that, don't you?' Natalie asked, smiling a little sadly as she let April go again.

'I remember you being born. It was so cold that day the bay froze over.'

'So you know that I didn't want this to happen. I didn't want to get divorced. I would never have married if I didn't think it was for life. Maybe the first time I was silly but this time…' She shook her head. Natalie gave the impression that she didn't care, that she treated her failed marriages like some kind of game, but Sadie – and to some extent April – knew her better than that. 'I was unlucky. I suppose you could say I was unwise. Does that mean I have to pay for that mistake for the rest of my life? That's what all those couples did; the ones who used to marry for life. They got it wrong and then they were stuck in misery. And for what? Because it was proper? Because that was what people did? Because the neighbours would gossip if they dared to do anything about it?'

April sniffed. 'I guess not.'

Natalie held her at arm's length and appraised her. 'Does this mean I'm not your favourite anymore?'

'You know you've always been my favourite, darlin',' April said, a smile blooming now. 'You're like family – you and Georgia; you know that. It's why it makes me sad to see things go wrong for you.'

Natalie kissed her on the cheek. 'Well I'm glad not to be in the bad books now. I don't think I could bear it.'

April laughed and wagged a finger as Natalie started back to the dining room, Sadie following. 'I didn't say that…'

Natalie and Sadie both started to laugh too as they went back to the table where Georgia was checking her phone.

'She seems like her old self again,' Natalie said.

'I thought that too.' Georgia looked up from her phone. 'Not at all what we'd expected.'

'Yeah…' Sadie replied carefully. 'I wonder if I jumped the gun a bit. I suppose it was bound to be weird being back here at first, but she seems a lot better today.' She smiled. 'I don't mind telling you I was starting to think I'd made a terrible mistake, but today I'm hopeful this might work out after all.'

Natalie got settled on a chair and took off her jacket. 'So you don't regret quitting your course now?'

'Oh, I regretted that as soon as I'd done it. You know me and my history of terrible decisions. I thought straight away I'd made another one, but whether I did or didn't, it's too late to undo it now.'

'It's never too late,' Georgia said.

'I'm proof of that,' Natalie agreed.

'Yeah.' Sadie nodded. 'Ewan said something similar last night when he dropped us off at home. He said I could always reapply for the course, but I'm not so sure.'

'I imagine you could,' Georgia said.

'Maybe, but even thinking that now is kind of already setting myself up for failure here – if you catch my drift. I shouldn't be making plans as if this isn't going to work out, I should be concentrating on making this work out.'

'It doesn't hurt to have a plan B,' Natalie said.

Sadie grimaced. 'No offence, but I don't want my life to be full of endless false starts and plan Bs.'

'Well, as you qualified that statement with the words "no offence" I think it has a meaning that will offend me,' Natalie said briskly.

'I didn't mean it to sound like that,' Sadie said. 'I just mean that… well, I feel I'm getting too old to keep on starting again because I've messed yet something else up. I need what I start now to work out or I'll run out of time for any more new starts.'

Natalie rested her elbows on the table and looked up at Sadie. 'Still offended. Some of us don't have any choice but to start again, whether we like it or not, and some of us aren't the cause of them. Some of us are on the receiving end of the messes.'

'I know, and what I said wasn't meant as a reflection on you. But you deal with it differently too. You bounce back and you're strong enough to start again. I don't think I am, not in the same way. And you've got a successful career, at least. You haven't messed that up. I haven't even got that… I'm nowhere right now.'

'You're happy,' Georgia said. 'You have the happiest life of anyone I know.'

'I'm not saying I'm not happy,' Sadie replied patiently. 'I realise I probably sound a bit ungrateful, and I know I'm lucky to live in a place like this with my brilliant family and brilliant friends but…' She sighed. 'Is it selfish to say I want more?'

'We all want more,' Georgia said, turning her gaze to the windows where a cornflower sky topped the sage of the waves. 'It's in our DNA; we can't help it – I read it somewhere. Some philosopher said it.'

'I don't know who said it,' Natalie replied, turning to Sadie, 'but even if it's true that doesn't mean we shouldn't still be thankful for what we've got.'

Sadie shrugged. 'That's just it. When I really take stock I don't feel that I do have a lot that actually means anything. I'm sorry if that sounds selfish and entitled, but there it is. I can't help what I feel and you are two of the few people I'd dare be honest enough to say that to. I have a nice home and family, but I don't have any purpose. I'm just floating around. Can you see what I mean?'

'Yes,' Natalie said, her tone softening again. 'And maybe this place will be your purpose if you just give it enough time to work.'

'Aristotle!'

Natalie and Sadie spun as one to look at Georgia.

Natalie grinned. 'Remembered it, did you?'

'No.' Georgia held up her phone to show them the screen. 'But Mr Google did!'

Sadie smiled. 'Well, things seem better already for knowing that.'

But then her attention was diverted by a woman who was approaching the unmanned counter. She glanced back at her friends. 'Better go; work to do. Catch up with you later.'

'That's OK,' Georgia said, angling her head towards the kitchen doors. 'Our food is here.'

Sadie looked to see April marching over with two plates piled high with waffles, fruit and cream, one topped with chocolate curls for Georgia and one with sprinkles for Natalie. Sadie smiled. From here their orders looked bang on what they'd asked for. Yes, it did look as if they might be on the right track now after all.

Sadie was humming softly to herself as she turned the key to lock the front door of the waffle house for the night. Her grandmother was cleaning tables and outside the sky was still bright and the air warm. Plenty of people were continuing to mill around too – walking the pier or sitting on the scrolled iron benches looking out to sea, or on rides or heading into the amusement arcade, and the beach was still dotted with families and parties of friends messing around on the sand.

'Gammy...' Sadie began slowly, 'didn't you ever think about staying open a bit later in the summer months?'

April looked up, sleeves rolled to her elbows. For a lady of her age, her forearms were strong and toned and the skin smooth, but then, she'd spent her whole life working, hardly still for a moment. Perhaps it wasn't a surprise that she was in such good shape when you thought about it that way, and April herself usually said so whenever Sadie gave her a compliment. She'd laugh and point out that it was down to nothing more than hard work and good genes, but Sadie often looked and admired her Gammy – as she did for so many other things – and hoped that those good genes would one day find their way to her.

'Never really saw the point. People don't want sweet things in the evening.'

'What makes you think that?'

'They just don't.'

'But restaurants offer a sweet menu—'

'For after your dinner... which is the most important bit. Nobody goes in there just asking for the sweet menu, do they?'

'Well, what about these dessert places that are springing up everywhere? They've got at least half a dozen in Bournemouth and Weymouth...'

'We're not Bournemouth or Weymouth,' April said briskly. 'Sea Salt Bay is nowhere near as big as one of those towns, and we just don't get the trade that those places do.'

'But they stay open into the evening,' Sadie insisted. 'We're only a small town but we'd only have one place like that open. I think the trade would come.'

April wrung out the cloth she was using into a bucket. 'Your grandpa always said we worked a long enough week as it was without working into the night and I happen to agree. Besides, in case you hadn't noticed, I'm an old lady now and it's a bit too late to start working all the hours the dear Lord has sent us.'

'But you've got me now.'

'Two of us is still just the same as it was before.'

'I can work longer… I'm younger.'

'I can't.'

'I could do it alone if it wasn't too busy.'

April shook her head. 'You couldn't – it's just not practical. And even if you could, would you really want to spend your whole life in here?'

Sadie didn't want to spend her whole life in the waffle house, of course, but she was beginning to think that since she'd committed herself, she might as well make a success of it. A good place to start might be to gently overhaul the way they did things. The way they did things now was the way her grandparents had always done them, and what worked when they'd first opened all those years ago – the days when shops didn't open on Sundays and pubs really were empty by 11 p.m. – didn't necessarily suit today's society. People now wanted things when they wanted things, and they expected their bars and restaurants and shops to be open for business for a lot more of the day. If the waffle house opened longer Sadie was sure they'd get enough custom to make it worth their while.

She was aware, also, that it might be too much to ask of April to put in longer hours, but Sadie was certain she could find a way to make it work for them. Her family had all said they were too busy to help, but part of that had been about making a point to Sadie because they hadn't wanted her to do this. But if they all saw how serious she was about making it work, how she could build the waffle house into a far more successful venture than her grandma or grandpa could ever have imagined, then perhaps they'd be more supportive and willing to lend themselves out for the odd hour here and there.

'What about trialling a few evenings to see how it goes?' Sadie asked. 'If it took off and we thought it would make enough money we could hire help—'

'No, darlin'. You have a life outside this place. How are you gonna meet a man if you're always working in here?'

Annoyingly, and without her permission, Declan popped into Sadie's head. And as fast as she shook away the thought, it was followed by a vision of Luke. One a man she had to force herself to forget and one she'd like to know better, even though the circumstances of her meeting with the latter were about as unromantic as it got. But Sadie couldn't let herself dwell on any of that; the waffle house had to be her first and top priority. Maybe the romance in her life would come when she least expected it, and maybe that was the best way to let it happen, but she sure as hell couldn't expect any business to run that way.

She folded her arms. 'I have plenty of time to meet a man and I don't need one to make me happy.'

April shook her head again and dipped her cloth back into her bucket.

'That's your final word?' Sadie asked, not angry or annoyed, but a little frustrated that she couldn't make her grandma see the potential in the waffle house she could.

April looked up. 'The day you own this place, Sadie... then you can decide the final word on whatever you like. Until then it's my business and I have the final word on everything.'

Sadie planted her hands on her hips and stared at her grandmother. She'd wanted the old April Schwartz back and – boy – had she got her now. Strong, but also stubborn. Sadie had given up a lot to be here – couldn't her grandma see that? She'd given up far too much and yet her grandmother was dismissing her like a child. Was that how April saw her still – like a little girl? Didn't she think Sadie was capable of making sound decisions? And couldn't she see how knowing her grandma saw her that way might hurt Sadie?

'So I don't get a say in anything even though I'm running the place with you?'

'You're helping us,' April said. 'We probably won't need you tomorrow.'

Sadie's eyes widened. 'Who won't?'

'He ought to be back tomorrow.'

'Who will?'

April rubbed at a stubborn spot on the table. 'If I know your grandpa he won't want to be away for too long.'

Sadie felt sick. She wobbled to a seat and dropped into it as she stared at her grandma. Just when she thought things were looking up, that they were on the path to happiness, the ground had collapsed from beneath her again. Was it always going to be like this now?

'Gammy,' she said slowly, her heart beating in her ears, 'where do you think Gampy is?'

April laughed lightly, her attention still on the crusted bit of sugar clinging stubbornly to the table. 'Oh, Sadie… don't tease your old grandma. You know just where he is as well as I do.'

'Gammy, I—'

There was a knock at the door. Sadie opened the blinds, ready to tell whoever it was that they'd closed for the day, only to see Declan standing outside. Quickly, she unlocked the door.

'Dec!' she cried with more emotion than he could have reasonably expected because he looked shocked by the greeting.

'Sadie…?'

'Come in,' Sadie added, ushering him inside before closing and locking the door again. Declan watched as she did so, perhaps wondering whether he was going to have to fight his way out if he needed to leave.

'I wanted to drop in yesterday to see how things were going but you'd locked up before I got here. And then I planned to come a bit earlier today to catch you but I got a bit held up at work…' He looked carefully at Sadie and dropped his voice. 'Is everything OK?'

'Oh, hello, Declan!' April called cheerfully. 'Come to take Sadie out?'

Declan shot a confused glance at Sadie.

'I'm afraid the kitchen's closed right now,' she added.

'That's OK,' Declan said carefully. 'Another time maybe?'

'That'd be just fine,' April said fondly. She dropped the cloth into the bucket of water and straightened up, rubbing at her back before reaching for the handle. Declan rushed over.

'Here… let me get that for you. Is it going to the kitchen?'

'Oh, yes, thank you, darlin'! That's so sweet of you.' April turned to Sadie with a gleam in her eye. 'My favourite,' she mouthed as he took the water away, and Sadie was more confused and scared than ever. How was it that Gammy could recall with perfect clarity a conversation they'd had the day before – one that she'd only appeared to be vaguely engaged with – but not the fact that Gampy was dead?

Declan rubbed his hands down his trousers as he came back in. 'Anything else I can help with? My muscles are at your disposal.'

Sadie didn't know whether to cry or run to kiss him. He always knew just the right thing to do in any situation, and he was doing it again now. It must have been obvious to him that something wasn't right here, but he wasn't making a big deal about it, instead doing his best to put April at ease and show Sadie that he was on her side. Not for the first time, along with gratitude that she had such a friend, Sadie was also assailed by regrets that she'd ever let a man like him go.

'And they are fine muscles,' April said, laughing. 'If you'd like you can stack the chairs on top of the tables so I can sweep the floor.'

'I can sweep the floor,' Sadie said. 'Why don't you go and tidy the fridge – you know better than me what needs to be thrown out.'

'Sure, darlin'; I can do that.'

April went into the kitchen. As soon as she'd gone, Declan turned to Sadie and the carefree expression he'd worn for her disappeared, replaced by one of urgent questions.

'I know that face,' he said. 'What's wrong?'

'Nothing,' Sadie said, wondering why she was even bothering to cover anything up. Declan had already seen for himself that things weren't right and she knew him better than to think he'd let it drop. But it wasn't right to involve him in her problems. Once upon a time maybe it would have been OK, but they weren't together now, and the burdens he needed to share weren't hers, they were Melissa's. It wasn't fair of Sadie to pile more on him. 'Why should there be anything wrong? I'm tired and it's been busy here – more than I'm used to. And sometimes I feel as if it's too much but I'm sure I'll get used to it.'

'And that's it?' he asked, his tone edged with obvious scepticism.

'Yes. What else would it be?'

'OK,' he said, still sounding unconvinced. He grabbed a chair while Sadie went to get the sweeping brush.

'I bumped into Ewan yesterday and—' Declan began. But he stopped short because Sadie was crying. She hadn't wanted to – not in front of him and not with Gammy in the next room – but she couldn't keep it in any longer. He put the chair down and rushed to wrap her in his arms. No questions, no waiting for permission, just an instinct to comfort her, and though she knew she ought to be grateful for his reaction, it only made things worse.

'I'm sorry,' she said, sniffing hard. 'Ignore me; I'm just tired.'

He held her tighter still. He still smelt the same, a special scent that seemed to have been created just for her. She closed her eyes and breathed him in.

God, how many years had it been since she'd been folded into his arms like this, and yet, how could it feel so painfully, heart-achingly familiar?

'You're sure that's all it is?' he asked. 'Nothing else?'

'No.'

'Nothing to do with your scare at the beach the other day…? Because nobody would think you were weak for admitting that it had affected you and sometimes it's a delayed reaction—'

Sadie buried her head further into his chest. She knew that she ought to push him away but she didn't want to. 'No, it's not that.'

How could she tell him what it really was? How scared she was for her grandma, how she was even more scared that she'd made the most terrible mistake leaving her teaching course to come and take the waffle house on?

Terrible mistakes, she thought ruefully, seemed to be her speciality these days – she'd certainly made enough of them over the last few years. Many of them were still being afforded the luxury of time to regret. One of them was standing with his arms around her now, making it worse than he could have ever imagined, and the fact that his intentions were nothing but pure made it all worse still.

'You need some help in here?' he asked. 'Until you get used to it?'

'You're far too busy.'

'It's a shame but I am really, even though I'd like to help. I was thinking Melissa might be able to, though. She has some afternoons free and I could ask—'

'No!' Sadie said, panic-stricken by the thought and with a tone that was probably a bit too revealing of that fact. Melissa was the last person she needed in here. It was hardly Melissa's fault that Sadie's emotions were all over the place, but her presence certainly wouldn't help.

'I'm sure she'd say yes.'

Sadie eased herself free and looked up at him. 'Everyone is busy and I wouldn't expect anyone to give up their time regardless. We have to manage, Gammy and me. We'll find a way to make it work; it might just take a little time.'

He smiled down at her. 'Everyone loves her, you know. Everyone wants this to succeed. And everyone knows why you're doing this, but not one of them would blame you if you decided it was too much. It doesn't have to be your battle, and you certainly don't have to fight it alone.'

'You say that, but it kind of is. I'm here now, I dragged Gammy back into this place and I persuaded everyone that it was a good idea, and now I feel I have to see it through. I could have left it alone but I didn't, and I have to take responsibility for that. It's only fair – I can't give hope and then take it straight away again, especially not when it comes to Gammy.'

He caught a tear with his sleeve pulled up around his hand, just like he used to do whenever she got upset, and, for a moment, she felt she'd stop breathing.

'Thank you,' she said, and she'd never meant those words more. And if he'd asked her what for, she wouldn't have been able to tell him. It was for too much, far more than she had words for. Most of all, that he could still be this kind and patient, this supportive, this much of a friend after all she'd done to him. She'd never felt so grateful and yet so undeserving, and like such a snake for the unwanted thoughts she had: that if she could see a way to removing Melissa from his life with no comeback and no recrimination then she might be sorely tempted to do that so the way would be clear for her again.

'Look,' he said, 'is there anything else I can help with while I'm here? I don't have to be anywhere in particular for a while.'

Sadie forced a smile. 'You've just done a full day at work – the last thing you need is to start again here.'

'I want to help; tell me what I can do.'

At that moment, April emerged from the kitchen. Sadie glanced at Declan, relieved that she wasn't still in his arms because who knew what kind of confusion that might cause.

'Oh, darlin'…' April said cheerily, wearing a broad smile, 'if you really want to help then we could sure use your muscles to take all that garbage out to the bins on the promenade. It's such a walk for me these days.'

Sadie hadn't heard Gammy coming back to the dining room, but her grandmother had clearly heard some of what they'd been saying. There was no way to know how much of the rest of the conversation she'd picked up without asking her straight out, and Sadie wasn't about to lift the lid on that potential nest of vipers, but, judging by her breezy attitude, it didn't appear to be much. So Sadie hurriedly rubbed her eyes and put on her brightest smile. Declan flexed his biceps with a grin that made April giggle like a teenager.

'Your wish is my command!' he said. 'Show me what you want moving and I'll be happy to do it for you.'

'Oh, you are just a dear,' April began. 'This way… I'll show you…'

They went through to the kitchen together. A moment later Sadie heard laughter from them both as she turned her attention to moving the chairs that Declan hadn't finished doing and sweeping the floor. Declan had always found it easy to charm April, even as an awkward boy. He was just one of those people who exuded warmth and kindness, whose good soul shone through. No wonder Melissa was so keen to keep any potential competition for his affections firmly out of the picture, and no wonder she didn't trust Sadie. And she didn't trust Sadie an inch – that much was evident. Sadie wouldn't trust Sadie either, and this evening was a dangerous reminder of those feelings that she constantly fought to keep locked away. Natalie would have said Sadie needed a distraction, though Lord knew that Sadie had been trying hard enough over the last few years to find one that might finally become more permanent than that, someone who could banish the regrets over Declan that she couldn't seem to shake – her long list of unsatisfactory boyfriends since Declan was testament to that.

She looked up as he came back from the kitchen lugging a large refuse sack, chatting easily to April as she followed to unlock the front door for him. He shot Sadie a smile full of sympathy and understanding that seemed to tell her not to worry, that she wasn't on her own, that she could share her worries and stresses with him whenever she needed to offload, and her heart gave a lurch like a ship tossed on an unseen swell.

God, she needed a distraction and she needed it pronto.

Chapter Eleven

As the sun went down, Sadie walked along the beach, the sun warm and friendly on her skin, the evening light mellow and pinky gold on the cliffs. After they'd finished clearing up at the waffle house Declan had given them a lift home before going back to meet Melissa from work. Sadie had been grateful for the ride for April's sake, but for her own, she'd wished he could find it in himself to be less than insufferably kind for one second of his life because she would rather – really needed to – have walked. So Sadie skipped dinner at home, incurring Henny's ire, but making excuses that she'd been picking at the fruit and sweets at the waffle house all day and had ruined her appetite and was going to take a walk to try to get it back.

The bit about the fruit and sweets wasn't true, even if the part about needing a walk was, because she'd hardly had time to pick at anything. She just wasn't hungry at all, even though an early start and a busy day ought to have meant she was. Maybe she'd get some leftovers later, or maybe she'd even stop by for fish and chips, which tasted better by the sea than anywhere else (even people who lived by the sea couldn't deny that). Although, that did run the risk of bumping into Declan's dad, who owned the fish and chip shop and, even though he had staff, sometimes worked a shift too. Or even Declan himself, who might be around, as he sometimes was, sitting at a table shooting the breeze with his dad if the restaurant was gifted a quiet moment.

But for the moment Sadie wasn't really thinking about food. She wasn't really thinking about anything, and yet, she simultaneously seemed to be thinking about everything in the world. Her head was full, but nothing seemed to stay long enough in there to fully process because as soon as a thought presented itself another would come along demanding her attention. The end result was a Sadie increasingly frustrated with her inability to make a decision about anything, a Sadie who had even less ability to actually begin addressing any of the things that were bothering her than a Sadie with no time to think of them at all. Walking the beach, the sea licking at the shoreline like a contented cat, was helping her to relax, but it didn't feel as if it was solving anything.

Toes dug into the soft sand, she stopped to gaze out to where the sunlight was sprinkled over the waves like glitter. Visibility was good this evening, the light just right so that you could see for miles, and on the horizon she counted at least three large ships and the distant headlands further along the coast. This view was the most perfect view in the world to her. She hadn't always thought so, but being away from Sea Salt Bay had taught her a lot of things, and how to appreciate her home was one of them. She couldn't understand how her sister Lucy could live so far from here and never want to come back, but perhaps that was because Lucy hadn't felt so connected to the people she'd left behind. One, in particular…

Sadie shook the thought away. She'd come out this evening to get away from those feelings, not ponder them some more.

'Would now be a bad time to say hello?'

Sadie almost visibly jumped. She turned to find Luke standing next to her, yet she'd been so lost in thought that she hadn't even noticed him approach.

'It's a good thing you're not a mugger,' she said, catching her breath. 'Although you'd be bloody brilliant at it because I never even heard you sneak up on me.'

He gave a warm chuckle. 'Sorry about that. But you can keep your money; I'm not a mugger.'

'We've got to stop bumping into each other like this,' she replied with a laugh.

'I know – it must look as if I'm stalking you and I promise I'm not.'

'Ah, well, I think I can believe you on that score. Sea Salt Bay is a very small place and it's inevitable that we'd keep running into each other really.'

He held her in a gaze that threw her for a moment. 'Is that so bad?'

'Um… No…'

He turned to the sea. Sadie glanced at his profile in the low sun. He was even better-looking than she remembered, everything in perfect proportion, his features not as soft as Declan's but…

Ugh, why did she keep on comparing people to Declan?

She began again. *Luke*, this was Luke, and he was like himself, nobody else. His skin was tanned, his hair dark, the faint beginning of crow's feet at the corners of his eyes that didn't detract from his looks but only gave them a sexy hint of experience and a life well lived. He was tall too, maybe around five eleven, six feet. His accent was that of a well-heeled Londoner though there were traces of other accents that suggested he'd lived in other places too. She'd never really noticed that before, or how his voice was mellow and full, like the notes of a well-loved oboe. She'd had plenty of distractions previously, but already she could tell that Luke might be different. And was he flirting with her? Yes, she decided, maybe he was. And maybe she might quite like it.

'It's a beautiful place,' he said, gazing out at the view she'd just been admiring. 'I suppose you take all this in your stride when you've lived here all your life.'

'All what?'

'This…' He swept a hand along the line of the horizon. 'I suppose it stops being so incredible to you after a while; you take it for granted.'

'No, it doesn't really. I was born and raised here, and I suppose I'm used to it, but I never take it for granted and it never stops being beautiful. It was one of the things I missed most when I went away to uni. Now that I'm back, I know I'd never get bored of it, even if I looked at it every day for a hundred years.'

'I can see why. I'm hoping I'll feel the same when I've been here long enough to start feeling I can call it home.'

'So you're planning to stay, even though you're being treated horribly by the locals?'

He laughed again, a warm, rich sound.

'I think the locals might have just cause. I think I might have got off on a very wrong foot with them. But if at least some of them can forgive me then I'd like to call this my forever home. I can't imagine now how anywhere else could compare after being here.'

'One of them has already forgiven you,' Sadie said.

He cocked her a sideways glance. 'And would that one be standing close by?'

'They would.'

He smiled. 'Then I'm grateful to know that not everyone hates me.'

'They don't, and even if they did it wouldn't last long. Even Ewan will come round eventually.'

Luke raised a disbelieving eyebrow.

'It might take twenty or so years,' Sadie admitted, laughing. 'But he will. He's not scary at all when you get to know him.'

'So I've been hearing. He seems to have a lot of fans around here.'

'Ah…' Sadie grinned. 'Would these fans be mostly female?'

'It does seem he's a bit of a local heartthrob.'

'God, it's enough to make a sister want to vomit.'

He looked at her again. 'That bad? If it's any consolation he didn't get all the good-looking genes in your family…'

Sadie burst out laughing and he shook his head, having the decency to look a little embarrassed.

'As chat-up lines go,' he said, holding in his own laughter, 'that was dreadful, wasn't it?'

'A chat-up line? Was that what it was – I hardly recognised it.'

'In my defence, it was off the cuff. You could at least cut me a bit of slack here – I'm trying to think on my feet to woo you in very difficult circumstances.'

'And what circumstances might those be?'

He rubbed a hand across his chin. 'Well… I can't imagine I'm your favourite person right now—'

'But I appreciate that you're working hard on that,' Sadie cut in with a smile.

'But still… I find myself trying to win you over anyway. Tell me honestly, is it a lost cause? Tell me I'm deluded and I'll sod off and never bother you again.'

Sadie's smile grew. 'You've got balls, I'll give you that.'

'Does that mean you admire my tenacity but I *am* deluded?'

'No. It means I like that you're trying and I could be persuaded to… what actually are you asking for?'

'How about a drink with a stranger in town who doesn't yet know anyone except the girl he almost drowned and who's apparently crazy enough to forgive him?'

Excitement bubbled up in Sadie – a mad, giddy kind of excitement that she hadn't felt in a long time.

'You want to take me out?'

'You don't want to go?'

'Yeah… yeah, I do. I was just making sure I was following the conversation because, you know, since that bump on my head I get kind of confused.'

He looked suddenly horrified, and Sadie started to laugh. 'Oh, God, I'm sorry! I thought you'd realise I was kidding!'

His hand went to his heart and he looked a little offended. 'No, I didn't!' But then his features relaxed again. 'OK, I probably deserved that.'

'In all honesty, though, I did need to check because I hadn't really expected things to go the way they are.'

'Can I be honest? Neither did I. Until five minutes ago it hadn't crossed my mind to ask you out. I mean, it had, because, you know, I find you very attractive, but I wouldn't have dared after…'

Sadie giggled. 'Just goes to show that sometimes life can surprise you.'

'It does.' He held her in a gaze lit by the setting sun. 'Is it forward to say that I've never met anyone like you before?'

'A little, but I can deal with it.'

'It's true. I meet a lot of people but none of them have ever caused me to spontaneously make myself look like an idiot.'

'You don't look like an idiot. I'm glad you felt spontaneous.'

'Can I be even more spontaneous then?'

'How?'

'That drink… what are you doing for the next couple of hours?'

Sadie smiled, her stomach doing delicious flips again. As distractions went, this one was looking promising.

'Nothing,' she said. 'But I have a feeling that's about to change.'

There were a few raised eyebrows in the Listing Ship as Luke approached the bar with Sadie by his side. Everyone knew he was newly arrived in town, but that wasn't the only thing they knew because by now everyone had heard about the incident where his boat had collided with Sadie's head. She could imagine that this latest turn of events might surprise a few of them.

Vivien, who by day was the lollipop lady for Sea Salt Bay's only school and worked the bar at Sea Salt bay's only pub at night, was on duty. Even though Sadie and Luke came in together and approached the bar together, after a swift, uncertain glance at him, it was Sadie she addressed first.

'Hello, Sadie. How's your gran doing?'

'Oh, she's getting better every day, thanks,' Sadie said. She wasn't about to give anyone outside the family any more information than that.

Vivien nodded. 'I heard you opened up the waffle house again.'

'We have. It's a trial run,' she added carefully. 'See how she copes, and I'm helping her.'

'Well I'm glad to hear it. The town's not the same without that old place.'

That was what Sadie kept hearing from everyone. She couldn't help but wonder whether, if it made her a hero now for trying to get this show back on the road, would it then make her the villain if it didn't work out? If they ended up having to close again for good, if it proved to be too much for Sadie, would everyone blame her for the failure?

Would they see April as the victim of an unsupportive granddaughter who'd decided that she'd rather please herself than keep the family business going?

But now wasn't the time to worry about that, and so Sadie decided she wasn't going to.

'This is Luke,' she said instead, gesturing to him.

'So I've heard,' Vivien said, regarding him closely now. 'You've moved into the Old Chapel, haven't you?'

'Yes,' he said cheerfully.

'Bit of a wreck up there, ain't it?'

'You could say that, but it's nothing I won't be able to sort out. Have you been up there lately? It's not looking too bad since I painted the outside.'

'Can't say I have. Never met the man who owned it before you either. He didn't drink in here,' she added, as if to say that fact alone made him someone every sane person would want to avoid.

'Oh,' Luke said, 'where did he drink then? I thought this was your only pub?'

'It is,' Vivien said, her tone even more distrustful now of the unknown previous owner of the Old Chapel.

'Can we get a couple of beers?' Sadie asked.

Vivien nodded. 'Pints or halves?'

Sadie glanced at Luke and grinned. 'I don't know about you but I'm having a pint.'

'Well if you're having a pint I can hardly wimp out and get a half, can I? It's lucky the old house is in walking distance because it might need to be if we have more than a couple of those.'

'Almost everything in Sea Salt Bay is in walking distance,' Sadie said as Vivien went to get their drinks. 'I don't know how it's even classed as a town at all – it's basically about three streets.'

'It doesn't seem all that small to me.'

'OK,' Sadie said, laughing. 'Maybe about half a dozen streets. Only just big enough to sometimes not feel like walking.'

'Ah. Well they're half a dozen very nice streets.'

'Oh, yes,' Sadie replied. 'I'm the last person to argue with that.'

Vivien returned and plonked two frothing glasses down. 'Will you be wanting food? Only the kitchen might be closing early tonight. Also, I don't know who eats the muck, but the halloumi is all gone. Only two burgers left an' all so if you want burgers you'd better get in quick.'

Sadie turned to Luke.

'I could eat a burger,' he said. 'Ask me any time about burgers and I'd always say yes.'

'Well, it's hardly...' Sadie began, but then paused. What she'd been thinking was that it was hardly first-date food and ordinarily she'd have gone for something a bit daintier. But she had skipped dinner at home and by now her black mood had lifted – even if only for the moment – and she was hungry. Not to mention that somehow this didn't feel like a first date, though she couldn't say why. The excitement was there, the newness, all the possibilities laid out before her. Would they get beyond tonight? If they did, how far could it go? The difference was that she felt far more relaxed today than she ever had on any first date. Conversation and even banter felt easy with Luke, and the desperate need to look like a girl who was more than she was just didn't trouble her.

Perhaps it was down to the spontaneity of it, the speed by which events had taken over. She hadn't had time to stress over what to wear or what she'd say. She was standing here, hair unkempt, sand in her shoes, wearing the same clothes she'd had on at work. But somehow, that was OK. Because Luke's hair was also windswept, and he had sand in his shoes too and paint on his old denim shirt. As first dates went, it was about the most casual one Sadie had ever been on, but there was something she liked about that – very much – something different and wild and a little bit sexy too. Like anything could happen. And age difference or not (which wasn't all that bad – in her opinion anyway), family disapproval or not, Luke was a little bit sexy too. OK, more than a little bit. He was what Natalie would have called sex on legs.

He looked at her, waiting for her answer with a mischievous, inviting look in his eyes. Burger first, and then what? She hardly dared imagine because the thought had her heart beating so fast it made her dizzy.

'Why not?' she said. 'I'm starving.'

'Me too,' he said. He turned to Vivien. 'We'll take those burgers if you don't mind.'

Vivien shrugged as she rung them through the till. 'No skin off my nose. One less item on the menu for me to worry about.'

'This' – Luke nodded at his burger, still chewing on the mouthful he'd just taken – 'is just the best burger I've ever had.'

'The best?' Sadie asked, laughing as she reached for her own. 'The absolute, undisputed best you've ever had in your entire life?'

'Yup.'

'Wow…' Sadie took a bite of her own. The patty was juicy, no doubt about that, the pickle-to-sauce ratio just about perfect and the brioche bun soft and a little sweet, but the best ever? She munched with a look of contentment as she contemplated his statement. Or rather, she contemplated him. God, he was good-looking, and he got better-looking the longer she looked. There was no doubt that tonight was turning out to be an unexpectedly good night, a distraction from her worries which, right now, seemed a lifetime away.

'So,' she said as she swallowed a mouthful, 'what made you choose Sea Salt Bay over all the other seaside towns you could have chosen?'

'I used to come here as a kid with my parents. Until I was about eight anyway.'

'Why did you stop? They got bored? You got bored?'

'My dad got bored… with my mum.'

'Oh… I'm sorry.'

He waved away the apology. 'Life, isn't it? He left her like so many do. Went off with his muse.'

Sadie frowned. 'His muse?'

'He was an artist. Mum was his muse at first – he drew so many incredible pictures of her. But after she'd had me she put on a little weight and he told her he'd have to find someone else to draw because she wasn't the right shape anymore.'

Sadie's frown deepened.

'I know,' he said, reading her thoughts in her face. 'It was cruel and I don't think my mum ever really got over it. And apparently Dad couldn't have a muse and not sleep with her. So, you see…'

Sadie's mouth dropped open.

'Yes,' he said, laughing and without a trace of bitterness in it. 'He was an arsehole of the highest order and, no, I don't really care for him all that much if I'm honest. I saw how it all left my mum and I didn't much like it.'

'Hmm…'

'Are you shocked? Sorry, was it too much too soon?'

'It's just… well, I was expecting more along the lines of "It has a nice pier" or "I like the beach."'

'Oh yes,' he said, laughing again. 'It does have a nice pier and I do like the beach. All of those things are true. And I do have a lot of happy memories of this place from before my parents split.'

'Do you see your dad now?'

'Not often. He moved to Majorca with *her*' – Luke made speech marks in the air with his fingers – '*where the light is better*. I pop over at Christmas and I try my best to get along with everyone but I find it quite gratifying that my mum has aged far more gracefully than either of them have.'

'So he's still with the woman?'

'Yes, so at least he didn't throw his marriage away on a fling, I suppose. I guess he must have loved her.'

'And you,' Sadie asked, 'you never…?'

'Married? No. A few close calls, of course. By thirty-five most people have had at least one, haven't they?'

'If it's not too personal, what do you mean by close calls?'

His expression closed. It was so sudden and jarring that it threw Sadie completely. She half expected him to stand up and walk out.

'I'm sorry…' she began, but he put up a hand to stop her.

'You have nothing to be sorry for. I should have expected you to ask questions like that – it's only natural given that we're here together now. It's just…' He let out a pained sigh. 'It's just that something happened and I still find it hard to talk about.'

'You don't have to. I shouldn't have asked.'

'You had every right to ask. If it matters to you then—'

'No.' Sadie shook her head. 'When you're ready. I can't say I'm not mad with curiosity but I'm happy to wait until you're ready to tell me.'

He nodded. 'Well, anyway, that's why I never married.'

Sadie wondered whether the way he referred to marriage, rather than simply to settling down or moving in with someone, was because marriage had been on the cards for him, and she wondered what on earth could have destroyed that hope – because looking at his face it was clearly something he'd hoped for once. But she'd meant what she'd said: she didn't want to force a confession from him of that sort – not while this was all so new between them – and part of her wondered if she wanted to know just yet. What if it was something that would put her off him? She was really beginning to think that she liked him a lot, and she really didn't want to hear something that would change that so she turned the conversation back to her own life (not that it was all that much safer) and she tried to make it light again, hoping the moment would pass.

'My family are always complaining that I haven't settled down yet,' she said.

'I'd have said you're far too young to worry about that.'

'Try telling my family that.'

'How old are you – if that's not an impertinent question?'

'It's not, and I'm twenty-six.'

'Twenty-six. I can't pretend I'm not a bit jealous – I wish I was still twenty-six.'

'My brother says you're too old for me.'

'Your brother says a lot of things…' He shook his head. 'Sorry, I didn't mean to sound… I realise he's just looking out for you.' And then he gave a cheeky smile. 'So, this conversation where your brother is telling you I'm too old for you… when did this happen? More to the point, why?'

It was Sadie's turn to smile, but it was less cheeky and more sheepish. 'I guess he can just see the tell-tale signs that I fancied you. Let's just say he won't be very pleased when he hears he was right.'

'We don't have to tell him – it's just one date after all.'

'No, but you can guarantee that Vivien will; she'll be straight over tomorrow hoping for brownie points.'

'What is it with this town and your brother?'

'I can't explain it, but everyone just loves him – and I mean everyone. You won't hear a bad word said about him. Imagine how it feels to be the little sister of such perfection.'

'I should imagine it's hard for everyone to compete. I'd hate to have been a teenage boy in this town if he'd been at my school.'

Sadie laughed as she reached for her beer. 'You'd have got my vote, if it's any consolation. Although, I could hardly date my own brother.'

'With one hand she giveth, then with the other she taketh away.'

Sadie's laughter rang out across the pub. 'Sorry, that probably sounds like a backhanded compliment, but it *was* a compliment.'

'Then thank you.'

'You're welcome.'

'What about you?' he asked. 'There must have been more than your fair share of boyfriends.'

'So I look like a slapper?'

'God no!' he cried, almost choking on his burger. 'God, is that what it sounded like? I didn't mean that at all!'

Sadie's laughter was louder still. 'Oh, dear, you're very easy to wind up, aren't you?'

'Hmm. I'll have to look out for that. But seriously, what I meant was that you're… well, you're gorgeous and I would have expected to see men queuing outside your door.'

'So now I sound like a prostitute, so thank you. I can see there was a compliment in there too though.'

'I mean it,' he said. 'I think you're stunning. After… well even after the boat accident I shouldn't have been thinking about you… well, not in the way I was, but I couldn't do anything else. And I was really hoping you'd call the number on my card because it would give me an excuse to talk to you again.'

'You have Ewan to thank for the fact that I didn't. He did his best to lose your card, although I've since found it. So I do have it and maybe I will call the number on it now I know all this.'

He smiled. But then it became a vague frown. 'Your brother really doesn't like me, does he?'

'Let's just say I'd better not take you to his house for a visit any time soon.'

'I suppose that's fair enough in the circumstances. Maybe one day in the not-too-distant future he might be able to forgive me?'

'If you're living in Sea Salt Bay now he has a very good reason to. The town is too small for people to have serious grudges; we make an effort to get along for that reason if nothing else. It doesn't mean it's all peace and harmony, but it means that we try maybe a bit harder here. Ewan will come round.'

He nodded. 'That's good to hear. So… what's the deal with your waffle house?'

'It's not my waffle house – it still belongs to my grandma. She and my grandpa have run it for as long as anyone here can remember, and when he died we – the family – were all set to close it. But I decided to help Gammy get it running again.'

'And that's a long-term plan for you? What did you do before that?'

'I was training to be a teacher, would you believe?'

'You've given it up?'

'I've quit my course, though everyone seems fairly sure that I could get another place if I needed to.'

'Do you think you'll go back to it?'

'I don't know. It depends what happens with the waffle house. I don't know that I'm cut out to be a teacher, if I'm honest.'

Sadie took a swig of her beer. She didn't much like the way the conversation was going; after the day – no, the week – she'd had, she just wanted to forget about the waffle house and her future for a while.

'Tell me more about you,' she said. 'What do you do?'

'It's a bit dull in comparison to what you've told me.'

'How can it be dull? You've already told me that your dad is an artist – that's not dull.'

He shrugged. 'I'm just a builder. By trade, anyway. Now it's just this and that.'

'Ah, so that's why you can be so blasé about restoring the Old Chapel! A handy guy to know actually, and I think people will suddenly start liking you a lot more around here when they find out you can fix their leaky roofs.'

He laughed as he reached for his beer.

'So, this and that,' she continued. 'What's this and that?'

'I don't just take on contracted work now; I invest a little here and there, buy to sell, that sort of thing.'

'You were right, I started to glaze over when you mentioned investing.'

'I did try to warn you. Even I think it's boring and it's how I earn my living.'

'So what's not boring to you?'

'Being on a date with someone who's incredibly attractive and makes me laugh into the bargain.'

Sadie blushed. She picked up her burger, mostly to hide her face, and took a great bite, causing relish to squelch out and drop onto her plate.

'Even when she's doing this?' she asked through a mouthful.

'Oh, the burger just adds an extra layer of sex appeal. I did say I couldn't get enough of burgers, didn't I?

'So, you have a pub and a beach here. What else do you do for fun in Sea Salt Bay?'

Sadie put her burger down and wiped her mouth. He might have said he found her eating her burger sexy but she wasn't taking any chances.

'There's the amusement arcade and the fairground rides on the pier – not exactly high-octane but families like them. I expect you've seen those, though. The bay here is really shallow and safe – that's why so many people dive here…'

He grimaced and she laughed.

'Maybe no diving for you just yet. And I guess hiring boats is out of the question now too.'

'Yes, I think it might be wise to stay away from boats for a while.'

'We've got a donkey sanctuary on the cliffs a couple of miles along the coast – Sweet Briar, I think it's called. It's very cute anyway.'

'Not really my thing, I'm afraid. I got bit by a horse once.'

'But they're not horses.'

'They look enough like horses to put me off.'

'Oh, well there's a seaside postcard museum.'

'Even less my thing if I'm honest.'

'Hmm, it is a bit crap to be fair but the tourists like it. There's the chip shop, ice-cream parlour, bingo hall…' She looked at him. 'I'm not really selling this place, am I?'

He laughed. 'I don't need you to sell it to me; I'm already sold – I have a house now, remember? I just wondered what there is I might be missing out on.'

'Well…' She paused, and then inspiration struck. 'Midsummer there's always a firework party on the beach – that's always fun.'

'Sounds like it. So that's…'

'A couple of weeks away. Not too long to wait now. Will you go?'

'Will *you* go?'

'Everyone does. And let's face it, if you live in the bay you might as well because you're sort of subjected to it whether you like it or not – you can see it and hear it from more or less everywhere in the town.'

'So, now you've told me what there is to do, what do *you* do for fun, aside from snorkelling?'

'Me?' Sadie took up her burger and gave it a daintier nibble this time. Actually, putting it like that, she realised that the answer was *not a lot*. It felt as if she'd forgotten how to have fun these days, outside of family pursuits at least. She'd go out on the boat with her parents, go swimming or diving with Kat or Ewan and the kids, maybe walk the beach, but that was about it. Sometimes she'd meet with Natalie and Georgia for a drink, but even that wasn't as often these days. These days she spent far too much of her time worrying about a future she couldn't yet see and regretting a past she couldn't change. 'This is pretty fun,' she said. 'Being here with you.'

'I'm glad to hear it. So I might be in with another date after tonight?'

'You never know.' Sadie raised her eyebrows and he laughed.

'I'm going to take that as a yes because I don't think my poor heart could take your rejection.'

'I would say yes, but I've got to retain a little mystery, haven't I?'

'Mystery is overrated. I prefer people to say what they mean – it usually works out better in the end.'

'OK, one hundred per cent yes then. I'd love another date. Is that direct enough for you?'

He grinned. 'That's more like it.'

*

Despite the ample food to mop it up, three more pints of beer had left Sadie a little tipsy when Vivien had eventually called time for the Listing Ship's bar. Luke had fared better, though Sadie was sure he'd drunk just as much as her.

'Are you deliberately trying to get me drunk?' she'd asked as he'd come back to their table with the last one. He'd just tapped the side of his nose and laughed, and Sadie had informed him that if that was his plan then it would probably work.

The moon was still low and full in the sky as they came out of the pub, a salt breeze rolling in from the sea that heaved and sighed as the tide crept in. It would never fully cover the beach, and that was one of the big attractions of the bay for many holidaymakers because it always felt safe. Tonight, though Sadie could see the shoreline, still only a dark, undulating line on the sand. Mellow streetlamps lined the promenade while the technicolour lights of the rides on the pier reflected back from the black mirror of a calm sea.

'I'll see you home,' Luke said as they stepped out onto the tarmac.

'There's no need. I've walked home a million times before.'

'Drunk?'

'I'm not drunk. And even if I was a little drunk I've walked home way drunker than this too.'

'Probably, but I'd still rather see you were safe.'

'I'm perfectly safe here. The only crime we have in the bay is committed by the occasional thieving seagull.'

'Well if you won't let me see you home to be safe, will you let me see you home because I want to spend a bit more time with you?'

She looked up at him with a soppy smile. 'You do?'

'Why wouldn't I? I've had such a great time tonight, why would I refuse the opportunity of a few more minutes of your company?'

'Me too,' Sadie said. 'But it might be a good idea not to come right up to the house.'

'Probably – at least for now,' he agreed.

As she turned to walk the promenade towards the cliff road that led home she felt his hand close around hers – not forced or unwelcome, just natural and right. It was the first actual physical contact they'd made that evening and it sent sparks shooting through her. She hadn't reacted to a man's touch like that since…

'Heads up,' he said, nodding towards a couple of figures up ahead. They looked as if they were arguing – at least the body language from this distance didn't look too friendly – though Sadie couldn't make out whether it was someone she knew or what they were saying.

'Perhaps we should hang back,' Luke said.

'Maybe…'

Sadie halted, staring along the road. Luke had a point, because if it was someone she knew that would probably mean a bit of an awkward exchange, at the very least, considering she was out with Luke. Even if that wasn't awkward, she didn't want to get in the middle of a dispute. But the couple had stopped too now, the flailing of their arms intensifying and the volume of their voices increasing. There was no doubt they were in the middle of a huge bust-up.

'They could be there all night,' Sadie said.

Then one of the couple changed direction and started to head towards Sadie and Luke instead of away. The other followed. Sadie still couldn't see who it was but now the voices sounded like… sounded like…

'Shit!'

Sadie looked closer. She couldn't make out anyone's features but she could now recognise the woman's long, graceful – if slightly agitated – strides, and the gait of the man who'd begun to chase after her.

'Oh shit…'

Sadie cursed under her breath and yanked Luke across the promenade towards the darkness of the beach, out of sight.

'Do you know them?' Luke asked as she marched towards the shadow of the pier's underside, taking him with her.

'Um, yes. It's just someone I don't want to talk to right now… Might be awkward…'

'Why? Is it your brother?'

'No, it's…'

My ex-boyfriend.

She couldn't say that, could she? That would sound weird, wouldn't it? Not weird that she had one, but weird that she was bothered he was there. Though that wasn't really it – the problem wasn't so much Dec being there but that she was certain Declan and Melissa had been having the most almighty argument, and even more certain that she'd heard Melissa screech her name. If Sadie had really been dragged into whatever the argument was about, to run into them at this precise moment would be horribly awkward – not only for her but for Luke too. Had he heard Sadie's name being angrily tossed out too? Even if he had, but had been too gallant to say anything, she certainly didn't want him to overhear any more. She didn't know what Dec and Melissa were arguing about but the last thing she wanted to do was give the impression that there was some weird love triangle going on – which there absolutely wasn't.

But why would Declan and Melissa be arguing about her? Sadie could only think of one reason – that Dec had decided to ask Melissa about helping out at the waffle house after all and she'd taken serious offence at the suggestion. If that was the case, Sadie could hardly blame her. Sometimes, for all his tenderness and charm, Declan could be dim-witted when it came to reading a volatile situation. Sometimes he'd just charge on in with his logic, judging everyone by the standards of his own openness and generosity, and it wasn't always that simple. He'd have given his time up for Sadie and the waffle house in an instant, but Sadie could see that it wouldn't be that straightforward for Melissa.

With the line of the sea just feet away, Sadie stopped beneath the pier, sure now that they were out of sight.

'What now?' Luke asked. His face was deep in shadow but, from the tone of his voice, Sadie thought he might actually be finding this turn of events funny. She wished she could find it amusing too, but right now she was only finding it mortifying.

'Um… I guess we just wait for them to go past?'

'You realise this is a bit weird, don't you?'

'Yes?' she said uncertainly. 'Sorry.'

'Don't be. I like weird.'

'Good… I think?'

There was no time to say anything else. The shadow of his face moved in and his lips pressed to hers, and the force of her reaction was such that it felt as if the midsummer fireworks had already begun. She kissed him back, hands creeping into his hair to pull him closer still. It might have been the drink, or the surreal nature of the situation, but God it was good. It might just have been the best kiss she'd ever had. Awkward meetings out on the promenade were forgotten in a fiery, sexy instant.

Eventually he broke off and she took a moment to catch her breath.

'Wow… I mean, just wow… I wasn't expecting that.'

His hand went to trace the line of her cheek. 'I wasn't expecting to do it. But the darkness under here by the sea and the excitement of having to hide and… I don't know, it just did something to me. *You* do something to me. I've never felt like this before, it's just... you're just incredible. Different and frankly nutty but incredible.'

'Nutty is about right,' Sadie said with a giggle that turned into a hiccup. But she was warmed by the rest of it, even if she was too humble and slightly embarrassed to say so.

'Do you think your friends on the promenade have gone?' he asked. 'It sounds quiet out there now and I think you might need to go home.'

'Why do I need to go home?'

'That's where we were heading, isn't it?'

'I changed my mind; I don't want to go home now. Not mine anyway.'

'What does that mean?'

'I want to go to your place.'

He paused, and when he spoke again there was the sound of a grin in it. 'You're drunk.'

'Says you.'

'I'm sober as a judge.'

'Me too. A little bit anyway. Sober enough to want to go and see your house. I want to see your nice painted front.'

'It's dark – you won't see much of it tonight.'

'Alright, you can show me in the morning then.'

'Then you'd have to come back tomorrow.'

'You know what I mean.'

'I'm afraid I don't,' he said, his tone teasing her because they both knew exactly what she meant.

'I want to look inside then.'

'There's not much to see.'

'There must be something. Where do you sleep?'

He let out a sigh. 'If I show you where I sleep I'm afraid we might do something that we'd both end up regretting.'

'We won't. I have self-control.'

'I'm not sure I do.'

'I wouldn't regret it,' she said softly, moving to kiss him again. This time as they broke off his voice was husky and full of longing.

'Oh, God, Sadie... I can't tell you how much I want us to go back to my place right now.'

'Then let's go.'

'It wouldn't be right. You're tipsy and this is our first date – we hardly know each other. I don't want a one-night stand from you; I like you too much for that. I want to see you again and I don't want to wreck my chances by doing something tonight that might make you rethink things in the morning. You understand? And you have to believe that it's taking some serious willpower to say this so that means I really do like you – a lot.'

She gave a slight shrug. She could understand it, though that didn't mean she wasn't a little disappointed and even more frustrated. But she loved that he had so much respect for her and that it meant so much to him to see her again.

'You're right,' she said finally.

'Home then?' he asked. 'It sounds like the coast might be clear now.'

'It does,' Sadie agreed. 'Kiss me again before we go to see though.'

'I don't think I can – I might explode. And I don't know if this amazing willpower I'm exerting right now could withstand another kiss like you give. I'd crumble under the pressure.'

Sadie giggled, and though she desperately wanted that kiss she didn't press him any further. 'Come on, then,' she said, taking his hand this time to lead him back out onto the beach.

The promenade was deserted now – it looked as if Melissa and Declan had either walked pretty fast to get to the other end or they'd veered off to take one of the many cliff paths back to wherever they'd been headed.

The walk back was much quieter. The night air was mild and still and scented by the broom and gorse that grew alongside the cliff road as they walked it, the sea down below breathing in and out. By the time they'd reached the point where Sadie felt it was no longer advisable for Luke to be with her, she'd sobered considerably, enough to see that he'd been right to refuse her a night at his place and for her to start wondering what the hell had been going on between Declan and Melissa.

She glanced at Luke, walking alongside her. For a moment he caught her eye and smiled.

'Alright there?'

'Yes,' she said, and her heart skipped a little. She liked him. She was beginning to think that she might like him more than she'd liked anyone since Declan – at least, the early signs were good. But if the gossip about her and Declan was out there, and if Melissa got to hear about it, did that mean eventually Luke would get to hear about it too? Luke interrupted her thoughts.

'Is that your place?' he said, stopping on the road. Maybe a quarter of a mile away Sadie saw her parents' house, lights burning in an upstairs window but the rest of the house in darkness. It looked as if Henny and Graham were on their way to bed and Gammy had probably turned in long before.

'Yes.'

'It's nice. Good spot up here. Must be worth a bit.'

'Probably, but I've never really asked. I think Mum and Dad had help paying for it.'

'From family?'

'My mum's parents. They're much posher than we all are.'

He laughed. 'I'll remember that if I ever have to meet them.'

'God, I would never let you meet them; they're hideously snobbish! You wouldn't want to see me again if you thought I was related to people like that!'

He hooked an arm around her waist and pulled her close to kiss her. 'I don't think so,' he murmured before his lips touched hers.

'I wouldn't risk it,' she whispered back as they broke off. She smiled up at him.

'When can I see you again?'

'I have absolutely no social life, so whenever you want to.'

'Tomorrow night?'

'Keen…'

'I have no social life either.'

'We're a good pairing then. Tomorrow night it is. What time?'

'What time can you be ready?'

'Depends how much effort I have to put in.'

'Come as you are – I like spontaneous you.'

'I probably ought to shower first – you must have noticed I smelt like waffle batter tonight.'

'Maybe I like waffle batter.'

'As much as you like burgers?'

'More…' He kissed her again and she wanted nothing more than to melt into his arms and stay there. But then he let her go and smiled down at her. 'Can I have your number?'

'Needy.'

'You have mine, so I think it's only fair.'

'True.'

She pulled out her phone and he keyed her number into his own before stashing it back into his pocket.

'Goodnight,' he said, and he began to walk back down the path. Sadie watched him, the imprint of his lips still tingling on hers.

'Goodnight, Luke.'

As distractions went, it hadn't been bad at all.

Chapter Twelve

'Somebody is burning the candle at both ends.'

Henny gave Sadie a stern look as she plonked a full toast holder onto the breakfast table.

'I decided to pop into the Ship last night and got talking to someone,' Sadie said. It was a half-truth – and her parents didn't need to know who she'd got talking to just yet. She was tired and not in the mood for a lecture, which she knew she'd get soon enough once Vivien had opened her big mouth and word had got round that Sadie had been out with the newly arrived owner of the Old Chapel.

'Well I don't know how you expect to do a full day at the waffle house if you stay out half the night. You'll be neither use nor ornament to your grandmother if it becomes a regular thing.'

'It was just once, Mum. I am allowed a social life surely?'

'I'm just saying that April is relying on you, and this was all your idea after all.'

'Where is she anyway?' Sadie asked. Currently there was only her and her mother at the table.

'Your dad has taken her to the cemetery to see… She wanted to go early because she's been too tired in the evenings.' Henny paused. 'Sadie, have you noticed anything… *off* about your grandma lately?'

'Like what?' Sadie asked carefully, teacup halfway to her lips.

'Little lapses of memory... judgement... that sort of thing. And little mood swings too. Nothing major but sometimes she'll say something quite unexpected...'

If any time was a good time to say something, now would be it, and yet Sadie could barely bring herself to. If all this came out now, would that mean the end of the waffle house? She wasn't ready to give it up yet, and she still clung to the belief that once Gammy was back into a routine all would be well again. April wasn't one of those old ladies who would fade from view and become someone they no longer recognised – not her Gammy. It wasn't possible and Sadie wasn't going to believe it. She was just a little lost right now, still struggling to come to terms with Gampy's death, that was all. She'd be fine in a few months with Sadie's help.

'Don't make me too much breakfast,' Sadie said. 'I'd better get down to the waffle house and start getting ready to open in case Gammy's a while at the cemetery. You can phone Dad and tell him there's no rush if she wants to spend a little time there; I can't imagine we'll be that busy first thing.'

'Your grandma won't be happy if you open up without her,' Henny said briskly.

'She might have to get used to the idea... Mum... I know you said just now that you thought she might be a bit off. Well I don't know about that but she is slowing down, isn't she?'

'She's been slowing down for years – they both were. The trouble is neither your grandmother nor grandfather would listen to anyone's advice on the matter. You know already that part of the reason we didn't want you to take that place on is that the books weren't looking good. It's why we're still against it, though you seem to be hell-bent on doing what you want.'

'I'm not stupid, Mum – I knew full well they weren't making as much money as they'd once been. For a start, there's a lot more competition in the bay than there was when they first opened. I can make it work again though. If I didn't believe that then I wouldn't have pushed to try.'

'So this isn't purely an emotional attachment?'

'It's that too. I thought we'd sorted this out – why are we going over it again?'

'Because we don't want to see you pouring your heart and soul into this only for it to fail and for you to be heartbroken.'

'It's lovely to have such a wealth of support from my family,' Sadie said, her tone dripping with sarcasm. 'Lovely to know you have such faith and belief in my abilities.'

'There's no need to be like that.'

'Dad's not saying this, surely?'

'There are no flies on you, are there?' Henny said with a faint smile. 'You know he's as resistant to the idea of the waffle house closing as you are but that doesn't mean he doesn't share my concerns about you.'

'I know you're just looking out for me but I can't give this up – not yet. I've already talked to Gammy about opening for longer hours so that would bring more money in.'

Henny raised her eyebrows as she poured herself some tea from her favourite Wedgwood pot. 'And she's agreed to this?'

'Not yet,' Sadie admitted. 'But given time I think she will.'

'Sadie, I know this has been discussed before, and I know you don't want to hear it, but don't you think it would be kindest to let your grandmother retire?'

'She'd never let someone else run the waffle house without her.'

'I know. I still think it would be best all round to let it close. Yes, it's been here for almost fifty years, and yes, the town would miss it, but all things come to an end, even the Sea Salt Bay Waffle House.'

'Ewan's put you up to this, hasn't he?'

'No, he hasn't. But now that you mention it he's just as worried about you – both of you. He told me that your grandmother had a *moment*… in the car the other day. Your father and I have noticed them, and you must have done too. She's an old lady and we have to accept that.'

'But if we put her somewhere to rot then she'll get old quicker than ever. We'll lose her inside a year, I just know it. We have to keep her active, give her something to live for. The waffle house is that thing – I know it.'

'I think you're letting your emotions cloud your judgement.'

'So what if I am? You say it like it's a bad thing!'

Henny sighed and fell silent as she took a sip of her tea. Sadie threw down the slice of toast she'd been eating and stood up.

'If you'll excuse me,' she began, always mindful of her etiquette where her mother was concerned, regardless of her mood, 'I'm going to get ready for work.'

It didn't take long for Sadie's mood to brighten. The morning was fresh and clear and promised cloudless skies as a night fog began to lift from the sea. Sadie walked the cliff road, keeping close to the rocks in case of oncoming cars, but she needn't have bothered because the road was quiet, as it often was. Her shoes crunched on fallen scree while gulls and curlews cried overhead.

When she arrived at the waffle house, Gammy and Graham were already waiting outside.

'I forgot my keys,' April began.

'But we knew you'd be down shortly,' Sadie's dad added. 'So we decided it was a nice day and, rather than go haring back up the hill, we'd sit here and look at the sea for a while until you turned up with yours.'

'Good plan,' Sadie said, smiling fondly at them both. Her dad wouldn't say it, but he was on her side. She knew he was always on her side, but often he'd struggle to stand up to her mum to say so, because Henny's personality was so forceful and often so formidable. It didn't make him weak; it made him an ordinary mortal man – when it came to it, most people struggled to stand up to Henriette Schwartz. The only person who could give her a run for her money was Kat, but she was so much fairer-minded and didn't often feel the need to. Even Ewan, as confident as he was, struggled to argue with his mother once she'd rolled up her sleeves and dug in, and, besides, he often agreed with her and so didn't need to argue. And as for Henny's own parents, they might attempt to cross swords with her but they never got far, as evidenced by the fact that Henny had married Graham, a man they'd viewed with about as much contempt as the groundskeeper they'd once had to sack for selling pheasants from their estate on the sly. 'It's a good job I brought mine.'

'I knew you would,' April said. 'You're learning so fast you won't need me soon.'

Sadie paused for a moment, key in hand, and turned to look at her grandma. Had she heard that right? Only an hour before Sadie had been telling her mum that grandma would never give up the waffle house. Why would she say this now? Was it just a flippant comment, or could it be that on some unconscious level, even April was starting to see that she couldn't keep it up for much longer?

Giving herself a mental shake, Sadie poked the key in the lock and gave the door a shove to open up. April went round the dining room to open the blinds and let the morning stream in while Sadie began to switch everything on.

'Want any help before I go?' Graham asked.

'You've got enough of your own to do,' Sadie said. 'Thanks though.'

'I'll be off then,' he said. 'Sea's looking good today – should get plenty of trips in.'

'It is,' Sadie said. 'Away with you then.'

Sadie could hear him chuckling even after the door had closed behind him. She turned to April.

'Mum said you went to the cemetery this morning.'

'Yes,' April said. 'It was such a lovely morning to go.'

'Hmm. Maybe next time I'll come with you.'

'I'd sure like that, darlin'.'

'Me too.'

'You always were his favourite,' she said, walking to the little office. 'You were his first granddaughter after all, and grandpas sure do love their little girls.'

Sadie frowned. 'Second granddaughter…'

'What's that, darlin'?' April called from the office.

'I'm the second. What about Lucy?'

April came back with a bag of change for the till. She stared at Sadie. And then she shook her head. 'Silly me. For a moment I clean forgot about your sister.'

Sadie stared at her, but April didn't seem fazed at all. Lucy didn't come home very often but she could hardly be forgotten. How could you forget a whole person, your actual first granddaughter? How could you forget she existed and not even be worried by that?

'Did you email Timpson's yet?' April asked briskly. 'We're gonna be clean out of batter by the end of today if it's as busy as I think it might be.'

'Yes,' Sadie said. 'They said they'd be here by nine.'

'Good girl. How about you count this change while I go and get mixing?' She handed the bag to Sadie as she waltzed past to the kitchen like she hadn't a care in the world, like a woman half her age who hadn't spent the morning at the grave of her recently passed husband. Sadie was beginning to freak out. Her conversation with her mother that morning hadn't helped either. If everyone was noticing April doing weird things, did that mean her condition was worse than Sadie had thought?

She turned her attention to the change in the bag. There was nothing else she could do except soldier on – at least for today. As for tomorrow, she couldn't even think that far ahead and there was absolutely no way to know what it might hold even if she could. Every day with Gammy right now was a crazy ride, as unpredictable as the rickety, twisting old Mad Mouse that rattled people around its tracks on the fairground nearby.

At least she had her date with Luke to look forward to. Her stomach fizzed as her mind went back to their night in the Listing Ship. And then afterwards beneath the pier... But then thinking about being beneath the pier also brought back the reason they'd hidden under there in the first place. She'd often fantasised that Declan and Melissa might split up and leave him free, so it was strange that this morning she found herself hoping that whatever they'd been arguing about last night had been resolved and that they were OK.

There was a knock at the window, and she looked up to see her current favourite distraction grinning through the glass at her. She ran to open the door.

'What are you doing down here so early?'

'I couldn't sleep so I thought I'd take a walk. Are you busy?'

'A bit.'

'Oh.'

'I am trying to run a business here,' she said, laughing. 'It's alright for you – you can start work whenever you like but I have to be open when the sign on the door says I'm supposed to be. Did you need anything in particular?'

'No, I just wanted to see you.'

'You're seeing me later.'

'I know; I'm greedy. I wanted to see you some more. I can't stop thinking about you.'

'Are you always like this?'

'Like what?'

'Going at a hundred miles an hour.'

His face fell. 'I'm sorry, I just…'

'I'm joking,' Sadie said with a smile, though she was aware that she might have said the wrong thing. The heartbreak he'd mentioned in the pub the night before came back to her and she had to wonder whether perhaps it had made him emotionally fragile. Maybe she should have gone ahead and heard the story after all, because maybe it was a story she really ought to know so she could act accordingly. Although, she wasn't sure if she herself was in any state to offer support to someone else as unstable as her.

Her reply seemed to help him find solid ground, and he returned her smile with one of his own. 'I have to move quick; I have a feeling there'll be plenty of competition.'

'Trust me, there isn't,' Sadie said. She reached to give him a quick kiss, but he placed a gentle hand on her neck to hold her for longer.

'Oh, Luke…' she murmured as he let go and she opened her eyes. 'You really can't do things like that to me when I have a full day's work ahead and hours before I can see you for more.'

Kissing him was like a magic spell, and whenever his lips touched hers she had to fight off the trance that she felt herself drift into. It was delicious, but it sometimes felt a little dangerous too, like she might lose control, though she wondered whether that might not be the sexiest bit about it. Would it be so bad to lose control with him? To let him do what he wanted? And what he wanted couldn't be so far from what she wanted.

Reluctantly, she pushed him back through the door. 'I have work to do.'

'Temptress,' he said.

She laughed. 'You're the one doing the tempting. Go and build a shelf or something – whatever it is you do all day. Come back later like you're supposed to.'

'I can't,' he said. 'Every time I try to do something I start thinking about you and then I get all useless.'

'Well you'll just have to try. If I've got to manage today then so can you.'

With a last shove and a laugh, she closed the door on him and locked it. He pressed his face against the glass with a forlorn look and she laughed even harder, so tempted to open it again and drag him in.

'Go!' she said and turned away. But when she got back to the counter she looked up and he was still there. 'For God's sake!' She let out a giggle that brought April to the doors of the kitchen.

'What's the matter?' she asked.

Sadie was about to answer, though she didn't know what she was going to say, then she glanced back at the window. At least Luke had had the good sense to see that April's appearance might be a good time to make his getaway, because he was already walking down the pier towards the promenade.

'Oh, just something funny someone said to me yesterday,' Sadie said, turning back to her grandma. 'I just thought about it and it's still funny.'

'That's alright,' April said. 'It's just that I thought I could hear someone else in here and I thought it can't be opening time already because I've only just started mixing.'

'Don't worry, Gammy, you can get back to it and you have a little time yet.'

April bustled away, and Sadie's gaze returned to the window. By now, Luke was out of sight. Gone, but definitely not forgotten, and she couldn't wait to see him again later.

During the morning, Sadie didn't feel too tired, despite her late night, but by the lunchtime rush she was flagging, and by two o'clock she was desperate for her bed. But she kept going and she kept smiling for the customers and, as her grandmother had predicted, the good weather brought them in larger numbers than other days. Most popped in for an ice cream to take away as the queues at the parlour were enormous, but many stayed for the full works. There wasn't a moment where the dining room was empty, and that only added stress to Sadie's day because, as the orders came in thick and fast, she had to keep checking on April in the back to see that she was managing and, more to the point, wasn't flying off to fairyland. It was a cruel way to look at it, but in the cold light of day and with a full restaurant, it was the only way Sadie could look at it. But, to her great relief, it seemed that April was having a better day than of late and handling the kitchen with cheery efficiency. That, and the fact that she was looking forward to meeting Luke later, was all that was keeping Sadie on her feet by mid-afternoon.

By three the customers were thinning a little, but the waffle house was by no means quiet, and by a quarter to four Sadie was thinking of getting a quick nap at home before she headed out again for her date. At four on the dot, after seeing out the last of their customers, she heaved a thankful sigh of relief and went to lock the door. Dropping the keys on the counter, she went to cash up the till. It had been a good day – even if it had been tiring – and she was looking forward to seeing how much they'd taken. If nothing else, at least it would prove to her mum that the waffle house was capable of making money.

'Gammy…' she called as she finished stuffing all the cash into money bags. 'Gammy… what time does the bank open tomorrow morning? I've got to be somewhere later and I don't think I'll have time to take this tonight – do you think I'll be able to stash it in the safe until I can get to the bank?'

There was no reply. Sadie picked up the money and wandered through to the kitchen. There, she found her grandma filling the mop bucket.

'Gammy… about the takings for today. Do you think they'll be OK in the safe for tonight?'

'Can't you take them to the bank?'

'I would, but I was hoping to get a nap this afternoon because I'm going out later.'

'Going out?' April hauled the bucket from the sink. Sadie ran to take it from her.

'Yes.'

'On your own?'

'No, I'm meeting… a friend.'

'Oh. Well, be sure to say hello to them from me, darlin'. I'm sure I could take the money along tonight.'

'There's a lot here. I think it would be better if I did it.'

'Ain't nobody going to mug me around here,' April said, laughing.

'No, I know but… well,' she said brightly, 'I wanted to walk up the cliff with you. I like it when we walk home together and we didn't walk in together this morning and I missed you.'

April smiled and reached to stroke a lock of auburn hair from Sadie's face. 'You are a funny one. Sure we can walk up together. I guess it wouldn't be the first time the takings have been left in the safe for a few hours.'

'And that's why it's called a safe,' Sadie said. 'Because it's safe.'

April laughed. 'Whatever you say.'

'OK, great.'

After putting the bucket down in the dining room and warning her grandma not to touch it because she'd mop up while April went to sort through the fridge, she went through to the little office to put the money in the safe. Once she'd locked the door, her phone pinged in her pocket. She got it out and saw with a smile that Luke had sent her a text. It had an image attached and for one horrible moment she thought it might be the sort of unwanted photo she'd had from many men. Her smile grew though as she saw it was a picture of the front of his house, newly painted in a pretty sage green.

You said you wanted to see it.

She tapped a reply:

And now I have. Very nice. I'm hoping to see the inside very soon.

Can't wait to see you later.

Me too. X

Putting her phone away, Sadie went through to the dining room. It was empty, the bucket and mop still standing against the wall, chairs still on the floor instead of stacked on top of the tables, rubbish bags still in the corner and one table even still had used crockery on it.

'Gammy...?' Sadie called.

There was no reply again. So again Sadie went through to the kitchen expecting to see her there, but she wasn't. With a frown, Sadie went back to the office. Gammy's handbag and coat were there so she couldn't have gone far. She went back to the dining room.

'Gammy!' she called again, louder this time. 'Gammy!'

She was greeted by silence, only broken by the hum of the fridges where they kept the chilled drinks.

'What the actual hell...'

And then Sadie's eyes fell on the counter where she'd left the front door keys. Only the keys weren't there. She ran to the door and pulled on it but it was locked.

'No!' she murmured. 'No, no, no...'

She ran from room to room again, as if her eyes might have deceived her the first time and she'd find her grandma after all, hiding in one of them. But she wasn't there, and neither were the keys, and the door was locked. Did that mean Gammy had wandered off, locked the door and taken the keys with her, leaving Sadie trapped inside?

Sadie wondered for a moment if she was the one who'd gone off to fairyland. Surely her grandma wouldn't do that. But if she had where would she have gone? She couldn't have got far, wherever it was.

Sadie checked around again one last time. And then she checked the front door. And the back door that was always locked and that, stupidly she realised now, she'd never bothered asking for keys for. Gammy had the only set for that door and she'd left all her keys at home that morning, which meant the only way to get out was to get some keys from Gammy somehow. Which meant finding out where she'd gone.

Pulling her phone from her pocket, she was forced to ignore the new text from Luke. Instead, she dialled Ewan's number. It went straight to voicemail. So she tried Kat and gave a thankful sigh as her sister-in-law answered.

'Hey—'

'Kat… I know this is going to sound a bit desperate but is Gammy there?'

'April? No, but—'

Sadie hadn't imagined for a moment that her grandma could have got to the dive school offices that quick but she hadn't known what else to say. The fact was she'd lost Gammy – or rather, Gammy had lost her – and there was no way to dress that up as anything except what it was.

'What's wrong?' Kat asked.

'Gammy's gone off somewhere and locked me in.'

'You're at the waffle house?'

'Yes. Is Ewan there?'

'No, he's on a lesson. But we don't have keys for the waffle house anyway so we can't let you out.'

'I know, but if you could find Gammy that's probably a bigger priority at the moment anyway. She just took off without a word, and she doesn't even have her bag or coat with her. I just can't imagine where she's gone but she can't have got that far because it was only a few minutes ago.'

'I can go and look for you. What are you going to do about getting out?'

'I suppose I'll have to sit tight until you find her. Unless someone can go home to get Gammy's set. She left them there this morning, which is why there's only one set here. I can only guess that she must have picked these up today thinking they were hers, but I still don't understand why she just left knowing I was still in here cleaning up. I mean, she'd never leave me to clean up alone and she certainly wouldn't go without telling me.'

'She wouldn't go without her bag either – she even takes that to the toilet.'

Sadie gave a tight smile. On any other day Kat's statement would have made her laugh, but not today.

'What about your parents?' Kat asked. 'Could they come down to you with the keys?'

'I think they'll be out on the boat. Dad said he thought they'd have a pretty full day. I'll try them, but if they are then there won't be much hope of getting hold of them.'

'I'll go and look for your gran now,' Kat said. 'Try not to worry; I'll call you as soon as I find her. Like you said, she can't have got that far in a few minutes.'

'Thanks, Kat.'

Sadie ended the call and put her phone on the counter. She looked around the still messy dining room. There wasn't much she could do, but at least, she supposed, if she was captive here, she might as well make herself useful rather than stand around worrying. But first, she ought to reply to Luke's text.

Don't eat too much dinner – I thought we could drive out of town to eat somewhere new.

Sounds good. X

After setting the ringtone to its loudest setting so she'd be sure to hear it if Kat called, she set about cleaning up. It would take longer than usual, and would probably mean she'd miss out on that nap she'd promised herself, but hopefully it wouldn't delay her too much. She was worried to death about Gammy, but she still couldn't help but look forward to her date with Luke, though she had to admit that this turn of events did put a damper on things a little. For now, she had to hold on to the hope that things would be resolved quickly.

A few moments later her phone started to ring. Sadie dropped the mop and raced to answer it.

'Sadie…' Her mum sounded tense on the line. 'What's this about April going missing?'

'Mum, how did you… never mind. Where are you?'

'About five miles off the coast but as soon as we've docked we're going to cancel the last trip of the day.'

'No, Mum, you can't do that.'

'We've got to look for your grandmother!'

'Kat's looking for her now.'

'I know, she said so, but she can't do it alone.'

'Has she told you that Gammy has only been missing for about ten minutes now?'

'A lot can happen in ten minutes to a confused old lady,' Henny said sternly, and Sadie's blood froze. She'd been worried, but she hadn't even considered that something truly catastrophic might happen.

'But…'

'What are you doing now?'

'Well, I'm cleaning the dining room.'

'You're cleaning the dining room at a time like this?'

'I didn't see what else I could do – I'm stuck here.'

'You didn't think to call the police?'

'Well, no…'

'I'm going to hang up now and call them because you—'

Sadie didn't get to hear the end of her mum's sentence because there was a rap on the window. She looked to see Declan standing outside with April.

'Mum!' she cried. 'Mum, Gammy's back! I'll call you later!'

Cutting short the call, Sadie ran to the door.

'It's locked!' she shouted. 'Gammy… do you have the keys?'

April looked confused and shook her head. 'How on earth have you managed to lock yourself in and lose the keys?'

Sadie held in a scream of frustration. She shot a look at Declan that silently pleaded for help. She couldn't say it in front of April, but she hoped he'd understand because he at least knew that something hadn't been right at the waffle house since it had reopened.

He turned to Sadie's grandma. 'April, maybe you want to check your pockets for those keys?'

'I've told you I haven't got any… Oh…' She held them up. 'How strange,' she added with a shaky laugh.

'Could you open up?' Sadie called through the glass.

'Why don't you have your keys?' April asked as she unlocked the door and shoved it open.

'They *are* my keys,' Sadie said.

'No, they're mine,' April replied serenely.

Sadie let out a long sigh. Without a care in the world, April wandered through to the kitchen, tutting as she stopped to pick up the dirty dishes from the still uncleared tables.

'Thank you,' Sadie said, turning to Declan.

'Want to tell me what's going on?'

'Have you got a week or two?'

'You could summarise?'

Sadie smiled. 'I could, but even that might take more time than we have. I'd better just call Kat first.'

Declan nodded and went to take a seat while Sadie phoned Kat to tell her that April had turned up and all was well. The only problem was that Kat had already sent Ewan a message to call when his lesson was done and he'd soon know about what had happened. When he did, and when the whole family got together, serious questions would have to be asked now about the wisdom of Sadie and April running the waffle house together when April clearly wasn't up to it. Once she'd ended the call she went back to Declan.

'It's lucky you found her. Where was she?'

'On the promenade. She was outside the ice-cream parlour asking when it had opened and why nobody had told her about it. I could tell straight away that something wasn't right when she said she needed to get back here to tell Kenneth about it. I thought you might be closed but I thought I'd better come with her just in case.'

'But the ice-cream parlour…' Sadie began.

'I know,' Declan said. 'It's been there at least five years.'

'And to be fair, she never got upset about it when it first opened up because she always said there was plenty of trade to go around and the waffle house had their loyal regulars.'

'She's not well, is she?'

'I don't think she is,' Sadie said, taking a seat next to Declan with a heavy sigh. 'I've been in denial this whole time but it's been staring me in the face. I didn't think she would do anything dangerous, though, but now I think that she might. I know my parents will think so and they won't want to take that risk.'

'Where does that leave you and the waffle house?'

Sadie shrugged. 'I don't honestly know.'

Declan leaned forward and took her hand. 'You love this old place, don't you?'

'There are a lot of memories here for me.' She smiled up at him. 'For all of us.'

'That's true,' he said slowly. 'But the memories are going nowhere, even if the waffle house does.'

Sadie shook her head, her eyes beginning to mist. 'What am I going to do?'

'Hey, hey…' Declan moved closer and pulled her into a hug. 'It looks bad now but it'll be OK. You're stronger and more resourceful than you think and you can get through this.'

'You think? I'm glad you can see that because I can't.'

'I've always seen it in you…'

He tipped her face to his and smiled down at her. For one stolen moment, she wondered if he might kiss her. But then she stood up and moved to the counter because she didn't want to know the answer to that question. It would cause more problems than it solved and she had enough right now.

'You want a coffee?' she asked, drying her eyes. 'It's the least I can do to thank you.'

'For walking along the pier on a sunny day with your lovely grandma?' he asked with a smile. 'I was hardly crossing the Gobi Desert on an epic quest – there's really no need to thank me.'

'You do seem to be there when I need you. Like my knight in shining armour.'

'I'm glad someone thinks so,' he said, and Sadie frowned at his tone. It had been a long time since she'd heard it, and even longer since it had been directed at her.

'Melissa? Is everything… Never mind, it's none of my business.'

'Out of all the people I could tell about it, you're the one who would understand the most.'

'But you can't? A burden shared… and after all, I've dumped enough on you these past few days.'

'I can't, Sadie. I would if I could.'

She nodded slowly as she went to the coffee machine behind the counter with two mugs. It hadn't been cleaned yet, along with a lot of other things, and if it had to wait a minute or two longer while she used it then it would have to wait.

'Well if you do feel you want to offload and it's something you can tell me about, you know I'll always be there, don't you? No matter what else happens.'

'I know that. You know, Sadie, I sometimes wonder…' He sighed. 'What's the point?'

'What it might be like if we'd stayed together? If I'd never gone away?'

'I love Melissa – you have to know that.'

'I do know that, but it doesn't stop you wondering. Just as it doesn't stop me from wondering either.'

'I think about it a lot more than I should. Especially at times like this.'

'I'd be lying if I said I didn't too.'

The coffee machine chugged and frothed as Sadie made the drinks and she watched it, silently contemplating what he'd said. What was happening here? Was something changing between them? This conversation – whatever it was – should have taken place a long time ago, when she'd first returned to Sea Salt Bay, but they'd both been too scared to have it.

So why were they having it now? What did it mean? Was it something to do with Luke? Was it because she found herself at some sudden and unexpected crossroads? She'd spent so long thinking that the only man who mattered was Declan, but someone new was in her thoughts now – and not as someone who was an idle prop to pass an hour, but as someone who might one day really mean something to her. Perhaps she had to deal with her unresolved feelings for Declan before she could give Luke the attention he deserved, and yet, dealing with her feelings for Declan meant accepting that she had given him up, and that he'd moved on, and that she had to move on too, and she wasn't sure she was ready for that reality just yet. Today proved it, because when the chips were down and she'd needed someone, it was Declan who'd been there, and she'd been glad it was him rather than anyone else.

Part of her wondered whether it would always be Declan. And part of her still didn't know enough about Luke to be certain that he was someone worth putting her faith in as the man who might change all that. She had a great time with him and they had such fun, and yet she felt the presence of some dark secret hanging over him, some heartache she hadn't yet been allowed to see. She had to wonder whether, if Luke's secret came out into the light, it might be something big enough to scupper anything she might hope for with him.

When the drinks were done Sadie went back to the table and handed a mug to Declan. As he took it, his hand brushed hers, sending a shockwave through her. It rested there, longer than it needed to, and his gaze caught hers and held it, and that was longer than it needed to be too.

Involuntarily, Sadie tore her eyes away and glanced at the windows. She should have closed the blinds, but to do it now might somehow imply that they were doing something wrong, something that needed to be hidden. But they were, weren't they? Even having this conversation was wrong. Declan had just said he loved Melissa, and in a matter of hours Sadie would be with Luke again. This conversation was very wrong.

In movies and books, right about now, Melissa would appear and catch them in the act, and she'd dump Declan on the spot and then Declan would fall into Sadie's arms and they'd live happily ever after – except for Melissa, who would prove to be a nasty person, and Luke, who would also prove to be equally nasty. They'd probably end up together and live in nastiness for the rest of their lives. But they weren't nasty. Melissa might have been cold and distant where Sadie was concerned, but Sadie knew she was a good person. As for Luke, Sadie didn't know all that much about him, yet she felt she'd got the measure of the man and that he was a good, kind, considerate one.

Instead of Melissa appearing at the window, April came back from the kitchen. She paused for a moment, taking in the scene, and then she smiled.

'You two lovebirds… where are you headed tonight? To see a movie? I don't know what's showing but I'm sure you wouldn't be seeing much of it anyway. Too busy kissing and hugging in the back row.' Chuckling to herself, April went to fetch the mop and bucket from where Sadie had left it earlier. 'Oh, if this water isn't cold. How did that happen?'

And just like that, the spell was broken. Sadie looked at Declan, tears once more in her eyes. This time he put down his coffee and leapt up to hug her, and there was no frisson of desire, just the warm, dependable support of a good friend, one of the oldest and most reliable she had. She dragged in a breath and, despite the comfort it gave her, pulled herself from his arms.

'I should get cleaned up.' She forced a smile. 'I've got a date tonight, you know, and I need to get ready as soon as I'm done here.'

'Is this with the guy who just bought the Old Chapel?'

'Ah.' Sadie laughed through her tears. 'Vivien told you?'

'Oh, no, my dad. I don't know who told him but you know what it's like around here.'

'Only too well.'

'He seems OK,' Declan said.

'Yeah, I think so too,' Sadie agreed. 'It's early days but… well, I like him.'

'Good.'

Declan smiled, but Sadie had to wonder if he meant it. Was that why the conversation had happened? But Sadie had dated loads of men since him and none of them had prompted Declan to say anything about any unresolved feelings he might have for her. She hadn't even been sure there had ever been any on his part, though today had told her otherwise. Was he feeling as uncertain as she was about that crossroads? Did he feel it was there for him too, the final chance to take a path that might soon be blocked forever? Was he testing the ground as Sadie felt she was, checking that it was the right way to go, terrified that she'd make the wrong turn and forever regret it?

He tipped his coffee cup to his lips and drank deep before taking it to the kitchen. When he returned he gave April a quick kiss on the cheek.

'Stay out of trouble,' he said with mock sternness.

'You know it, darlin',' April replied with a laugh. And then Declan turned to Sadie.

'You know where I am if you need me,' he said.

Sadie nodded. She knew alright, and maybe that was the problem. Maybe she knew too well where he was, what made him tick, and that, no matter what, if she called he would be there. Maybe all that needed to change.

She let him out of the doors, and before he'd gone ten feet she saw Melissa come from the direction of the amusement arcade to catch up with him. Melissa threw a last glance back at the waffle house, and Sadie felt her cheeks flare. It was obvious where he'd been, and Melissa made certain that Sadie could see that she knew. Sadie quickly dropped the blinds, feeling as guilty for a crime she hadn't committed as she would have done for one she had.

Chapter Thirteen

Of course, the thing that Sadie had most been dreading happened. There was no way it wasn't going to happen but she had hoped for a stay of execution, if she couldn't hope for anything else. But moments after she and April had finished cleaning (later and with more urgency than usual after the drama of the afternoon) and locked up for the night, Sadie looked up to see Ewan's car screech to a halt on the promenade. Well, as screeching as a station wagon could be – it was hardly Starsky *&* Hutch.

'Oh, hello, darlin',' April said as he strode down the pier towards them. 'Come to take us home? You are a sweet dear.'

'Yes, Grandma,' he said, giving her a tight smile and reserving his death stare for Sadie. She pouted in return, ready for a fight. And if he wanted a fight he was going to get one. It was hardly her fault Gammy had decided to go walkabout, and she wasn't going to take the blame. And she was even less inclined to stand for one of Ewan's lectures.

He led them up the pier and the three of them drove home in almost perfect silence. April fell into a doze, but she wasn't sleeping deeply enough for anyone to start a conversation about her, and they arrived at the house to find Henny, Graham, Kat and the kids sitting in the kitchen. Sadie grimaced inwardly and braced herself for the onslaught.

'Oh!' April said as she saw them all assembled. 'Is it someone's birthday? Did I forget?'

'No,' Kat said, giving the most natural, reassuring smile of any of them. In fact, the only smile at all. 'Ewan and I just thought we'd stop by and say hello.'

Sadie looked to see her brother had taken a seat next to his wife.

'Well, it sure is wonderful to see you,' April said, settling on a chair herself.

'Mum...' Graham began gently, 'what was going on this afternoon?'

April blinked at him. 'Whatever do you mean?'

'You left the waffle house and locked it up with Sadie still trapped inside.'

'Why, I...' April looked confused. But then she brightened. 'I don't exactly recall – I was so busy today I was just whizzing around doing everything without thinking too much. I expect I went to the bank because Sadie couldn't go... Yes, that's it. I went to the bank. Sadie didn't have time – did you, darlin'?'

'You left the money in the safe, Gammy,' Sadie said. 'We'd agreed to leave it in there until tomorrow because it was getting late.'

'Did we? In the safe? I was certain I had it in my bag when I left you.'

'Your bag was in the office too. You didn't take it. You didn't take your coat either.'

'It was warm enough.'

'I know, but...'

Sadie's sentence simply ran out of energy. It was sort of how she was feeling right now. This was beginning to feel like swimming against a very strong tide. April looked at all the faces around her in turn, and then a shadow crossed her own.

'Why are you all so angry with me?' she cried, her voice wavering. 'I've done nothing wrong!'

Freya looked up from the ubiquitous book clasped in one hand with a shocked frown, while Freddie simply stared down at his feet. A fleeting thought crossed Sadie's mind that perhaps this wasn't a place they ought to be right now, but she wasn't about to say it to Ewan, who was already ready to blow, or to Kat, who must have thought otherwise and was their mother after all.

'Nobody is saying that you have,' Graham said patiently. 'Nobody is angry with you.'

'Well it sure as heck feels that way with everyone staring at me,' April retorted.

'Nobody is staring at you either,' Ewan said, his tone as soft and patient as his father's.

April swept a hand around the table. 'Well, what do you call this?'

Ewan glanced at Kat, who nodded immediate understanding.

'April…' she began. It seemed to Sadie that Kat was the most reasonable, rational voice at the table right now, and certainly the calmest and kindest. She always was, which was why Sadie herself had more often than not over the years gone to her when she'd had a problem before anyone else. 'I think the strawberries on the bushes out in the garden are about ready – I noticed it the other day and I think the kids would like to go and pick them. I wonder if you could help them recognise the ripe ones – you're so much better at these things than I am.'

'And where are you gonna be?' April asked cautiously.

'I'll come with you if that's OK. That way I'll know for next time – if we have to pick them without your help.'

April didn't look convinced, but when Freddie and Freya looked hopeful at the thought of strawberry-picking (and strawberry-eating, probably) she seemed to quite forget she was supposed to be angry at them all for something.

'How can I refuse those darlin' faces?' she said with a smile. She reached for her handbag and followed Kat, Freddie and Freya out of the room.

'Now she takes the bloody bag,' Sadie muttered as she watched them go. But the moment they were out of earshot her mother rounded on her.

'I knew something like this would happen!'

'How could you have done?' Sadie shot back. 'How could any of us have really seen this coming? There's a difference between being a bit confused and what happened today – I know that! And if I'd thought for a minute that Gammy was as ill as she seems to be I would never have pushed to reopen the waffle house – even I'm not that pig-headed!'

'Sometimes I wonder…' Henny said brusquely.

'Well,' Sadie said, her tone just as cold, 'if I am then you must know where I get it from. Why am I suddenly the villain here?'

'Nobody is saying that,' Graham put in.

'You just never listen to anyone,' Ewan said.

Sadie threw her hands into the air. 'Oh, here we go! Saint Ewan has spoken and everyone has to listen!'

'Oh, grow up, Sadie!' her brother shot back. 'And maybe you could listen once in a while; you might find that people aren't always out to get you or stop you from doing what you want when they're giving you good advice. They're just trying to protect you.'

'Well maybe I don't need protecting. Maybe I can be left to look after myself and make my own mistakes like everyone else does, and maybe it will work out just fine.'

'Like the waffle house? Because that's worked out just fine, hasn't it?'

Sadie crossed her arms over her chest and looked out of the windows. She could hear murmurings coming from that direction; the voices of Kat, April and the kids as they pottered about in the greenhouse. If only she could have volunteered to take April out of the way and let everyone else have this horrible conversation instead of having to be a part of it.

'Nobody is blaming you,' Henny said, her tone more measured now.

Sadie turned to her and jabbed a finger at her brother. 'He is.'

'That's because—' Ewan began, but their mother jumped in.

'Enough!' she snapped. 'You're not children anymore – either of you – but you're bickering more than I've ever seen Freddie and Freya do.'

Ewan's mouth clamped shut. Henny turned to Sadie.

'We realise your efforts at the waffle house came from a place of love for your grandmother, but surely you can see now that the kindest thing to do is to call it a day. Your grandmother will be unhappy at first, but it will take her less time than you imagine to settle into a new routine without it.'

Sadie turned back to the windows. She sniffed hard.

'Sadie…'

When Sadie looked back at the table, Graham had left his chair to sit on the one now vacant next to her. He took her hand.

'Nobody loves that old place more than me, and nobody is more proud of what you've been trying to do there than me, but sometimes you have to know when to throw in the towel.'

'But that's just it, Dad, it feels like I'm always throwing in the towel. With my teacher training, with…' She stopped, paused, took a moment to recognise that some things she'd given up probably shouldn't be mentioned. 'I don't want to throw it in this time. Just once, I want to see it through. I could make a go of that place, I know it.'

'Everyone told you not to chuck in your teacher training,' Ewan said, and Henny glared at him.

'That's not helping, Ewan.'

He shut his mouth again.

Sadie looked at her dad. 'Maybe I could buy the waffle house from Gammy? Then I could take most of the responsibility in running it; that way we'd keep it in the family and she'd sort of be retired but she could lend a hand when she felt up to it. Could that work?'

Graham shook his head sadly. 'Where would you get that kind of money from? And don't forget that it represents your future inheritance – yours, Ewan's and Lucy's. We couldn't allow it to be sold for anything less than the market value in light of that fact – not even to someone who would stand to be one of the beneficiaries of that legacy. It wouldn't be fair to the others.'

Ewan spoke again, but his tone was much warmer this time. 'I wouldn't insist on my share, if that helps. If it meant Sadie could keep it running I'd give my inheritance up… I don't need it all that much anyway.'

Sadie's eyes filled with tears again as she looked at him. 'You'd do that?'

'Yes. What else are big brothers for?'

'That's very noble,' Henny said, 'but I rather think Kat might have an opinion on the matter and I think it would be disrespectful not to seek it. She is your wife after all.'

Ewan shrugged. 'Maybe, but I think she'd agree with me. We could certainly have the conversation if it helps.'

'What about Lucy?' Henny asked.

'I think she'd be a different matter,' Graham said, and on that Sadie had to agree. The sliver of hope Ewan had offered to her had been raised and dashed in the same breath. Lucy had allowed herself no ties to Sea Salt Bay and no interest in what happened at the waffle house, save that one day a share of it would come to her. She'd want her inheritance or she'd want Sadie to buy her out and Sadie couldn't afford that. She couldn't even afford a third share, even if Lucy did give hers up, as Ewan had said he would, though it was easier to find a solution that might get her the money for a third than the whole of it. And she secretly harboured a hope that the family might come to some arrangement over the money that might make it happen, because, despite this conversation, everyone around the table cared as deeply about the old waffle house as Sadie did.

'Could we talk to Lucy?' Sadie asked.

'I could phone her later,' her dad said. 'See what she thinks.'

'You could fill her in on the situation but I wouldn't press her on it,' Henny put in. 'The decision must be entirely hers.'

'Of course it would be,' Graham said. 'There would be a lot of other things to work out anyway so I'd only be testing the water to see how she felt about it.'

Sadie nodded – she could hardly argue with that, and she was grateful that her dad would try, even though she wasn't all that optimistic about what the outcome of the conversation would be.

'One thing's for certain,' Henny added, 'April can't go to work again; goodness knows what dangers she might pose. To herself and to others.'

'We can't just close the waffle house again,' Sadie said.

'We don't have a choice.'

'But... if it turns out I can take over properly, surely it's better that it's kept open in the meantime?' Sadie said.

Graham nodded. 'I have to admit, Hen, she's got a point. Even if we do decide to sell up I'm sure it would make more money as a going concern than as a run-down empty building. In this climate, that close to the sea, standing empty would soon have the building deteriorating.'

'Yes!' Sadie said.

'How do you propose to keep it going without your grandma?' Henny asked.

Sadie shrugged. 'I can't just magic up a solution – I know that. I wasn't expecting I'd have to. Give me a couple of days and I'll talk to people.'

'And what couple of days would these be?' Henny asked. 'As presumably you'd need any help you're going to ask for by tomorrow morning and you'd also need them to have some catering knowledge. Do you know anyone who ticks all those boxes?'

'I have catering knowledge,' Sadie said. 'They wouldn't need all that much.'

Her mother raised disbelieving eyebrows.

'OK, I have a bit,' Sadie admitted. 'And maybe they'd need a bit. But I could just tell them what needs doing and we'd muddle through somehow. And they do say that the best way to learn is on the job.'

'Well, we shan't have to worry about keeping it open until we get a sale, because with that solution I should imagine you'd be bankrupt inside a week,' Henny said acerbically.

'Well,' Sadie shot back, 'that's what you want anyway so there's no harm in me trying it, is there?'

'Your mum's trying to help,' Graham said gently.

Sadie glanced at the clock. She couldn't help but feel that they were going round in circles. Just when they were on the brink of a solution, someone would shoot it down and they'd be right back where they'd started again. She didn't have time for a discussion that would go on like this the whole night and end with them going to bed with nothing decided at all. And she still had to get ready to meet Luke – about the only good and certain thing she had to look forward to right now.

But then, it occurred to her that she might just have the answer after all, from a most unexpected place.

'I might know someone who can help,' she said. 'I'm almost certain he's free tomorrow – at least, I don't know of any solid commitments he's got right now and I'm sure he'd be willing to lend me a few hours.'

'Who?' Ewan asked. But then he grimaced. 'No way!'

Sadie pouted. 'But you don't even know who it is.'

Her brother folded his arms. 'Luke Goldman, by any chance?'

'Who?' Henny asked.

'The new owner of the Old Chapel,' Ewan said. He looked at Sadie. 'Did you think I wouldn't find out about your night out with him?'

'You went out with him?' Henny asked, looking from Sadie to Ewan and then back again. 'This is the same man who—'

'Yes,' Ewan said. 'The nutter who nearly killed her in his boat.'

Sadie slapped her hands on the table. 'For the last time, it was an accident! And if you don't like it, have you got a better idea for staffing the waffle house?'

Ewan looked as if he would argue. But then he let out an impatient sigh. 'You're really this determined?'

Sadie nodded.

'Right.' Ewan glanced at his parents in turn and, when nobody stopped him, he looked back to Sadie and continued. 'I don't want Goldman anywhere near the place, but I'll talk to Kat and we'll see if we can work out a way to help you. It wouldn't be ideal and it wouldn't be a permanent solution, but…'

Sadie broke into a broad smile. 'Sometimes you're not so bad, you know. As stinky brothers go.'

'I'm not making any promises,' he warned. 'And, like I said, it's a short-term solution. You do need to make some other arrangements as soon as you can – and it had better not involve Boaty McBoatface.'

Sadie's smile grew. For the time being she wasn't about to challenge Ewan's disapproval of Luke, thankful that she'd finally got his support with the waffle house. It was a small victory but she'd take it. If she was totally honest, she wasn't sure Luke was the answer and even if he'd agreed to help she didn't know how much use he would have been. She'd really been clutching at straws there because Luke knew next to nothing about catering – as far as she was aware – though she could hardly deny that it might have been fun having him around.

She glanced up at the clock again.

'Is there somewhere you need to be?' her mother asked haughtily. 'Because you seem to be very interested in the time.'

'Well… I do have to be somewhere, actually, a little later on…'

'Could you postpone or cancel it?' Henny asked.

'Actually, no,' Sadie said, not daring to look at Ewan because she was certain her face would give the game away. Ordinarily she wasn't one for secrecy, particularly where her family were concerned, and she had no issues with them knowing who she was dating. But this was different. Even setting aside their intense dislike of Luke, there was still a lot going on here. Sadie wasn't stupid – she knew it looked bad that she was planning to be elsewhere while so much still needed to be discussed. But in the end, what would hours' more discussion achieve that hadn't already been agreed?

'Jesus Christ,' Ewan muttered. 'Let me guess…'

'You'll have to cancel whatever it is,' Henny said, apparently not catching on quite as fast as Ewan and confirming what Sadie had been afraid she'd say. 'There's far too much going on here and we need you.'

'Haven't we already sorted it?' Sadie's shoulders slumped.

'No. We've sketched the plan but we've yet to fill in the details.'

'Mum's right,' Ewan said. 'We're nowhere near finished.'

'But…' Sadie gave a look that pleaded with her brother to back her up, just once more and despite the fact that it would be going against everything he thought was good for her. 'I know you don't like Luke, but I really do. If you gave him time you might even change your mind.'

'I doubt that,' Ewan said.

'Actually, so do I,' Sadie replied in a tone that suggested she really didn't care. She looked at her parents. 'I won't stay out late and when I get home I promise I'll have a plan for tomorrow. In fact, before I go I'll make some calls.' She turned to Ewan. 'I know you're going to talk to Kat but I wouldn't expect you two to take up all the slack.'

Ewan leaned forward and rested his arms on the table as he surveyed them all. 'This is all very well, but what are we going to tell Grandma? I don't know about you but I don't want to be the person who tells her she can't go to work tomorrow because it might be dangerous for her.'

Henny and Graham exchanged a look. They hadn't thought of that – that much was obvious.

'How about this…?' Sadie began. 'If I can get someone to be in the kitchen with her all the time she can still go in? We'll pretend she's training whoever it is and, in a way, she will be.'

'Who's going to be in the kitchen with her?' Henny asked. 'You keep coming up with these bright ideas but you still haven't said who you're going to ask.'

'I know,' Sadie said, trying to keep her voice even despite the fact that her patience was wearing thin. 'I told you I'm working on it.'

'Well you'd better hurry up,' her mother said.

Sadie gave an uncertain nod as she ran through a list of possibilities in her head. There was no shortage of names, the trouble was – for various reasons – they'd all said no before. But maybe if she could ask again, cherry-pick a little time from each, persuade them of the urgency of her request, just until she could figure out something more permanent… maybe she could make it work.

She got up from the table. 'I know it's not good timing but I really do have to get changed. I'll mull it all over as I get ready.'

Henny took in a sharp, hissing breath of disapproval, but Graham and Ewan were silent. Sadie shrugged. What else could she do?

'I'll be back in a tick,' she said as she rushed out of the room before anyone could pile any more guilt on her.

Chapter Fourteen

'So, what are you going to do?'

Luke lifted his glass to take a drink of the mineral water he'd ordered so he could drive Sadie home as soon as she felt she needed to get back, and get her home quickly. She'd told him her predicament on the phone just before they'd been due to meet and he'd offered immediately, no questions asked, and they'd arranged to stay more local too rather than go further afield. She'd left home promising to come up with a solution to the staffing problem at the waffle house but she had absolutely no clue what that might be. She had about twelve hours to find out, and it had felt natural and easy to share her worries with Luke. She found herself telling him the whole story, perhaps more of it than she'd meant to and perhaps more than her parents would want her to. He'd been understanding and sympathetic and happy to listen, but he didn't have any suggestions to offer. It wasn't that Sadie had really expected him to – after all, he didn't know the business and what it needed like she did – but she'd still harboured a little hope that he might come up with something she hadn't thought of.

'That's just it,' Sadie said. 'I don't see I have any real options. Every time I think of something I think of a reason why it wouldn't work. I know Ewan said he and Kat would try to help but I don't really think that's going to work out.'

'I'm sure you'll come up with an answer. It's a shame I can't help.'

'Ewan would have an actual aneurysm. And to be honest, he's right about one thing – you don't know the first thing about running a food business. If I'm honest I don't know all that much but at least I have Gammy to guide me. Nobody else I know who might have time on their hands would know their way around the business either. I suppose they could work front of house and I could be in the kitchen, but then I'm afraid that my cooking would be so much worse than Gammy's that everyone would be able to tell and we'd lose customers.'

'I'm sure you couldn't be that bad. Couldn't your grandmother show you how to make things as well as she does?'

'She has shown me a little over the years, but she just has a special talent, you know? And you can't learn that, no matter how hard you try.'

'Maybe you're being a little hard on yourself there? It's tempting to compare yourself unfavourably with someone who's very, very good at something, but just because you may not be quite in their league doesn't mean you're necessarily bad at it.'

'Trust me; I'm nowhere near Gammy's league.'

'And you couldn't afford to employ someone on a temporary basis until you've got a better solution?'

'There's very little in the kitty to pay a decent wage. And anyway, I don't really have a clue how long I'd need them for. Not many people would agree to work on those terms.'

He nodded thoughtfully and Sadie let out a long sigh. 'My mum is right about one thing: I'm so stubborn about this stuff. I stand my ground and refuse to listen to reason and I wind up with egg on my face because my family turn out to be right. I guess it's happened again, hasn't it? If I can't have Gammy working with me and I've got nobody else then it looks as if I won't be able to open for business tomorrow after all. Or for the foreseeable future until I can sort something out. And if I can't…'

'It seems like a crying shame to me and a sure way to lose a lot of valuable custom.'

'I know.' Sadie's gaze went to the bar of the Listing Ship. Vivien was on duty again, and though she'd given them a knowing look as they'd walked in, Sadie didn't see the point in indulging her by addressing the fact that her gossiping had caused trouble between Sadie and Ewan. She wasn't going to give her the satisfaction of knowing she cared and, when it came down to it, that was what people in Sea Salt Bay did. Someone did something and by the next day pretty much everyone knew about it. Vivien was never going to be any different and she certainly wasn't ever going to keep her juicy tittle-tattle to herself. Crows crowed and sheep baaed, and the residents of Sea Salt Bay talked about all the other residents of Sea Salt Bay. It was just the way things were.

'It seems to be the story of my life… watching good things slip away from me and being far too useless to do anything about it. Grand schemes that come to nothing…'

She probably sounded a bit whiny and a bit too sorry for herself, and so she stopped.

'I don't think you should write it off so quickly,' Luke said.

'I'm not; I'm just being realistic. There's a long way to go for a solution and will there be any point in the end? If everyone is determined that the waffle house ought to be sold then what am I doing this for?'

'You might have to delay your opening but I wouldn't abandon the whole thing. You're right about one aspect – it's a far more attractive prospect as a going concern, especially with the reputation it has in the area and the volume of trade it could attract in a town like this. Someone would take your hand off for the chance to buy a business like that, something that's already up and running with so much potential. In the right hands it could be a little goldmine.'

'But those hands aren't mine?'

'I didn't say that. They could be, but right now you don't even seem certain of that yourself.'

'You can see why that might be – I haven't been very good at it so far.'

'You've been dealt bad cards. You weren't to know your grandma's health would deteriorate in the way it has.'

'That's just it – I should have spotted it sooner. I guess I did really – we all did – but none of us wanted to admit it was happening.' She forced a bright smile. 'I'm sorry this is turning out to be such a terrible date. I thought coming out with you would help me to forget all that and we'd just have fun, but that hasn't happened at all. I bet you wish you'd stayed at home with a tin of paint right now, done something useful with your time.'

'No,' he said, holding her in a warm gaze. 'I don't wish that at all.'

'But it can't be much fun with me.'

'I think you're gorgeous and intelligent and interesting company. And although I'm sympathetic to your plight and happy to lend an ear, there is an ulterior motive.'

'What's that?'

'I get to sit and look at you and think about kissing you. Don't imagine you have my undivided attention for a minute because those lips of yours are very distracting.'

Sadie laughed, tension draining from her in the warmth of his words.

'Don't laugh,' he said, 'I'm being serious. It actually makes me a terrible person and I do feel a bit guilty about it.'

'No,' she said. 'It doesn't. I like it and thank you for making me feel better.' She took a deep breath and sat up straighter. 'I'll write a note for the door of the waffle house explaining that we have to close for a few days and pop in there first thing to put it up. It's all I can do. Hopefully it'll mean people won't think we're gone for good and they might keep checking back to see if we're open, so when we do – *if* we do – the customers will still be there.'

'And does it mean you can stay out a bit later with me tonight?' he asked with a mischievous smile. 'As you don't have to work tomorrow?'

'As tempting as that is, I do still have to work tomorrow. I need to find a way out of this problem.'

'But you could do that after an extra hour in bed?'

'Well,' she said, relaxing a little more still, 'I suppose I might think more clearly on a fun night out and a bit more sleep.'

'My thoughts exactly.' He looked at her glass. 'So how about we top up that gin and tonic and I try to take your mind off your troubles for a while?'

She leaned across the table to kiss him. She could have done so much more, and she wanted to, but there were people waiting at home to talk to her and things that still needed to be resolved.

'I'd love that so much,' she said. 'But I really should get back after this one. I'm sorry... You're not upset, are you?'

'I'd be lying if I said I wasn't disappointed, but I understand that you need this. Of course I'll take you home. Just' – he glanced at her glass again – 'just don't drink that one too quickly, eh? I'm not ready for the evening to be over just yet.'

Even though Sadie ought to have been tired, sleep didn't come easily. Luke had dropped her off shortly after ten thirty, and though the passion of their first date had been evident again in their goodnight kiss, it had been gentler, more understanding and respectful this time. It was clear to him that she wasn't in the mood for anything more (though she'd enjoyed his company and had appreciated the time out from complex family discussions) and that she had more important things going on.

That wasn't to say that she hadn't still been thinking of him, even as her parents had tried valiantly to pick up where they'd left off earlier that evening, and even as she'd tried very hard to concentrate on what they'd been saying. Scenes and snatches of the night spent sitting close to Luke in the snug of the Listing Ship came back to her though, filling her with a dreamy sort of longing for what the next evening and the one after that might promise. If she was very lucky, luckier than she felt she deserved, could this even be the second chance at something meaningful – even love? The second chance she'd begun to give up all hope of having? With all that racing around in her mind, she was finding it hard to make room for the more pressing matters that she knew she really had to get to grips with.

So she'd tossed and turned during the night, awake to hear an owl's soft hooting and then another in reply, and then, as the sun crested the horizon, the chattering of gulls on nearby cliffs. Just after the sun had bled through her bedroom blind she got up, dressed quickly and headed down to the pier.

The town was still quiet and sleepy, and Sadie had often thought that there was something melancholy about the way it looked so early in the morning, as if the soul of it had departed the body for just a little while and had yet to return. It was sort of like a toddler still stirring from a long night's sleep, content to slowly and silently greet the new day, blinking out at the world but still confused by it. Only later, when it had woken properly, would it be a happy whirlwind of manic activity, of noise and energy and fun, making everyone around it happy too.

At the door of the waffle house, Sadie poked the key in and shoved open the door. Once she was in, she locked it again. She didn't put on the lights – there was enough daylight if she opened a couple of blinds, which she did before going through to Gammy's little office to find paper and pens in the absence of a computer and printer. She could have printed a sign at home, but she'd forgotten to do it before she'd gone to bed the night before and this morning she was afraid that the noise would wake the house so, instead, she wrote a note in blue felt-tip.

Sea Salt Bay Waffle House will be closed until further notice. We apologise to all our loyal customers, but we will be back soon!

A little optimistic? Maybe, and Sadie was beginning to feel in her heart that it was a little white lie, not only to herself but also to the people of Sea Salt Bay. Maybe the waffle house would open again but, even if it did, she was beginning to see that it wouldn't be in its current guise. In fact, she was more certain than ever that it simply couldn't be.

When she'd hung the sign in the window she sat at a table for a minute, head in hands. She needed time to think in peace, without someone breathing down her neck, demanding immediate answers. But even now, her thoughts were muddled and her heart wasn't really in it.

An unexpected yawn caught her. There was nothing else to do here – nothing with any kind of time pressure anyway. If her misfiring brain would let her, the most sensible thing would be to try to grab a couple of hours' sleep back at home. Her parents would be on their way out to the boat by now to get it ready for the day. Gammy would likely be awake, though they'd explained to her the previous night that the waffle house wouldn't be open the next day because Sadie was unable to help out and inventing some excuse that she didn't feel well.

It wouldn't be a stretch to keep up that pretence because fatigue was making her feel quite unwell anyway. It meant that Gammy would probably find something to do in the house – she liked to make herself useful where she could – and hopefully, in the house, she couldn't get into too much mischief. Sadie could set an alarm and she wouldn't sleep for too long and then she'd be around to keep an eye on things for the rest of the day.

It was as she was leaving that she saw Luke, almost racing down the pier towards the waffle house. She locked the door and then turned to him, squinting in the now bright sunlight.

'What are you doing here?' she asked. 'Not that I'm not pleased to see you, but it's early and—'

'I was hoping to catch you; I need to talk.'

'OK,' Sadie began slowly, wondering what on earth would need such urgent attention. 'I have a phone, you know.'

'Yes,' he said with a breathless laugh. 'I know, but I can't kiss you down the phone, can I?'

Sadie smiled and walked into his arms to claim what he'd promised. He smelt incredible and his lips were warm and responsive, and suddenly she didn't feel quite so tired or despondent.

'Is that all you've come for?' she asked as they broke off.

'Not really,' he said, and for the first time since she'd started to date him he seemed a little anxious.

'Then…'

'I've had an idea.'

'Oh. Well, is it something you can convey in small words? Because I'm very tired and right now I have a very short attention span.'

'OK. So…' He paused. 'So, I was thinking… why don't I buy the waffle house?'

Her forehead creased into a deep frown. 'What?'

'If I buy the waffle house, does that help you? I have some money spare to do it.'

'And do what with it?'

'Exactly what it's doing now.'

'Who's going to run it?'

'You. I thought that was what you wanted. You said—'

'I do want that, but you buying it doesn't change my predicament. I still don't have anyone to run it with me and I can't do it alone. Besides, why would you do something like that? You hardly know me; we might hate each other this time next week and then where would we be?'

'That's not going to happen.'

'Even if it didn't, the fact remains that I can't afford to employ someone – I'd have to pay you back… Or will this be your business?'

'It'd be yours. And I'd work with you – at first anyway. I can't promise I'd be much good but you can teach me and it'd just be until you started to make enough money to hire help.'

'You can't work with me – you have enough of your own to do. And you're not exactly the most popular person in town as far as my family are concerned – they'd never sell to you.'

'But surely they'd see things differently if I was doing you all a favour? They surely can't be that stubborn? And I do owe you big time, don't forget.'

'Oh, God, not the boat thing again. Isn't anyone going to let that drop?'

'Well then, I want to do it because I like you and I want to help.'

'But, Luke… you don't know the first thing about the business. I mean, I know you know about business in general but this is so different from property…'

'You're saying I can't learn?'

'Of course you can, but why would you want to? Don't you have work of your own to be getting on with – an existing business that needs you?'

'Well, yes, but—'

'Then why make promises to me that you won't be able to keep?'

'I would keep them.'

'You'd mean to but then something would happen. And I love that you want to help, I really do, but…'

'I don't understand…'

'It's another false start for me, isn't it? You'll decide in a few weeks that you don't have the time to spare because your house isn't finished as quickly as you need, or because people are asking you to build them an extension or whatever and you need to do it because you need to earn, and then you'll leave me to it. And I'll be exactly where I started, except with the possibility hanging over me that if you get bored or need cash you'd be able to sell the waffle house on without a bit of consultation.' She shook her head. 'Where would you even get that kind of money from, anyway?'

'I have some I made from property sales in London,' he said, a defensive note creeping into his tone. 'It would be enough.'

He took a single step back from her, but in that step was all Sadie needed to know. She'd offended him. She didn't want that but there was no point in being anything other than straight with him – his plan was plain madness. She drew a breath. She was tired and tetchy but she didn't want to upset him.

'It's a sweet offer and I'm really touched, but it's too much and I can't even consider it. You'll look back on this conversation in a few weeks and realise that it would have been a horrible mistake and you'll be glad I said no.'

He chewed on his lip for a moment, head down, hands in his pockets.

'Right,' he said in a low voice, eyes still on the floor. 'Well, now I feel pretty stupid.'

'I didn't mean that.'

Sadie reached for him, but he took another step back.

'I have things to do,' he said stiffly. 'I just wanted to catch you before… I'd better go and leave you to it.'

Any energy Sadie might have had was quickly leaving her, and though she cared that he was so offended and perhaps felt stupid, she was too tired to see a way to rescue the situation. And even if she hadn't been, would there have been one anyway?

'Walk to the end of the pier with me?' she asked.

'Sure,' he said, but it was obvious his heart wasn't in it.

They carried on in silence, which had not been Sadie's intention at all, though it felt impossible to prevent it. As they reached the point they'd have to part she looked up at him.

'When will I see you next?'

He shrugged. 'Whenever you like.'

Sadie didn't press for anything more specific. 'OK, maybe you want to let me know when you're next free? You know, whenever. My evenings aren't exactly wall-to-wall social events so I'll probably be free.'

Her joke didn't even raise so much as a faint smile. As attempts at humour went, even she had to admit it had been feeble, but she'd hoped to soften the sharp edges of the situation a little.

He just nodded. 'Will do.'

She wondered if he'd kiss her but he didn't, and she watched as he walked away, torn between being annoyed at him for starting this and annoyed at herself for the way she'd handled it. But at the end of the day she was certain that no matter how much the idea might seem like a silver bullet for her problems, it wasn't. Someone would buy the waffle house from them, of that she was certain, but it couldn't be Luke.

Chapter Fifteen

Sadie was back on the cliff road when she saw a familiar figure walking towards her.

'Oh, God...' she muttered, quickening her step to meet them. As she got closer she recognised instantly the comfy shoes Gammy always wore to work.

'Why didn't you wait for me?' April asked tersely.

'What do you mean?'

'And who's minding the waffle house if you're here?'

'Nobody... It's not open, remember?'

April slapped a hand to her chest, eyes wide with shock. 'Not open!'

'Gammy... we agreed this last night. You must remember the conversation?'

'I most certainly agreed nothing of the kind,' April snapped. 'I've never heard such nonsense!'

'But, Gammy...'

April looked at her watch. 'Oh, my – it's almost nine! We'll never be ready in time to open!'

Sadie started after her as she continued her march down the hill. 'Gammy, wait!'

'There's no time to dawdle,' April said. 'We've got hungry people to feed!'

'Gammy, please!' Sadie cried, grabbing her grandmother's arm to stop her. 'Please, think back! Yesterday we sat with Mum and Dad and Kat and Ewan and we agreed that… well, that you needed a little break from the waffle house…'

'I would never agree to that,' April said, looking hurt and bewildered. Sadie could understand why she might be a little confused because a few short days ago it would have seemed so unlikely for her to agree to something like that. But she had agreed, and Sadie had to make her remember.

'Just let me…' Sadie began, letting go of her grandmother's arm to get her phone out. She started to dial her mother's number. It went to voicemail, and then her father's did the same, and so she got to poor Ewan, who already had enough on his plate.

'Oh, thank God!' she said as he picked up. 'You have to come and help me with…' She glanced at April, who was watching her carefully. 'You know last night when we said the waffle house… you know… that Gammy needed a break? Well she's got other ideas.'

Ewan's reply was tense. 'Where are you now?'

'On our way down from the house.'

'Going to the pier?'

'Yes,' Sadie said helplessly.

'Can't you explain it to her?'

'I've tried but she's… I've tried. I can't stop her.'

'She's going there right now?'

'Yes!' Sadie said. 'If she wasn't I wouldn't be calling you! She's got keys to open up. She's determined to go and I can't just let her get on with it, but I'm not supposed to be taking her there either.'

'What on earth are you talking about?' April asked sharply. 'We don't have time for this.'

'It's Ewan, Gammy… he…'

'Tell her I need her at the dive school,' Ewan said into Sadie's ear. 'Tell her we need her to help out with one of the kids. Say they're ill or something. As long as we keep her away from the waffle house for a bit longer. Once she's here I can take her home.'

A bit of Sadie wondered still whether it might make more sense to let April potter about in the waffle house with Sadie keeping a close eye on her. But she supposed that plan would only work if they didn't get very busy and they might. But trying to stop April from going there to work was only making her distressed and Sadie didn't see a way out of this that didn't make that worse. And Sadie hated all this lying and subterfuge. She hated telling all these stories and manipulating Gammy into doing everything they wanted her to do. Even though it was with her best interests at heart, it didn't feel right and Sadie didn't enjoy being a part of it. But she bit her tongue and did as her brother asked.

'Gammy… Ewan says he needs us to go to the dive school. He needs you to help with something.'

'With what?'

'One of the kids.'

'Shouldn't they be at school about now? What do they need me for?'

Sadie had to smile. April might have been confused but she wasn't stupid.

'I'm sorry but he'll have to get someone else. Where's Kat? Isn't she right there with him? What is it that only I can do? They've never asked me for something like this before.'

'I…' Sadie flicked back to Ewan. 'This is hopeless. She's determined to go and I can hardly stop her.'

'Why are you telling Ewan all this?' April snapped. 'It's just like sports commentary – April's doing this, April's doing that…' She raised her voice so that Ewan would be able to hear. 'Grandma's putting one foot in front of the other to walk down the hill… is that OK? Do you need any more information? Perhaps you want to know what coat I have on?'

Sadie didn't know whether to laugh or cry, though she did have to appreciate April's wit.

'Sorry,' she said to Ewan, 'but it looks as if we're opening up this morning. You'll have to come to us and try to persuade her, but I don't fancy your chances the mood she's in.'

'I'll meet you down there,' he said, and then hung up.

Sadie fell in step with her grandma. There wasn't much else she could do.

April wasn't very pleased when she saw Sadie's sign up in the waffle-house window. In fact, she didn't even wait for the door to be unlocked before she started to tear a strip off her and was in full flow when Melissa walked past. Sadie glanced at her and they exchanged a look of awkward recognition, Sadie flashing back to the night she'd heard Melissa shouting angrily at Declan in the street and she'd heard her own name mentioned in the tirade. She was still convinced that the conversation had been something to do with a request from Declan for help at the waffle house.

Melissa hurried by, at least having the decency to be embarrassed for Sadie at the sight of her being scolded very publicly by her grandmother. Sadie watched her go, wondering vaguely what had brought her this far long the pier, all that she knew about that night very much on her mind. She was dragged back by her grandmother's voice as she shoved the front door of the waffle house open and went inside, immediately removing Sadie's notice and putting it in the bin.

'It's just plain crazy to let this place stand empty,' she said. She set about switching the lights on and taking chairs from the tables. 'I don't know what you were all thinking!'

As she began to help, Sadie wondered if she could get away with sneakily locking the front doors, putting another discreet sign up and letting April potter around in the kitchen, thinking they were open but just having a slow day until closing time. But her grandma wouldn't be so easily fooled. After ordering Sadie to get the till ready, she went through to the kitchen to start in there, muttering all the time about how they were running late and would never get the doors open for customers by ten, and how crazy and annoying everyone else was. Sadie gave a mental shrug and turned her attention to getting the front of house in order. What she wouldn't give for her bed right now, but it looked as if bed was a long way off.

It was then that she saw Ewan at the door. He must have rushed over at top speed, judging by how quickly he'd arrived.

'What exactly are you proposing to do?' she asked in a low voice as she opened up to him. 'You heard her this morning – she won't be persuaded to go home. God knows I've tried everything.'

'You'll have to try harder. We all agreed that she isn't safe to be here.'

'We did – but tell her that! Actually, don't, because she's in a stinker of a mood and you'll only make her worse!'

'She can't be here!'

'She *is* here! And trust me, she's not about to go anywhere – at least not today.'

Ewan narrowed his eyes. 'And you haven't put her up to it?'

'Don't be a dick!' Sadie snapped.

'I'm just saying because you're keen to keep the place open and it would suit you to—'

'At the expense of Gammy's safety? Credit me with some humanity, Ewan!'

He ground his teeth and stared into space for a moment. 'As far as I can see, the sooner Grandma sells this place the better.'

'I know that. But first we've got to persuade her it's a good idea.'

'A quick sale and a good price might do that.'

Sadie wasn't so sure but she didn't say so. She wasn't sure any price would be enough for Gammy to let it go, especially not to a stranger.

'Does it matter who buys it?' she asked.

'Why?'

'No reason,' Sadie said, though she didn't know why Luke's offer had popped into her head at that exact moment. She could probably put it down to desperation. They needed a quick solution and he had one. But she'd already dismissed it because it wouldn't work, and her opinion hadn't really changed on that. It was just too easy to reach out for the nearest life raft, even if that raft had holes and too many people on board already. And no matter how desperate things became, her brother would never agree to Luke buying the waffle house anyway and chances were – the way things stood – that April would never agree to sell it either. Sadie was convinced that the only way her grandmother would sell was if it stayed in the family, but they'd already established that wasn't practical either because the only family member who wanted to buy it couldn't afford to. They really were looking at the most impossible puzzle.

'Ewan,' she continued, 'you can't go in all guns blazing this morning, telling Gammy all this; you'll only upset her and she's already unhappy. For today we're going to have to let it be and then talk to her again tonight. It might take time to get there and we're going to have to be patient.'

'We could talk to her again tonight if you could sit in the house for longer than ten minutes with us.'

Sadie put her hands to her hips. 'What's that supposed to mean?'

'I don't know… Don't you have a date with an axe murderer or serial killer or something?'

Sadie scowled at him. 'Oh, Ewan, you're *soooo* funny…'

'I'm not trying to be. Will you be in?'

'For what it's worth, yes. But I hardly think it matters. I'm hardly more persuasive than anyone else and nobody's got through to her so far.'

'That's where you're wrong. If you tell Grandma you won't work in the waffle house any longer she'll have no choice but to close up because even she knows she can't run it alone.'

Sadie stared at him. 'You want me to do *what?*'

'You heard me,' he replied, lowering his voice and casting a glance at the kitchen door.

She gave her head a vigorous shake. 'I'm not doing it.'

'Why not?'

'Because Gammy will hate me.'

'You'll be doing her a kindness in the long run.'

'Easy for you to say – you're not going to look like the bitch who lost her lovely waffle house for her. She'll still love you when it's all over.'

'Don't be ridiculous – she'll still love you too.'

'She'd always blame me and that's not fair because it wouldn't even be my fault. Why should I take the rap? It's a horrible idea and I'm not doing it.'

'You don't have a choice. It's either that or she does herself an injury here. Or worse, she does someone else an injury. Maybe even you.'

'You're overreacting – she's not *that* dangerous.'

'Sadie, she locked you in this building and then wandered off with the keys! And I'm worried this might only be the tip of the iceberg – it could get worse. She could blow the place sky-high and then nobody would have it.'

Sadie let out a long sigh of defeat. 'I hate you.'

'I know, but you'll get over it. Stay here today and I'll get whoever's free to come and check in from time to time. Tonight we have to sort things out because you just can't open again tomorrow.'

Sadie gave a grim nod. As if her day wasn't already bad enough, there was that to look forward to. What a start – it was hardly conducive to service with a smile.

Sadie had to wonder if they'd had more family and friends in checking up on them than actual paying customers at the waffle house that day. After Ewan had gone Kat called, having a couple of hours between lessons, and then late morning Henny dashed over, taking a break from the boat and letting Ewan (who now had an hour free) go out with Graham instead.

At lunch Natalie called in (after being filled in by Vivien at the pub, who'd heard it from Melissa's mum, who'd been told by Melissa, who'd been told by Declan that he'd found April wandering the day before with Sadie locked in the waffle house). Natalie demanded to know why Sadie hadn't approached her for help, and though Sadie appreciated the sentiment, she suspected that if she'd asked for help, Natalie probably would have been too busy to do very much at all. But she was here now, concerned for the welfare of all involved, and Sadie was grateful for that. Natalie went through to the kitchen and sat on a stool, chatting to April while she drank tea and ate crepes. While Sadie appreciated that her friend was keeping Gammy company and keeping an eye on her, she also had a little wry appreciation of the fact that her friend was getting a pretty good deal out of it. Then Natalie had to dash off back to work and Sadie was left in relative peace – for an hour at least.

The day saved the best (or worst, depending on how you looked at it) until last. About an hour before closing, Declan came in. He seemed tense, not quite his usual self, but he denied this when Sadie asked him about it. She wondered whether problems with Melissa were at the root of it, and whether perhaps the row she'd overheard the night she'd hidden beneath the pier with Luke was still rumbling on. But he hadn't taken an hour off work to talk about himself, he said, he'd come to check if Sadie and April were OK, and to see if he could lend a hand. He also expressed some surprise that they were open at all.

'You're not the only one who's surprised,' Sadie said in a low voice. 'We weren't supposed to be open but it got a bit tricky. I suppose Melissa told you she saw us this morning?'

'Yes, though when she told me I thought maybe you were just checking the place over. And then Ewan called me about an hour ago to see if I could come by.'

'Hmm. Well, basically, Gammy was determined that we'd be open no matter what anyone said about it, and you know how difficult she can be.'

He gave a slight smile. 'The stubbornness doesn't surprise me – it runs in the family.'

'I hope you're not alluding to me.'

He shrugged. 'Take it how you like, but if you recognise it…'

'Oh!' she cried with mock annoyance. 'So rude!'

He held his hands up in a gesture of surrender. 'I'm just saying I might have seen it before.'

Sadie couldn't help a warm smile for him. 'Even though it does look as if you've taken an hour off just to come and insult me, thanks for looking in on us anyway. But you needn't have worried – we're just fine. We have a plan, apparently. At least, Ewan does.'

'Doesn't sound as if you're overly keen on it.'

'I'm not, but I don't think I have a choice.'

'Want to fill me in?'

Sadie glanced at the kitchen door. 'Not now – you never know who's listening.'

He nodded. 'You don't need anything from me while I've got an hour? Anything at all – name it. As long as it doesn't involve human sacrifice or lime jelly I'm all over it.'

She let out a giggle that had the half-dozen diners they had in looking for the source of the noise, and she had to clamp a hand over her mouth, a sheepish grin on her face.

'Jelly?'

'You don't recall the jelly incident? Or Jelly-Gate, as I like to call it.'

'You don't eat jelly.'

'No, and there's a good reason why. Come on now, think back.'

Sadie paused, and then she giggled again. 'Oh, God, yes… that time…'

'I never used to eat it and you couldn't understand why and I couldn't remember why, so one day you made me have some with custard and I broke out in hives almost immediately.'

'And you had your headshot for student council the next day.'

'And I looked like I'd got some horrible disease and nobody could ever recognise me from that photo. I spent three bloody years explaining to people that it was me and why it didn't look like me at all. Three years stuck with a portrait that made me look like a bowl of tapioca pudding!'

'Oh, God,' Sadie snorted and again put a hand to her mouth to stifle her laughter. 'Does it make it better that I'm still sorry about that?'

'It would, only there's so much else for you to be sorry about that I think you'd have to pay penance for the next twenty years to make it all up to me.'

'You can talk!' she squeaked.

He put a hand to his breast and feigned an expression of newborn innocence. '*Moi*?'

'What about that time you phoned me to say Robert Downey Jnr was drinking in the Ship? I rushed down there and when I got there you were just sitting in the bar with one of those celebrity masks on, laughing your head off. You have no idea how disappointing it was!'

'Serves you right for racing down to see another man.'

'It was no man – it was Robert Downey Jnr! My free pass! What else did you expect me to do?'

'I wouldn't have done it.'

'Not even for Blake Lively?'

'OK, maybe…' He grinned. 'But free pass or not, you wouldn't have really gone there, even if it had been the man himself?'

'Yeah, because he would have totally gone along with that,' she said with gentle sarcasm in her tone.

'I wouldn't have, not even for Blake Lively.'

She smiled up at him. 'I wouldn't have either – you know that.'

He smiled too, and for a moment they held each other's gaze.

It was too easy to be like this with him, and alarm bells should have been ringing but they weren't. The fact was, no matter what else happened, where else life took them, nobody knew the soul of Sadie like he did and that was hard to resist, especially on days when she felt lost and out of her depth and needed a little understanding.

But then the door to the waffle house opened and Sadie tore away her gaze to greet a new customer.

Only it wasn't a new customer; it was Luke, and he was wearing the expression of a man who'd just seen something he wished he hadn't. There was a glance loaded with questions shared between Sadie and Declan, until it settled back on Sadie again.

Declan cut into the stark and sudden silence.

'If you don't need anything,' he said to Sadie, 'I'll get back to work.' He cast a wary glance Luke's way, as uncomfortable as the other man's had been distrustful.

'OK,' Sadie replied, determined not to let the moment get the better of her. 'Thanks for dropping by; it was thoughtful of you.'

Declan hooked a thumb towards the kitchen. 'Maybe I'll just go and...'

'Yes,' Sadie said, her smile brief and reserved now. 'That would be great; Gammy would love to see you and you could... you know...'

'Check on her?'

'Exactly. Kill two birds with one stone.'

Declan went through to the kitchen and Sadie forced a bright smile for Luke.

'Have you met Declan properly yet?'

'No, but I know of him.'

'Right. Of course. Small town and all that, of course you do. He's an... old friend.'

'I gathered,' he replied, and Sadie didn't know how to respond to that so she ignored it.

'I didn't expect to see you again today. Is everything alright?'

'I didn't expect to see you open today.'

'No; a lot of people seem to be coming in to say that. It's a long story. Did you just come in because you'd noticed or...?'

'Well, yes. But I thought I'd just come in to take the opportunity to catch you anyway. About this morning—'

'I'm sorry,' she said. 'I handled it very badly.'

'No, no you didn't. It was a stupid suggestion and everything you said made perfect sense. I just wanted to say that and clear the air. After we left things the way we did I haven't been able to settle all day.'

'Me neither,' Sadie said. 'Honestly, I'm so glad we've been able to speak again this afternoon.'

'Me too,' he said, and he seemed to relax a little. 'I was so worried that I'd blown it this morning.'

'Me too. We might be as daft as each other.'

'We might.' He glanced around the dining room before taking a step back towards the door. 'You're busy, and you don't have time for all this now. When you said you'd be free later…'

'Could we make it tomorrow? I know I said that this morning but things have changed. We have to talk to Gammy again, sort this business out once and for all, and I have to be there giving it my full attention. My parents will flip if I rush off again, not to mention my brother will want to come over and punch your lights out.'

'He'd probably be quite efficient at it too,' Luke said with a laugh. 'He looks handy.'

'Don't be fooled. He looks as if he could handle himself but all those muscles are just decoration. He wouldn't really hurt a fly.'

'Easy for you to say – he's probably never wanted to knock you out.'

Sadie smiled. 'How about tomorrow? That's if you're free.'

'My evening schedule is a bit like yours – pretty empty right now. I think tomorrow could work.'

'Tomorrow then. About…'

But Luke's attention had been drawn to the kitchen, and Sadie looked to see that Declan was walking across the dining room. She felt the temperature in the room drop by degrees once more as the two men regarded each other. Declan aimed a careless nod at Sadie.

'Don't forget, call if you need anything. Me or Mum or Dad – we'll all help if we can.'

Sadie smiled gratefully. 'Thanks, Dec. I appreciate it.'

'See you around then.'

'Yeah.'

He held his hand up in a casual wave and left. Sadie was aware that she wanted to watch him walk the pier for a moment or two, as she always did when he left the waffle house, but that she shouldn't. Instead she turned back to Luke.

'I'm looking forward to it already.'

'I'll text you later to see what time suits you. Where do you want to go?'

'I'm content just walking on the beach if you're there.'

'Really?' He grinned, and he looked so much happier now than when he'd arrived that it warmed her to see it. She was tired, and she had more trouble waiting for her at home, but at least there was this to look forward to.

'Absolutely,' she said. 'If the weather is good, that's what we'll do.'

Chapter Sixteen

Sadie had never seen her grandmother cry – at least, not like this. She'd seen her cry at Gampy's funeral, of course, and for other family members they'd lost over the years. She'd seen her cry at films and she'd seen her cry with happiness, but she'd never seen such bitter, hateful tears, and she'd never imagined in her wildest nightmares that she'd be the cause of them. April had called her a flake, lazy, disloyal, selfish… and that was despite Henny and Graham's staunch defence of her. It had cut into her very soul to see her grandmother look at her with such betrayal too, and yet, despite how much it hurt, she knew that Ewan was right and that the only way they'd get Gammy to step away from the waffle house was for Sadie to withdraw her help. It didn't mean that she was any less hurt by the fact that her brother had chosen to throw her under the bus to achieve it, and that he was now the golden boy while Sadie was the girl her grandma could hardly bear to look at.

In the end, Henny had been forced to take April to bed, and they'd been gone for a solid hour before she came back down to the drawing room, where Sadie was curled in her father's arms, her own tears falling now that her grandma wasn't there to see them. Ewan was in the garden with Kat, who was almost as distressed as Sadie and April about the whole thing.

'I'm so sorry,' Henny said, coming to sit with her husband and daughter on the sofa. 'I never imagined it would be quite this ghastly.'

'It's not your fault,' Sadie sniffed, sitting up and dabbing her eyes with her dad's clean hanky.

'I can't help but feel it is,' Henny said. 'We shouldn't have let things get this far… We should have put that old place on the market the moment we'd buried poor Kenneth.'

'I pushed it, Mum,' Sadie said. 'I don't want you to feel bad about it.'

Henny gave her a mournful look and reached to catch a tear as it tracked Sadie's cheek. 'How can I feel anything else? No mother wants to see her daughter cry like this. If anything, I'm angry at April.'

'Angry?' Graham looked sharply at his wife.

'I can't help it,' Henny said. 'I know I shouldn't be but look at the disharmony between us at the moment and it's all over that blasted waffle house.'

'You can't be angry at Gammy,' Sadie said. 'She doesn't know what she's doing.'

'That doesn't make it any easier to see you so upset.' Henny let out a sigh. 'Well, it's done now. Tomorrow morning we'll instruct someone to put the waffle house on the market. She'll have to sign the papers, of course…' She looked at Graham. 'That's going to be your job, I'm afraid, because I don't think she'd do it for anyone but you.'

Sadie gave her father a look of deepest sympathy. It seemed that she wasn't the only family member who was going to have tyre marks across their back by the end of tomorrow.

He nodded grimly. Sadie sank into the sofa and closed her eyes. She was drained – not only physically but emotionally too. She'd done a full day's work on little more than two hours' sleep, not to mention the added stresses of troublesome boyfriends and ex-boyfriends and brothers and mothers and grandmothers. All in all, she'd had better days.

With the sounds of her mother and father still talking, she let herself drift away. She didn't care that she was on the sofa – she'd have slept on a barbed-wire fence right now. And she might wake with a crick in her neck, but it was just another problem she'd have to deal with when she got to it. They were racking up quite nicely these days anyway.

She couldn't remember going to bed but Sadie woke around eleven the next morning in her bedroom. The house was silent, but her parents would have gone down to the harbour by now and would probably be getting ready to take out the second boatload of tourists that day.

She pushed herself up and stretched, and then suddenly remembered with a nauseous twist of her stomach that her grandma would probably be somewhere downstairs and that she would have to face her. Perhaps April would have forgotten the conversation, or perhaps she might have had a change of heart overnight and would be willing to forgive Sadie and put the whole thing behind them. Sadie wasn't sure she wanted to find out, because neither of those things might be true. And she couldn't just run away and go out, because if Gammy was in, Sadie felt duty bound to stay in too and make sure she stayed safe. Henny and Graham would expect that of her as well, as the only member of the family under retirement age and without a job.

She shuddered, yet another cold truth dropping onto her. She was officially unemployed. Twenty-six, living with her parents, unemployed, unfinished education and with no real prospects. If she hadn't felt miserable before, she did now. Natalie and Georgia might have complained that their jobs had no prospects but they were doing a damn sight better than Sadie. She'd have to address it, but it wasn't something she could face right now. Instead, she decided that she'd no choice but to get up and get dressed and face her grandma. It would have to happen sooner or later – might as well get it over and done with.

But when Sadie got down to the kitchen, there was no sign of April. There was, however, a note on the table telling Sadie that Henny and Graham had taken her to the boatshed with them to help (which meant they were keeping an eye on her and keeping her out of Sadie's way) and she had to heave a sigh of relief, even though it might not have been the most appropriate reaction. She also knew that this wouldn't be something they'd be able to do every day and that they'd probably have to enlist the help of someone they knew from the harbour community to enable them to do it today.

Instantly she felt lighter and surprisingly hungry too. She grabbed a slice of toast and a coffee and then headed upstairs for a shower. A freshen-up, another coffee and a walk out in the sun… it was surprising what the small things could do to lift a low spirit. And who knew, maybe her feet would take her in the direction of the Old Chapel, and maybe the owner would be around to say hello. There had to be some advantages to having unexpected time on your hands.

An hour later she was walking the road to Luke's house, on a mission to surprise him. The weather was cooler today, the sky a patchwork of fast-moving white cloud, and she'd thrown a cotton sweater over her vest top and jeans to stave off the chill coming in from the sea. But the sun, when it broke through, was still warm and comforting on her skin and she was happier and more optimistic just for being in it. She was looking forward to seeing Luke's reaction when she showed up unannounced, and to more than just that. She was hoping that he'd be able to down tools to spend an hour or two with her.

When she arrived at the Old Chapel twenty minutes later he was on the roof, stripped down to his waist. She stopped and watched for a while as he worked to replace a row of tiles, partly because she didn't dare shout up in case she spoiled his concentration and made him fall, and partly because his tanned and muscular back was a pretty good view, one she was content to drink in for as long as she could. In fact, she perched herself on a large boulder at the side of the rocky lane that led up to the house. It wasn't until he stopped and straightened up, standing atop the roof with impossible balance and admiring the view in the sunshine, that he suddenly noticed she was there.

'Wow.' He grinned. 'Must be my lucky day!'

She stood and walked to the garden gate as he scooted down the roof and negotiated the scaffolding like a mountain goat.

'What are you doing here?' he asked as he met her on the garden path. 'I thought we'd agreed to meet up later for that walk on the beach?'

'Oh, you know, I didn't have much to do and it was a nice day so I thought I'd throw the schedule out of the window and surprise you.'

'You certainly did that.'

'You don't mind, do you?'

'God, of course not! I needed an excuse to take a break and you're perfect.'

She shielded her eyes and surveyed the house. It was low level, one floor like a bungalow, with beautiful arched windows. It had once been Sea Salt Bay's tiny chapel, where the hundred odd parishioners got together on Sundays to worship. The last time it had been used for that purpose had been many years ago – certainly longer than anyone alive in the bay today could remember. It had been deemed too high up on the cliffs and too old and draughty to continue using, a Victorian red-brick church taking its place, and for many years it had stood empty, until someone had attempted to turn it into a house. They'd given up, and then someone else had had a go and decided it was too much for them too. Sadie hoped that Luke would be a bit more tenacious in his attempts – for purely selfish reasons, of course. She wanted him to stay in the bay, and he was far more likely to do that if he had a beautiful, completed home there.

'It's looking good,' she said.

'Coming along,' he replied, wiping his hands down his jeans and reaching for a shirt he'd left hanging on a gatepost. Sadie was almost sorry to see it cover his chest as he buttoned it up, but maybe she'd work on getting it off again before too long. She'd had a horrible few days and this morning, being handed a reprieve of sorts, had put her in a strange and mischievous mood. She felt like having some fun – in fact, she *needed* some fun because she felt as if she hadn't had fun for a hundred years.

'Can I get you a drink?' he asked. 'There's not much of a choice I'm afraid – it's either tea or orange juice. If I'd known you were coming I could have got more in, but…'

'Orange juice sounds nice.'

She followed him inside. The sunlight was swallowed by shade. The windows were beautiful in here but they were small and the frames worked with a heavy criss-cross design that kept out a lot of light. But, despite this, it wasn't a dark or unpleasant space because the ceilings were so high and the rooms so spacious. The walls were still bare plaster and the original floor boards – with some new replacements here and there – were on show. Almost everything was in one room – the kitchen, living space and dining room – except for a master bedroom and a small bathroom which were off to one side. He went to where the kitchen was separated from the main space only by a breakfast bar and opened the fridge.

'Want some ice in it?' he asked.

'Ice is good if you've got it.'

He nodded, and a few seconds later the clink of ice on glass could be heard. Sadie could see only two old armchairs, but she supposed there was no point in having loads of fancy furniture when you were still building around it. She sat down on one of them, and though it looked threadbare, it was surprisingly comfortable. Then he stood before her, two drinks in his hands, and he offered her one before taking the other chair.

'So…' he said, looking at her as he took a sip of his juice. 'Does seeing you today mean I don't get to see you this evening?'

'I don't see why we can't do both,' Sadie said carelessly, though her heart was thumping and she didn't really understand why. She only knew that today was going to change their relationship somehow. She didn't know why she felt that either, but something was telling her it was true. Was it that old, scary psychic ability again? Or was this going to be something of her own doing? Either way, it almost seemed inevitable. 'In fact, I don't have anywhere to be today. I know you have things to do but… I don't know… maybe you feel like taking a day off?'

'I do now,' he said with a smile. 'You're a bad influence.'

'I do my best.'

'OK,' he said slowly, drinking from his glass again, 'what do you want to do? I could show you around my house but it wouldn't take long.'

'I don't mind that. I'd like to see. You can explain your plans to me.'

'I'm sure it would bore you stiff.'

'I don't think so.'

He paused for a minute, regarding her carefully. Finally, he spoke. 'You haven't told me how it went last night.'

'I thought you'd be bored hearing about it. Even I'm bored of hearing about it and I'm involved.'

'I'm involved with you so that makes me involved too and I'm all ears if there's anything you need to get off your chest. I just want to know that you're OK.'

'Oh, it wasn't great,' she said. 'Gammy hates me.'

'She'll come round, won't she?'

'Yes… I don't know. Maybe, in time. You know what really scares me, though? Given enough time she would forgive me, but what if she doesn't have that? What if she dies suddenly and I never get that forgiveness and I have to live for the rest of my days knowing she died angry with me? I don't think I could deal with that.'

He was thoughtful again for a moment. 'I wish I could do something to help.'

'You are helping, just by listening.'

He put his drink on the floor and came over to her. Lifting a lock of hair with a light touch, he smoothed it behind her ear and bent to place a soft kiss on her lips.

'I can see you've been crying,' he whispered. 'I wish I could make that better.'

'Oh God, it's still that obvious? I spent most of last night crying over it, but what will crying do to fix anything? It's over and done now,' she said. 'I don't want to think about it.'

'Never?'

'Not now. Kiss me again.'

He did as she asked, and she was seized again by that strange, unnameable premonition that something huge was about to happen, that something was about to shake her world and turn it upside down. But she wasn't scared; she was excited, and she wanted it to come.

He pulled away and took her glass from her, placing it on the floor. And then he offered his hand. She rose from the chair and took it.

'Where are we going?' she asked, nerve ends tingling, veins full of fire.

'To start the grand tour,' he said. 'Where do you want to go first?'

'Where would you suggest?'

'Well,' he said with a smile that made her molten, 'the bedroom's rather nice at this time of day.'

She almost squealed with excitement, but she held it in and did her best to look sultry. 'Then show me the bedroom, and don't worry about rushing it – I've got all the time in the world.'

Sadie was sleepy, but she didn't want to sleep. She didn't want to miss a moment of this day, of being here in Luke's arms, in his bed for the first time. Scenes replayed in her head, of him lifting her onto the bed, of him ripping off his shirt, him taking her face in his hands and kissing her. His scent and his touch were all over her and she never wanted to lose it. She'd had sex since Declan, of course, but it had always been drunken, or rushed, or plain boring. It had been functional, at the end of the day, to fulfil a need. Even with Declan, even though it had always been good, it had become routine by the end of their relationship. Luke was something else, something that Sadie quickly recognised could become addictive if she let it. Already she wanted him again, but it seemed he wanted to talk and so, for now, she'd have to let him.

'Tell me about your life before I came to the bay,' he said as she nestled into the crook of his arm.

'There's not that much to tell. I was born, went to school, went to university – outside the town – came back, started teacher training and then quit teacher training. All pretty dull and most of it you know already. Never mind that – tell me about you. I don't know anything at all, Mr Enigma. Come on – spill the beans.'

'You really want to know? It's such a tale of tragedy you might regret asking.'

Sadie laughed lazily. 'Well, I've asked now so it will serve me right. I do want to know. Why did you really come to the bay? Tell me about your family, your childhood, all your near-misses.' Her smile faded as she recalled something darker that had been hinted but never explained. 'Back in the Listing Ship on our first date you said you'd had your heart broken but you never said what happened.'

'As I recall you told me not to tell you about it.'

'I did, but that was because it didn't seem as if you wanted to talk about it. But now…'

'You really want to know?'

'Yes; I do. I think we're at that point now, don't you?'

He let out a sigh and shifted slightly next to her. 'Maybe you're right. Her name is Christa.'

'Right. So where is she now? What happened?'

'She's living with my brother in Kensington.'

'They're together?' Sadie leaned up on her elbow to look at him. He nodded.

'I was engaged to her, but she decided that the other Goldman boy looked like a more attractive prospect. I don't mind telling you it tore my life apart. Everything changed, not just that. The business that I had renovating and selling properties – I was in partnership with Jacob; that's my brother – and so you can see that had to end; I could hardly work with him after that. I can't see him now because I can't see him with her and I don't want to see her at all. So one day I remembered this little place where I was happy for a few summers and I decided to chuck it all in and move away from London. I was going to have a quiet life, do up a house, swim in the sea every morning, go out on a boat, learn to fish and maybe surf... I wasn't intending to meet someone and certainly not as quickly as I did. But you just... well, you know how it went.'

'Yes, you should be careful fishing in these waters; you never know what you might catch.'

He chuckled softly.

'What about your mum? Is she in London? Was she upset about all this, because didn't your dad...?'

'Exactly. She was. I'd always vowed never to do that to someone because I saw first-hand what my dad's infidelity did to my mum. Maybe it had the opposite effect on Jacob – maybe those events somehow normalised it all for him. Or maybe he just didn't have the strength to resist the temptation.'

'She must have really thrown herself at him.'

'I don't know about that. I don't know any of the details and I don't want to. It's enough that it happened and now I'm separated from half my family and the life I used to know.'

'Are you sad that you've lost all that – the big glamorous life in London and the girl?'

'I'm mostly sad about Jacob. I can make a life anywhere but I hate that he's no longer in it.'

'And there's no way you could make up?'

He shook his head. 'Not right now; it's still too raw.'

'What if you moved on enough? Found someone new, fell in love again?'

'Maybe then. It would never be the same as it was before, though, because she'd always be there to remind me of that pain.'

'But you must think it would be nice to speak to your brother again. I can't imagine what life would be like without Ewan or Lucy.'

'Lucy? I'd almost forgotten you had a sister.'

'She's this big-shot theatre agent in New York; she doesn't come home that often. It sounds mean, but it's easy for people to forget her because she's never here. I think sometimes people who've lived their whole lives in the bay and watched her grow up here forget she exists now that she's gone.'

'Is she like you?'

'God no! When she plans to do something she makes a success of it. She'd never be suddenly unemployed with no money and living with her parents at the age of twenty-six.'

'But you could go back to teaching?'

'Everyone keeps saying that. Honestly? Probably. But I'm not sure I want to. There's a reason I gave it up so willingly, even if that reason isn't completely clear to me, and I think it's because, really, teaching's not what I'm meant for. And I say that with a heavy heart because I gave up a lot to try for something that ultimately turned out to be a complete waste of time.'

She settled back into his arms and contemplated the old plaster on his ceiling. It was cracked in many places, discoloured and crumbling, and she supposed that it was another thing he'd be replacing, but she kind of liked it the way it was. How many people had prayed and sang and found their peace beneath it during the years it had been a working chapel? And today, maybe, Sadie had found peace beneath it too. It felt that way right now, and even hearing Luke's story at last didn't put her off. If anything, it attracted her more strongly to him. He had a past, just like her – a complicated, messy past that would never fully be resolved, one where reminders would lurk around every corner. That made them the same, didn't it?

'Can I ask you something?' he said.

'Ask away.'

'When I came to the waffle house yesterday – the second time – and you were with—'

'Declan. Yes, we did used to be together and yes, I did once love him very much. Is that what you were going to ask me?'

Sadie rolled up to look at him again. There was no point in covering any of it up because even she knew that it was obvious to anyone who cared to look hard enough that she and Declan still had a connection too strong to deny. And even if she did deny it, the whole town knew their history – sooner or later Luke would get to hear it and then it would look much worse that she hadn't set him straight when he'd asked.

'Do you love him now?'

She flopped down again, her gaze going to the ceiling once more. 'That's a more complicated question than you might imagine.'

'Is it?'

'I love him, but it's not like it was. We're friends, best friends, and we care about each other. If he ever needed me I'd be there for him, and if I ever needed him he'd do the same. We're on a different wavelength from the rest of the world, a special one just for us two; at least, that's how it's always felt for me.'

'That sounds intense. I feel like the other man already.'

'It's not like that, not now. I can't explain it. You can't have the kind of connection we once had and not have any of that left behind when it ends. But he's with Melissa now and they're happy. They're going to buy a house together and then I expect marriage will follow, and kids. He's very traditional in that way – wants the whole set. Partly, that was what finished it for me and him in the end. He wanted to settle down but I didn't.'

'Do you regret that now?'

'I didn't at first; I was having too much fun – at least I thought I was. And then I did. But I decided I couldn't change it so there was no point in regretting it.'

'Sadie… I don't know if I dare ask this. Where are we at now? It's just, I promised myself I wouldn't get too close, not after what happened with Jacob and Christa, and I tried, I really did. But then today happened and I feel I'm already in too deep. And then you go and tell me about this other guy that you never really got over and—'

'Don't you think we're at a good place? I don't want to be with Declan now; maybe I didn't explain it very well. He means a lot to me – I can't deny that – but I don't want to be with him. Right now, I want to be with you. Is that enough? Can you live with that for now?'

'I don't know.'

She paused. 'Do you want me to go?'

'No – no I don't. I want you here and that's what scares me. I don't know if I can deal with you and this other guy being so close. I've been hurt once and I don't think I can take it again. But I want you here so badly right now that I can't think straight.'

'Then don't think at all. Just be here now with me and we'll take it a minute at a time.'

'I need to be able to trust that you won't hurt me like Christa did.'

'I'm not going to hurt you.'

'I don't believe for a minute that Christa meant to hurt me; it just happened. You might not mean it either but you might still do it.'

'You have to trust someone eventually. Or are you planning to spend the rest of your life alone just in case?'

'I'd hate that, of course I would. But it's so hard to do otherwise. I can have fun with you and I can enjoy your company, but to let you into my heart that way, knowing what I know about you and Declan—'

Sadie put a finger to his lips.

'Please don't. I wouldn't be here if I planned to mess you around like that.'

'That's just it – nobody plans it. I can't have that waiting in my future again, planned or not.'

'You're right – nobody does plan these things, and perhaps it's a good thing that we don't see what's at the finishing line; maybe it's better just to make the most of the journey. I sometimes think that's where I've always gone wrong. I've always been racing towards something, so fast that I've missed what was under my nose – and often those things have been more important and valuable than what I was running towards. If nothing else, the last few weeks have shown me that life has a way of tripping you up, but the successes might just be in the way you get up and dust yourself down.'

'Hmm.'

'You have absolutely no idea what any of that just meant, do you?'

'Not really.'

Sadie giggled and leaned in to kiss him. 'Don't worry about it. I've had enough talking for now anyway.'

He broke off and held her gaze for a moment, his expression intense, searching, even a little scared, as if he was standing on a cliff edge and pondering the wisdom of diving into the sea below.

'But I do worry about it. I can't go on with this if I can't be sure I won't get hurt again. Christa and Jacob… I never thought I'd get over their betrayal and I can't go through something like that again – it would break me.'

'I promise I would never do that to you.'

'But how can I know that for sure?'

Sadie was silent for a moment. 'I don't know,' she said finally. 'I don't suppose there is any way I can prove it to you. Maybe you'll just have to take a leap of faith.'

'That's easy for you to say.'

'Not as easy as you might think.'

He ran a hand down the length of her hair, his eyes locked onto hers, and she saw his uncertainty, the battle with his own doubts. He wanted to believe her, to believe *in* her – she could see that. And she could see how much he wanted *her*. She wanted him too, and she wanted to be able to show him how much, but she couldn't do anything to settle his doubts or undo the events in his past that would perhaps always make him doubt. But then his expression cleared and, for now at least, his desire to be with her seemed to have melted the doubts away.

'Am I going to regret this?' he asked as his hand trailed down to her back to pull her closer.

'No,' she said, kissing him again. 'Neither of us is.'

Chapter Seventeen

Sadie might have been in a rebellious mood by the time she was walking back after spending the afternoon with Luke, but she did realise that she would have to show her face at home, regardless of how much she didn't want to. There was still much to discuss and a fractured relationship with her grandma to fix, and she wanted to do that as soon as she could. The idea of Gammy holding a grudge against her, of being hated by her, was more than Sadie could bear. And she felt braver now, buoyed by the time she'd spent with Luke, which had made her feel more special and wanted than she had in a long time.

On the way back she stopped at a florist to pick up a bouquet of summer flowers. She'd give them to April with an apology and beg for forgiveness, and maybe her grandmother, having slept on things, would be in more of a mood to forgive. It didn't matter whether any of it was Sadie's fault or not; it only mattered that she and Gammy got back to where they'd been before all of this blew up.

Nobody was home when she got there, so Sadie set about cleaning (not that the place needed it because Henny kept everything spotless) and making a start on a fish pie for everyone. Her grandmother, in particular, loved a pie full of juicy salmon, fat prawns and chunks of fluffy cod

and creamy mashed potato – she called it food for the soul, God's gift
from the sea – and Henny had all the ingredients in, clearly planning
to make one herself at some point. And by the time everything was
bubbling away, the kitchen smelt so good that Sadie was beginning to
think that Gammy might be right about God's gift from the sea – it
was certainly a heavenly scent, and her mouth was watering already.

An hour later Henny, Graham and April returned. Sadie's parents
had cut down their trips so they could finish early, and it had turned
out to be a wise decision because the sea was getting frisky, or so her
dad said, and there would be a storm before the night was out. That
was OK, because before she'd left Sadie had told Luke that she probably
ought to be with her family tonight in the hope of sorting out the mess
they seemed to be in. As they'd spent the afternoon together he'd been
OK with that. He had a house to build anyway, he'd said, and he was
hardly going to do that with the sexiest woman alive distracting him.
That had made her want to jump back into bed and show him just
how sexy she could be, but she'd done a remarkable job of resisting the
urge and here she was, ready to make peace with Gammy. Or, at least,
she hoped so, because Henny wasn't the only woman in the Schwartz
family with a stubborn streak.

'Something smells good.' Her father took a seat in the conservatory
and Sadie put a cold glass of his favourite ginger beer in front of him.

'Fish pie,' she said.

'Oh, and what have we done to deserve such manna from heaven?'
he asked, taking his drink with a warm smile.

'Nothing. I just thought I was here doing nothing and you were all
out working hard so I might as well cook.'

'If you're going to cook every night then we might just keep you
on as a parlour maid.'

'Oi!' Sadie admonished with a laugh. 'Don't worry, in light of that comment I won't be cooking tomorrow night!'

Her mother came through, after freshening herself up, and gave Sadie a kiss on the cheek. 'How's your day been? Did you manage to get some rest?'

'Yes. Thanks for taking Gammy with you...' Sadie looked around. 'Where is she, by the way?'

'She's gone for a lie-down – she said she had a headache.'

'Oh. I got... never mind, I can give them to her later. How has she been today?'

'Complaining. I've never heard anyone complain so much. And I'm afraid her memory has been quite sharp today, because she's told just about everyone who would listen what happened in our house last night, word for word.'

'So everyone thinks it's my fault the waffle house is closed?'

'Don't worry, we set the record straight where we could. But I think we're going to have to grin and bear it for a while, until things settle and she's a little happier.'

'You mean *I'm* going to have to grin and bear it? She's not blaming anyone else.'

'Oh, she is,' Graham said. 'Apparently it's our fault for bringing up such an ungrateful brat.'

'Oh, Mum!' Sadie cried. 'What are we going to do?'

'We're going to do what we agreed last night. As soon as the waffle house is sold things will settle again. She'll see in time that what appeared to be cruel was in actual fact a kindness.'

'I don't think I can last that long with her hating me.'

'You really are worrying too much,' Henny said, heading towards the kitchen. 'Smells divine, by the way. Shall I go and check on it?'

Sadie collapsed into a chair and nodded. 'If you like.' She turned to her father. 'I can't bear it, Dad. There must be some way I can get Gammy on side again.'

'If you find what it is please tell me; I could do with a bit of help too.' Graham let out a sigh. 'You're never prepared for the death of a parent, but you're certainly never prepared for what comes afterwards.'

Sadie watched as he closed his eyes for a moment and sank into the chair. He looked exhausted, and she suddenly felt like the most selfish person alive. She'd been so wrapped up in what was happening to her she'd forgotten that at the heart of all this was the fact that her dad had lost his own dad. She couldn't imagine what life would be like without her father, but he was living it now, having lost Kenneth not so long ago. They'd all concerned themselves with how April was coping without her husband and nobody had stopped for a moment to consider how Graham was coping without his dad because he'd seemed so strong, so stoic that it was like he hadn't been affected at all. But if he'd loved his dad half as much as Sadie loved hers, then he must have been keeping a lot of hurt locked up tight and that couldn't be a good thing.

They ate dinner without April, who'd fallen asleep, and they saved a portion so she could eat when she woke. Though Sadie was relieved not to have to face her, she was also frustrated because she'd worked herself up to that meeting and she'd been ready for it, and then it hadn't happened. Now it was hanging over her still, and the longer she waited the more anxious she became, the more impatient to get it over and done with. In fact, she was all for waking April, and did her best to make more noise than usual as she washed up with Graham, though it didn't work.

After dinner she went into the drawing room to watch TV with Graham and Henny for a while. They were all full and content and happy to sit, though Sadie's mind wandered a lot and she found it hard to concentrate on the complex plot of the police drama they were trying to follow.

And then she jumped as the phone she'd balanced on the arm of the sofa next to her began to ring. Natalie's photo came up on the display.

'Hello,' Sadie said, taking it out into the hallway so she didn't disturb her parents' viewing, 'I was just thinking about you.'

'You'll never guess what I've just heard!'

No preamble, just straight in there. Natalie sounded breathless, almost as if she'd run to get her phone, or perhaps it was just excitement. Whatever it was, it must be huge news.

'Go on,' Sadie said, ready to hear some tawdry gossip about someone in the town or someone Natalie worked with, or even some new sexual conquest she'd fallen instantly in love with who was probably going to become husband number three.

'Declan and Melissa have split up!'

Chapter Eighteen

Sadie took the phone out to the garden. 'Who's told you that?'

'Vivien. She got it from Nessa at the chip shop; says he came to see his dad in a right state. She overheard them talking in the back and then Dec's dad took him home because he was drunk and couldn't drive.'

'She overheard them? What did they say?'

'Just that Melissa did the dumping. I don't know any more than that.'

Sadie was silent for a moment, processing what she'd heard, desperately trying to figure out what she was supposed to do – or even if she was supposed to do anything at all. Declan needed her, and if it had been the other way around, he'd have done what he could for her. She knew that, but if she got involved, might that make things worse? What if it was a temporary spat and Sadie getting in the middle of things turned it into something permanent? She knew Declan and Melissa had been having problems but she never imagined they were this serious. At least, she hadn't got that impression from Declan, but then, perhaps even he hadn't realised they were this serious. It was often the way with these things – that one partner saw the problems as bigger than the other did.

'Do you know how long ago this was?' Sadie asked finally.

'Not long. I think early this evening – at least, that's when Nessa would have finished her shift and gone for a quick one at the Ship before she went home.'

'So Declan could be at his place?'

'He could. His dad came back to work though, as far as I know. I don't know if his mum is with him or if he's alone. What are you going to do? Wait until the dust settles and then reclaim him? I would if I were you. This is it – your perfect opportunity. You two were meant to be together – everyone knows that. Melissa was never going to be the one for him, not while you were in the bay.'

'He loves Melissa – he said so, loads of times.'

'Well he was going to say that, wasn't he? He wasn't going to tell you that he was still pining for you and Melissa was just there to keep the bed warm, was he?'

Sadie shook her head to clear it. Of all the complications she might have seen coming, this wasn't one of them. As if her life wasn't complicated enough right now.

'I should probably call him to see if he's OK.'

'You're going to go to him, right? Strike while the iron's hot?'

'I don't think…'

'Sadie, he's ripe for the plucking. He's yours – he always has been! Don't let Melissa get in first and get him back!'

'Natalie, I'm seeing someone else.'

'Oh, I know. That man who's got the Old Chapel. Everyone knows, although you never told me and, frankly, I'm a bit offended about that. But he doesn't matter. You've been out with loads of blokes since Declan and they've all been crap. That's because Declan is your soulmate. He's the one.'

'What if he isn't? I like Luke. I like him a lot, and maybe Declan was never the one. Maybe I only thought he was because the real one hadn't come into my life yet.'

'Of course he is! Sadie, I don't think you realise just what you've got here. Hardly anyone finds their real soulmate, the one they were destined to be with. God knows I've made plenty of mistakes looking for mine. Yours is there, right in front of your face, and if you don't go to him you'll regret it for the rest of your life.'

Sadie didn't doubt that Natalie was right – perhaps her soulmate was right in front of her face. But which man was it? Her feelings were strong for both of them, despite having known Luke only a short time, but in very different ways that were difficult to compare. And only a matter of hours ago, hadn't she promised Luke that she wouldn't hurt him as Christa had done?

She took a breath and made a decision.

'I'd better phone him,' she said. 'Can I call you later?'

'You'd bloody better! I want to know everything!'

'Don't worry, I will.'

Sadie ended the call to Natalie and dialled Declan's number. She hadn't really expected him to answer so it was no surprise when he didn't. So if she couldn't speak to him, what next? Perhaps Melissa would be on duty at the arcade. Could Sadie talk to her to find out exactly what had happened? Would Melissa even give Sadie the time of day? It was a long shot but worth the risk, because other than going to Declan's house to see him (and she wasn't sure that was wise given the conversation she'd had with Luke that day) she had no other choice – she had to find out exactly what the situation was. And if she could help, then she owed it to them both to try.

Melissa was sitting behind the little glass window in the booth where people got their change for the slot machines. If she hadn't looked happy when Sadie walked in she looked positively murderous when she spotted her. Sadie had to concede pretty quickly that coming here might have been a mistake, but it was too late to back out now.

'Come to gloat?' Melissa asked sourly.

So, she knew that Sadie knew, or at least she'd taken an educated guess. The amusement arcade wasn't one of Sadie's usual haunts and certainly not since Melissa had started to work there. There would be very few reasons that would take her in there.

'Of course not…' Sadie said, keeping her voice level. 'But it's true?'

'Yes.'

'Why? What happened?'

'You really have to ask?'

'Well, yes… I'm asking.'

'I don't feel like talking about it. Why don't you go and ask Declan about it; I'm sure he'll be happy to fill you in. I mean, you run to him for everything else so this is like all your birthdays at once, isn't it?'

'Melissa, I—'

'Oh, get lost, Sadie, otherwise I might be forced to come out of this booth and throw something at you and I wouldn't want to break one of the fruit machines on your head.'

'Look, for what it's worth, I'm sorry.'

'You're sorry?' Melissa's laugh had no humour in it. 'You're *sorry*? Don't tell me you're sorry. Maybe if you'd stopped making gooey eyes at him for five minutes, sharing your private little jokes and giving him your private little looks and making the whole town believe that you were some fairy-tale couple that only ended because I broke it up – which I didn't – then you could talk to me about being sorry. Otherwise, save it, because you're wasting your breath.'

Sadie was about to say something else, but then stopped. What was the point? Melissa clearly wasn't in the mood to listen to her and she could hardly blame her for that. Perhaps Sadie had been too familiar with Declan and perhaps they'd been too close for comfort at times. But it was hard to explain to anyone else why that was; she'd even struggled to explain it to Luke as she'd lain in his arms, so it was no wonder Melissa didn't understand. And perhaps she had given the town cause to think that one day she and Declan would end up back together, and sometimes she'd even wished for it herself. But things had changed now, though it felt too late to undo what had been done. Was it?

'I really am sorry,' she said again.

'Save it,' Melissa said. 'He's yours if you want him, and good riddance to the both of you.'

'I don't—' Sadie began, but Melissa simply scowled at her, and Sadie realised that there was no point in continuing this conversation. So she simply turned and headed for the exit.

Uncertain what to do next, Sadie headed for the beach. There were so many pressing things that needed addressing she hardly knew where to start. She hadn't yet been able to make things up with Gammy, for one thing, who had still been sleeping when Sadie had left the house. And though she still wanted to go to Declan, she knew she shouldn't. She pulled out her phone to check it, but he hadn't returned her call and she didn't know whether it was a good idea to try again or not. One thing was certain: she was public enemy number one as far as Melissa was concerned, and that worried Sadie, because she had to wonder now how much of what had led up to the split had happened because of her. The thought filled her with guilt and sadness because she hated to think that she might be the cause of Declan's current unhappiness.

Dusk was fast approaching, the beach enveloped in a grainy light, like a photo taken on the wrong setting. The sea was choppy, whisked into grey peaks, and the sky was steely; though the storm her father had predicted had yet to materialise, Sadie could feel it in the air. There was something she'd always loved about the sea when it was like this. It was dynamic, dangerous, something entirely different than the clear blue swell of a summer's day – though she loved that too. As a child she'd imagine being a mermaid beneath it, swimming like a fish as it churned and boiled above her, just like a child safe inside a house while the rains fell and the wind howled outside. And because she didn't know what else to do now, she sat on the sand to watch it for a while, careless of the fact that the beach was damp and clammy. Part of her wished she could swim away now, if only for a while, to swim away from her problems and give herself real time and space to think.

'Mum said I might find you down here.'

Sadie whipped round to see Ewan behind her. She stood up.

'Is everything OK?'

'Of course. I could ask you the same question – Mum said the phone rang and then you rushed off on a mission that you couldn't tell her about. So what's happened?'

'Where do you want me to start?'

'Is it anything to do with that Goldman guy? Because if it is—'

'No.' Sadie gave a small smile. 'No, it's not him.'

'This business with Grandma then? She'll come round, you know.'

'I know,' Sadie said, although it was part of it and she wasn't entirely convinced that Gammy would come round. 'It's not that either. It's nothing really, nothing that should concern me.'

'Clearly it does. Want to tell me about it anyway?'

'Not really. You'll only say I'm an idiot for getting involved, and you'd be right.'

'I might, but when have you ever cared about that?'

Sadie had to laugh, despite herself. But then she noticed a figure on the pier. He was walking – or rather weaving – along towards the amusement arcade, and it looked like he had some kind of bottle in his hand.

'Oh…' she said in a small voice. Even though she couldn't make out his face from this distance, she knew the gait and the build well enough. The figure stopped outside the arcade and started to shout, waving his bottle in the air.

'Gotta go!' Sadie said and broke into a run.

'Where are you going now?' Ewan shouted, but there was no time to reply.

A few breathless minutes later Sadie was on the pier, running towards him.

'Dec!'

He turned to her, bleary-eyed and slurring. 'She won't come out and talk to me!'

'She's working, that's why.' Sadie grimaced as she got closer. 'And you stink! How much have you had?'

'I don't know… Get Melissa for me.'

'She won't come because I say so, trust me.'

'But you can try.'

'Why don't you pull yourself together and come back for her later?'

'I need her now.'

'Now is not the time to talk to her. I'm telling you, Dec, you need to sober up.'

He swayed for a moment, looking at Sadie. 'She says you wanted us to split up.'

'I didn't.'

'She says you still want me for yourself.'

'Dec, you're drunk and this is silly.'

'Do you?'

'No.'

'But if… I love you.'

'I love you too but it's not the same, is it? We're best friends, aren't we? Declan, do you love Melissa?'

'With all my heart. She's my world and I can't go on without her.'

Sadie felt her own world crack, just a little. She'd spent so long thinking that he might hold a candle for her, a spark, however small, in the same way she had for him, that to hear him proclaim real and proper love for Melissa suddenly made her understand just how much of her life she'd wasted on some silly fantasy. Declan was never going to come back to her, no matter how much she or the people of Sea Salt Bay might have been convinced of it. The strange thing was, she now realised that it had never really been what she'd wanted either. A few weeks ago she might have jumped at the chance to persuade him that they belonged back together, but that had changed.

'But you're my world too, Sadie. She says I can't see you if I get back with her. What am I supposed to do?'

Sadie swallowed the sudden, hot tears that sprang to her eyes and took a step towards him. 'If you love her, then you know what you have to do.'

'I have to stop talking to you?'

'Yes.'

'We can't even say hello?' he slurred, confusion etched into his features.

How Sadie wanted to reach for him, even now, to fold him into her arms once more and kiss him, if only to say goodbye. But she knew that would be a terrible mistake. If they had to do this, then they had to do it properly.

'Maybe we can say hello from time to time, but we can't sit and talk like we always did. But that's OK. You'll have Melissa for that, and that's how it should be.'

'And you have your man now.'

'Yes,' Sadie said, smiling through her tears. 'I have my man now.'

'And he makes you happy?'

'He does.'

Declan nodded to himself and staggered backwards, then reached for the railings of the pier to steady himself. The wind was picking up, the sky heavy and grey, and the first drops of rain fell into Sadie's hair.

'Go and sober up,' she said. 'Shall I go and get your dad from the chip shop to take you home?'

'You're not going to take me home?'

'I can't. Not now, can I? What would Melissa think about that?'

He nodded again and sank to a seat that wasn't there before setting himself upright again.

'I bet you can't still balance on here,' he said, slapping his free hand on the pier railings before taking a swig from the wine bottle in his other.

'I doubt it. We were idiots to try balancing on it all those years ago.'

'But it was funny.'

'It was funny,' Sadie said. 'But we were silly kids then.'

'A long time ago.'

'Yes.'

'Sometimes I wish we were still like that. I loved you. I would have married you one day.'

'I know.'

'Life was easier then, wasn't it?'

'Yes, but things change and we move on.'

'I love Melissa now.'

'You'll work it out – she loves you too. All you have to do is talk to her.'

With great care, he placed the wine bottle on the wooden boards of the pier and began to haul himself up onto the railings.

'What the hell are you doing?' Sadie cried, filled with sudden horror.

'Just one more time,' he slurred. 'I'll be a kid one more time and then I'll grow up and get Melissa back.'

'Dec, get down!'

He grinned and gave himself a last pull, but before Sadie could get there, he lost his balance and disappeared over the edge.

Chapter Nineteen

Sadie ripped off her jacket and ran for the railings, but before she got there another figure had already flown past her and leapt into the sea after Declan.

'Ewan!' Sadie screamed, leaning over the railings to stare down into the water.

'I'm on it!'

She spun around to see Ewan racing down the pier towards her, pulling off his jacket too.

'Get the coastguard!' he shouted.

Sadie froze. If her brother hadn't just jumped into the water after Declan, who had?

'Coastguard!' Ewan roared as he clambered onto the railings. 'What are you waiting for?'

'You can't go in!' Sadie cried. 'It's too rough!'

He shrugged, and then he lifted his arms above his head and tipped into an elegant dive. Instinctively Sadie grabbed for him, though she'd no more be able to stop his fall than catch fog. All she could do was watch him go like a dart into the waves. Then she saw two heads above the water where there should have been three, and she couldn't tell who they belonged to. She pulled out her phone with trembling hands and dialled the emergency number, willing the third head to appear.

'Coastguard,' she cried, tears of absolute terror choking her so hard she could barely talk. 'Sea Salt Bay – the pier. Three men in the water – one's drunk, the other two have gone in after him! Please hurry!'

'Stay on the line,' the voice at the other end said, and Sadie kept the phone clamped to her ear as she ran the length of the pier towards the beach. Even in her current state she understood that to dive in after them was folly, but if she could get down to the beach she might be able to swim out to help.

By the time she got there she could see that it was Luke who'd gone into the sea after Declan, and that he was dragging him onto the beach.

'Oh my God!' Sadie screamed, running to them. 'Oh my God he's dead!'

Luke collapsed onto the sand, panting and dripping wet and unable to reply. He just gave a faint shake of his head, and then set about trying to revive an unconscious Declan. Sadie looked out to sea again, for the spot where she'd seen Ewan go in.

'Where is he?'

Luke glanced up at her before returning to Declan.

'Luke! Where is he?' she cried.

In the next moment, Declan heaved and spluttered and a stream of water came from his mouth and he opened his eyes. But Sadie didn't have a moment to be relieved. Her brother was still missing and she had to find him.

He's a great swimmer; he's a great swimmer, she told herself as she went into the icy waves, and she tried to believe that being a great swimmer was enough, but even she knew better than that. Plenty of great swimmers had drowned in the sea. The sea didn't care if you were a great swimmer or not, because it had plenty of tricks to catch you out if it was in the mood.

The water was up to her knees and then up to her thighs as she struck out against the heaving rollers, icy and sharp, and then she felt an arm close around her wrist, yanking her back.

'I'll find him,' Luke shouted over the booming waves.

'I'm coming too!'

'No! Go back! Declan needs you! Go back – I'll find Ewan!'

Sadie shook her head, and Luke must have decided there was no time to argue because he let go and they struck out together, water smashing Sadie in the face at every stroke, filling her mouth and stinging her eyes so she could barely see a foot in front of her. Everywhere was raging grey murk. The sea didn't want her to find Ewan; the sea wanted him for itself, and she grew desperate and tearful, and now it wasn't just waves choking her but grief as well.

You can't have my brother! You can't have him!

And then she saw him. He was barely keeping his head above the water, fighting a current that had him trapped.

She turned to see Luke still swimming towards him. He didn't understand. He didn't see that if he went where Ewan was he'd be trapped in the current too and they'd both get pulled away from the shore. She tried to call out but her mouth filled with water the moment she opened it. Even if she'd been able to he wouldn't have heard. The sea was shouting and in her head Sadie screamed back.

You can't have them!

She began to swim again, trying to see a way she could get to them without getting caught in the current, but her arms were tired and her lungs fit to burst and she could barely make out where they were from one second to the next. On the shore, Declan was waiting for them, and she could only hope that he was OK, but she couldn't think about that. Right now, all she could think about was that all three of the people in the sea at this moment might not get out again. And she didn't even care that she might be the one who didn't make it – she only cared that the other two did.

Her muscles screamed and her limbs were so heavy she could barely get them to move, and yet she did, straining for every stroke, legs almost numb with cold but still kicking. But she was slowing down and she was getting weaker and she knew she couldn't keep going for much longer. She saw that Luke had reached Ewan and they were both trying to make a break for one of the huge struts that supported the pier, hopeful, perhaps that the current would sweep them in that direction and that they could cling on until they were rescued. Sadie could only hope they'd make it, because she had nothing left now.

She turned herself round and tried to get to shore. She could either trust that Ewan and Luke had done enough to save themselves and try to save herself too, or she could keep going and die here – because she was certain that if she carried on swimming out she would drown. But she hadn't been prepared for how strong the current would be, and how much the sea wanted to keep her from the shore, and how weak she was now, because no matter how she flailed and reached, she didn't seem to get any closer. Then she saw Declan wading into the waves and her heart sank. They'd just saved him and he was coming in again to get her and now all four of them might die. If things hadn't been quite so desperate it might have been funny, and in her half-delirious state she felt like laughing. She would have too, if opening her mouth wouldn't have caused her to swallow half the Solent.

Then she saw him get closer, and she felt his hands grip her and he started to pull her back. He was stronger than her – perhaps stronger than all of them – and right now she was glad of it. If he hadn't been so strong he might not have survived at all. But as he hauled her onto the shore she began to sob.

'Ewan…' she wept, exhausted, utterly wretched. 'He's out there with Luke.'

Declan wrapped his arms around her and pulled her close. She leaned against him as they sat on the sand together, too tired and weak to do anything else, and she cried.

'Don't worry,' he said, his voice husky and exhausted too, all traces of his drunkenness gone. 'Coastguard's here.'

Sadie looked out to see the lights of the boat, and she uttered a silent prayer of thanks for their arrival. But Ewan and Luke weren't safe yet.

'Dec!'

Sadie looked vaguely for the source of the new voice and saw Melissa running towards them.

'What the hell is going on?' she shouted.

Declan didn't move, and he didn't let go of Sadie.

'What are you doing with her? Why are you both wet? What's the lifeboat doing here?'

Declan shook his head. 'Now's not the time, Melissa.'

'It bloody well is!'

'No! It's not! For once stop thinking about yourself and look at the bigger picture! Two men might be dying out there as we speak and all you care about is the fact that I'm sitting here with Sadie! You've always been obsessed with Sadie, convinced that she's out to get you. Did you ever stop to consider that you might be the problem, not her?'

Sadie opened her mouth to say something, but her thoughts were sluggish and she couldn't form the words. All she could think about was that she might be about to lose her brother and the man she'd begun to believe might be her future. She glanced down the beach, beyond Melissa and out at the sea where the coastguard's boat had now stopped and was bobbing on the water, its engines silent. A small crowd of onlookers was beginning to gather and one figure broke free and ran towards them.

'Andy,' Declan said wearily.

'What's happened?' Andy asked.

Sadie looked up at Sea Salt Bay's part-time lifeguard. His face was in gloom now, obscured by the dusk that had settled over the beach, but she could make out the lines of concern.

Declan nodded towards the water. 'Ewan and that Goldman fella are out there.'

'Looks to me like you've been in there too.'

'Yes. Idiot me started it. Long story. Safe to say there are many regrets right now.' He glanced at Melissa but she looked awkwardly away.

'Are either of you injured?' Andy asked.

'I don't think so.' Declan looked down at Sadie, and she craned her neck to look round at him. She gave her head a small shake – it was all she had the energy to do.

Andy cast his gaze back to the water. 'Unless I'm very much mistaken it looks as if they've managed to pull someone out.'

Sadie heard the boat engines coming to life again, confirming Andy's statement.

'Where will they take them?' she asked.

Andy shook his head slowly. 'Depends on what state they were in when they fished them out.'

Declan's arms folded tighter around her. For once, he wasn't who she needed, but he was all she had right now.

Chapter Twenty

There had been four ambulances lined up on the promenade, one for each of them. Sadie couldn't help but feel it was a bit surplus to requirements, though she didn't doubt that her brother and Luke, at least, needed theirs.

Miracles did happen, though, and she'd never been so relieved to see the evidence of that. She'd been deemed fine, if a little cold and wet, by her paramedic, and Declan had quickly been given the all-clear too. Ewan had a slight case of hypothermia and dehydration and Luke a marginally more severe case, but it was nothing that a night under observation in hospital wouldn't fix for the both of them. Declan had gone home with Melissa. They had a lot to talk about, and Sadie was hopeful that in light of the evening's events Melissa would be a bit more inclined to listen to what he had to say.

At the hospital she went to Ewan first. By now, Kat and the kids were there too. Henny was on her way down, but Graham had stayed at home with April, having been reassured on the phone by Ewan that he and Sadie were fine and there was no point in distressing his grandma over it.

'Hey,' Sadie said, sitting next to Kat on the spare seat by the bed. 'How are you?'

'Fed up,' Ewan said. 'I don't see why I have to be in here.'

'Because you almost drowned?' Kat said, arching her eyebrows.

'I didn't almost drown. I would never have drowned – everyone's getting carried away with this drowning business. And to be rescued by the lifeboat – I'm never going to live it down.'

'Well,' Sadie said, 'perhaps living full stop is better than just living it down. You'll just have to suck it up, Aquaman, because it happened and everyone in the bay will know by tomorrow.'

'Nobody will come for diving lessons from a man who needed to be rescued by the lifeboat,' he said, pouting.

'Of course they will,' Kat said. 'By tomorrow everyone's going to think you're a hero.'

'A crap hero, granted,' Sadie cut in. 'But they'll probably book diving lessons just the same.'

He scowled at her and she gave a tired grin. She could joke about it with him now, because ribbing and banter was their default sibling setting, but it was harder to wipe from her mind the image of the boat hauling his floppy body out of the sea. Things could so easily have been very different and far more tragic than they'd turned out to be, and Sadie couldn't forget that either. Family meant everything, and sometimes that truth got lost in the noise; it took something like today to bring it back into focus again. No matter what else happened from this point on, her brother was here with them and she'd always be thankful for that.

'Have you been to see Luke yet?' Kat asked.

Sadie shook her head. 'I'm going in just a minute. I wanted to see Ewan first.'

'Don't you think you ought to? After all, he's got nobody else here and Ewan has all of us. I think we could spare you for a minute if you wanted to go along the corridor.'

'Yeah, and I'll see you at home in a few hours anyway,' Ewan said.

'Luke will see me too.'

Ewan looked at her carefully for a moment. 'Want to tell me what was going on tonight?'

Sadie gave a small smile. 'I could, but by the time I'd finished the story it would be time for you to go home. It'll wait.'

He nodded, content to let things go for now.

'Want to tell me why you were looking for me?' she asked.

'Well...' he began, and he shot an awkward glance at Kat.

'He came to tell you,' Kat cut in, 'that he's put your grandmother straight on a few things. Namely, that it was his idea you should withdraw your services from the waffle house. She wanted to talk to you about it. I think she wanted to apologise so Ewan came to find you.'

'Couldn't you have phoned me?' Sadie looked at him now.

Ewan shifted awkwardly. 'It was sort of...'

'What he had to tell you he wanted to tell you in person,' Kat cut in again.

'Why?' Sadie asked, looking from Kat to Ewan and then back again.

'Because your grandma was talking about cutting you from her will. Ewan realised that he really had thrown you under the bus because he'd been a total pig-headed dick about everything and he needed to apologise and you can't make an apology of that magnitude on the phone.'

'She was doing *what*?'

'It's sorted now,' Ewan said. 'I've put her straight and she loves you again. It's me she's not quite so keen on now.'

'Well, I'd tell you I feel sorry for you but I don't.'

'I thought it was the right thing to do. And don't forget Mum and Dad agreed to it too.'

'True. In that case, and in view of the fact you nearly died I'm going to forgive you.'

Ewan smiled. Even now, when he'd been lost at sea and dragged out with mild hypothermia and shock, his smile could still light up a room. 'He's alright, you know.'

'Who?'

'Goldman.'

'You mean Luke?'

'Yeah. Lucky he was passing.'

'I wish you'd stop calling him Goldman. And I told you so.'

'For once, I'm going to admit that you were right and I was wrong – but don't get too used to it. I'm sure it won't happen again.'

'I'm sure it won't,' Sadie said, her smile spreading as she got up from her chair. 'I'll try not to let the dizzy wine of success go to my head.'

She left the room and made her way along the corridor, her brother's laughter fading with every step, and a few doors later she came across Luke's room. She knocked lightly and then went in. He was sitting up in bed, looking as annoyed to be there as Ewan had earlier. She took a seat beside him. Neither spoke; they simply looked at each other for the longest moment. Sadie didn't know what to say and it seemed Luke didn't either. Eventually, she broke the silence.

'I'm sorry.'

'For what?'

'For all this. You shouldn't be in here right now; it's my fault.'

'I chose to jump in.'

She was silent again. 'And did you know who you were jumping in to save?' she asked finally.

'Of course I did.'

'And yet you still did it?'

'What else was I going to do? Leave him to drown?'

'Some people might have done.'

He frowned. 'Would they? I don't like the sound of them. He'd done me no harm.'

'But what I told you about him—'

'Made him even more important. If he meant that much to you then I had to try to help.'

She smiled. 'I'm glad you didn't die.'

'I'm fairly chuffed about it too. How is he?'

'Dec…? He's OK. He's gone home with Melissa to work things out.'

'What needed working out?'

'That's kind of what was happening on the pier when you saw us. Melissa had dumped him and he wasn't handling it well.'

'Oh. I had wondered…'

'Whether it was a thing between us?' She shook her head. It had been that too, sort of, but she felt certain that it had been resolved, once and for all. For her, it had, and she didn't see the point in raking it all up now. Whether Declan and Melissa worked it out was up to them but, as far as Sadie was concerned, with Melissa was where he belonged. And if that meant she couldn't spend time with Declan as Melissa had demanded, she wouldn't like it, but in time she supposed she'd get used to it. And she had Luke now, and he deserved better than that anyway. At least, she thought she had Luke. Right now she wasn't sure if that was still true.

'What about your brother?' Luke asked.

'Oh, he's fine. Smarting that he had to be rescued; thinks his reputation is in tatters now.'

'You know, for a few scary minutes out there I thought…'

'So did I. I thought I'd lost you both. I thought I might go with you. Let's just say I'm not in a rush to repeat the experience.'

'Me neither. There's nothing like a near-death experience to focus the mind.'

'One good thing has come out of it – Ewan can hardly be grumpy with you now for the boat thing because he owes you big time for tonight.'

'I didn't exactly do anything useful in the end except keep him company until we got rescued.'

'But the intention was there and that's what counts. You went in for him. You went in for Dec too and that makes you a hero.'

'Does it?'

She nodded.

'I've never felt much like a hero before.'

'You just needed the right circumstances to bring it out in you. After all, most of us never need to be heroes, so how do any of us know if we're up to the job? It's only when the moment comes that you know if you're capable or not.'

'Hmm.' He closed his eyes for a moment.

'You're tired,' she said. 'Maybe I should go so you can sleep.'

'No. Not yet.'

'I'm tired too, come to think of it. And I need to shower; my hair is full of sea.'

'Like a mermaid…' he murmured. 'Sexy.'

'I don't think sexy is the word I'd use to describe it. I look like I've been through a washing machine with a load of very muddy trousers.'

He opened his eyes. 'OK,' he said.

'What?'

'If you need to go that's OK.'

'Now I feel bad.'

'Why?'

'Because you looked so sad when you said it.'

'I will be sad when you've gone; I like having you here.'

'Oh,' she said. 'Well then, I suppose I ought to stay.'

'It would make me happy,' he said with a tired smile and closed his eyes again. 'And it's the least you can do. After all, I *am* a hero…'

Chapter Twenty-One

By the time the day of the annual midsummer fireworks party arrived, it was almost as if nothing out of the ordinary had happened in Sea Salt Bay. There had been gossip, of course, when the news first broke of the drama in the sea the night Sadie, Ewan, Luke and Declan had all gone in. There had been speculation aplenty about what might have happened between them all to cause such a disaster, and the stories that had emerged from that speculation had grown and grown, until they were a world away from the actual events of that night.

Everyone involved had their own reasons for not bothering to put anyone right. Melissa didn't want anyone to know what had happened between her and Declan because, in light of the events that followed her dumping of him, she felt a bit stupid. Declan didn't want to tell anyone because he felt stupid too. Getting blind drunk and falling off the pier wasn't a good look. Luke didn't say anything about it because he didn't feel it was his place to, and Ewan didn't want to look like less of a swimmer than he was, still concerned that if people found out he'd needed rescuing when he was supposed to be the sort of man who did the rescuing he'd be a laughing stock. Kat simply rolled her eyes and told him not to be ridiculous, but they all knew that it wasn't going to change anything. And Sadie didn't put any of the gossipers straight out of respect for all the others.

The important thing was that a week had passed and everyone was getting on again. Except, things were different than they had been before it had happened. Melissa and Declan were back together, but Melissa looked at Sadie differently than before. Sadie didn't know why, and Declan didn't tell her, but perhaps that was because he'd kept his promise to Melissa and kept his distance. She'd thought about phoning him to talk about things and see if he was really OK but decided against it. Sometimes you just had to let it go, even if it went against everything that you believed ought to happen. Gammy had forgiven Sadie, and after the drama in the sea she had found it in her heart to forgive Ewan too. And, a few days later, she had clean forgotten that she had ever been annoyed at either of them in the first place.

As for Sadie, she'd barely spent a moment out of Luke's company, and he seemed to like things that way. Their relationship had even been given the seal of approval from the Schwartz family, but then, they could hardly have withheld it because, as Sadie pointed out, he was a hero and they owed him even if they didn't like him. Then Ewan decided that he did like him and, to Sadie's great shock, took him for a pint at the Listing Ship. Sadie had grilled her brother and then Luke afterwards to find out what they'd talked about, but both of them had simply grinned and told her to mind her own business, which made her more insanely curious than ever and, thus, even funnier to them both. If she'd featured heavily in the conversation (and it stood to reason that she would) then she was never going to find out what they'd said. But the main thing was that they were finally getting along and perhaps that was all that mattered in the end.

In fact, the only thing still hanging over her, unresolved, was the fate of the waffle house.

The fireworks party always started with a barbeque that was organised by Declan's parents. Tonight, Declan's dad had left the chip shop in his assistant Nessa's capable hands (she hated fireworks anyway, and didn't care for most of the people in attendance that much either) while he came to set up. Declan's mum, Declan and Melissa were both helping him. By the time Sadie had arrived there with Luke, her parents, Ewan and April (Kat was following with the kids), the coals were already smoking and the first of the burgers were on the grill, the smell of cooking meat rising on the gentle breeze that rolled in from the sea. The weather was being kind to them too, far kinder than it had been the week before, and Sadie still gave an involuntary shudder whenever her eyes happened to settle on the spot beneath the pier where four of Sea Salt Bay's residents had almost drowned.

As they wandered over to the barbeque Declan left his station at the salad bar and jogged over to greet them. He shook Luke's hand and then Ewan's in turn. His smile for Sadie was rather less certain.

'How are you all doing? On the road to recovery?'

'Fine,' Ewan said. 'How about you?'

'Ah…' Declan shoved his hands into his pockets and hunched his shoulders. 'I still feel like a total dick about the whole thing, but…'

'We've all done stupid things from time to time.' Ewan clapped him on the back. 'I wouldn't let it worry you.'

Declan gave a sheepish grin. 'Easy for you to say.'

'It is, but I'm saying it anyway.'

Sadie glanced across at the barbeque. Melissa was standing with Declan's mum, and although she was talking to her, she was watching them now. More specifically, *Sadie*. Or at least, it felt that way. Perhaps she was being paranoid. In the week since the incident (the *second* incident, Luke had christened it, the first being the boat accident that had caused them to meet) she hadn't spoken to Melissa, and to Declan only in passing. But Melissa would have known what had passed between Sadie and Declan that night because, Sadie assumed, Declan would have told her everything in a bid to fix things with her. Well, almost everything. Sadie hoped that some things they'd said that night would forever stay just between them because they weren't for anyone else to hear and nobody else would really understand them. Some of the things they'd said might cause a lot more problems if other people got to hear them too.

As the men exchanged pleasantries, Sadie broke off and went over to Melissa, who'd just left Declan's mum to cut some lettuce.

'Hi,' she said. 'How's the barbeque going?'

'Oh, it's early yet,' Melissa said. 'I expect we won't be able to cook fast enough in a couple of hours.' She paused, thoughtful for a moment. Sadie waited for what might come next, aware that anything was possible right now and wondering if she'd be ready for it. 'You're with Luke Goldman now?'

'Yes.'

'And it's going well?'

'I think so.'

'Good.'

Sadie wanted to ask if things were OK between her and Declan but she didn't dare because she didn't know what that would unleash.

'I think I owe you an apology,' Melissa said.

'You really don't.'

'No, I do. I told Declan that he wasn't to speak to you again and that was wrong. It's just… you have no idea how hard it's been knowing that you two had this special bond. I've always felt like the face at the window, you know?'

'Well,' Sadie said. 'If there are apologies to be given, then I owe you one too. I should have respected that things had changed and that we couldn't be like we were anymore because his priority should have been you. I gave him up all those years ago and he moved on…' She shrugged. 'I guess it took me a while to deal with the fact that I couldn't just come back and have everything the same as it was before I went. He loves you more than life itself and it was always going to be you.'

'He told you that?'

Sadie nodded.

'Wow…' Melissa shook her head. 'I don't know what to say.'

'There's no need to say anything. I just wanted you to know. I hope maybe we can be friends now. Of sorts, anyway.'

Melissa gave a small smile. 'Sure. I think that would be OK. And if you… you know, if you feel the need to talk to Dec once in a while…'

'Thanks. I'll try not to make it too often if I do.'

Melissa looked at the salad spread out before her, still waiting to be prepared. 'We're not ready yet but… can I get you something to eat?'

'Not just yet, but thanks. I'm sure we'll be popping back later. Burgers happen to be Luke's favourite food.'

'Right. So we'll see you later.'

Sadie smiled and turned to rejoin the others. Declan gave her a curious look but he didn't ask what she'd discussed with Melissa. Perhaps he'd been reassured by the fact that they'd both been smiling as she'd walked away.

'I'd better get back to it,' he said. 'I'll see you later?'

'You can count on it,' Luke said. 'Those burgers look amazing.'

'Oh, they are,' Ewan said. 'Dec's dad makes them every year and you've never tasted anything like them.'

As Declan went to rejoin his parents on the barbeque stand, Ewan went to chat to Henny, Graham and April, who were standing with

Vivien from the Ship. Luke slipped his hand around Sadie's and smiled down at her. 'Doing a bit of fairy-godmothering over there, were you?'

'How did you know?'

'Just a wild guess. And have you fixed everything?'

'I don't know about that. I've done what I can to put her mind at rest, but there are some things only they can fix. I hope I've done enough though.'

'You care about him a lot, don't you?'

'Yes, but before you get all jealous I'd just like to remind you of some rather vigorous exercise we enjoyed this afternoon before we left your house to come here.'

'House? It's more like a building site. It'll never be finished if you keep coming round with your distractions.'

'You can always tell me to leave.'

'You're joking, right? That's never going to happen.'

Sadie grinned, but then she heard a squeal and saw Natalie and Georgia rushing over to them.

'Look at you! Where have you been hiding? We haven't seen you in ages!' Georgia called.

Sadie laughed. 'Yes you have. You saw me last week.'

'That's ages,' Natalie said. They both turned to Luke.

'Hi, Luke,' they said as one, voices loaded with mischief.

'Hi, ladies,' Luke replied with a mischievous look of his own.

'How are you?' Georgia asked. 'Still working hard on that house?'

Sadie let out a guffaw and both Georgia and Natalie stared at her.

'Yes,' Luke said. 'So, so hard… at it day and night, hammer and tongs. Screwing and screwing. I'm exhausted.'

With every syllable he uttered Sadie's giggling became louder and Natalie turned to her with a grin. 'Oh, now I get it. And I suppose you're at the house all the time now that you don't have any other commitments… *helping…*'

'I might be,' Sadie replied, trying to straighten her face.

'Jammy cow,' Georgia said, and Natalie gave a sympathetic nod of solidarity.

'My thoughts exactly.'

'I am doing other things too,' Sadie said. 'Like trying to find a job.'

'It sounds like it.'

'No, really, I am. In fact, I'm working on Ewan right now to find me something at the dive school because technically it's his fault I'm unemployed anyway.'

'Oh…' Natalie winked at Georgia and smoothed a hand over her hair. 'Talking of Hercules, where is he?'

'Hercules?' Sadie laughed. 'Hardly!'

'Not from where you're standing, sweetie,' Natalie said, 'but we wouldn't expect you to understand.'

Sadie rolled her eyes. 'He's over there with my mum and dad.'

'Oh.'

'I thought that might put paid to your flirting,' Sadie said. 'And Kat's due any time now.'

'There's another jammy cow,' Georgia said. 'The world's full of jam for everyone but me.'

'And me,' Natalie said.

'Yes,' Georgia replied, 'but you've had two blobs of jam already – it's not my fault you picked the wrong flavours when you had the chance.'

Natalie looked across the beach towards the promenade. 'Talk of the devil.'

Kat was just arriving with Freddie and Freya. But then Sadie saw that she had someone else with her.

'No!'

In the next second, she was haring across the beach to meet them, throwing her arms around the newcomer.

'Lucy!'

Sadie's older sister laughed and hugged her tight.

'Oh my God!' Sadie cried. 'I can't believe you're here!'

'To be honest it was a last-minute decision. Kat phoned me and told me about a few things that had been going on here and then she reminded me that the fireworks would be on and… well, I had a couple of days to spare and I thought, why not drop in?'

'Wait until everyone sees you!' Sadie said, laughing. She held her at arm's length and regarded her fondly. 'You look amazing!'

'So do you,' Lucy said. 'Your hair looks pretty piled up like that. And you've lost weight too.'

'Oh, I look like a country bumpkin compared to you.'

'You look like a natural beauty; you always did. Like someone who's been able to walk by the sea in the fresh air every day. I spend most of my time cooped up in an office and any glow my skin has comes out of a very expensive bottle.'

Sadie beamed at her. Then she looked at Kat. 'How did you keep this a secret?'

'With great difficulty,' Kat said, smiling. 'And Ewan found it even harder. But with all that's gone on we thought it would be a good time to bring our little family together properly, remind ourselves of how important it is.'

'And there's always one person missing, I know,' Lucy said.

Sadie grabbed her hand. 'Come and meet Luke.'

'Who's Luke?' she asked, having no choice but to go with Sadie, who was pulling harder than an excited Labrador.

'My boyfriend.'

'And how long has this one managed to last?'

'Not long,' Sadie said with a laugh. 'But the difference is, I think he's gonna.'

'Going to what?'

'Last.'

Lucy raised her eyebrows. 'Really?'

'Yes. He's… well, he's pretty special.'

'In that case,' Lucy said with a grin, 'this is a guy I have to see!'

Natalie and Georgia had already abandoned Luke, and now he was standing alone waiting for Sadie to return. He smiled broadly as she did, taking Lucy with her.

'This is my big sister!' Sadie squeaked. 'All the way from New York!'

Luke stuck out his hand. 'Lucy, right? I've heard all about you.'

'Well,' Lucy said, 'I haven't heard about you at all, but I think I need to. Sadie seems to be very excited about you.'

'Right,' he said. 'So that's good.'

'I'm sure I'll be grilling you as the night wears on. I'll wait until you've had a few drinks and then the secrets will be much easier to extract.'

'Oh, there are no secrets,' he said. 'I'm a bit boring really.'

'No you're not,' Sadie said. 'You're amazing.' She turned to Lucy. 'This is the man who saved Ewan and Declan and me from drowning.'

Her sister's eyes widened. '*That* guy?'

'It wasn't like that at all,' Luke said. 'We all sort of didn't drown together.'

'Yes, but if you hadn't jumped in after Declan then he'd definitely be dead. Me too, probably, because I would have jumped in to get him and drowned with him. And then you went back in for Ewan—'

'So did you.'

'Yes, but I was crap. You were the real hero.'

'I think the lifeboat crew were the real heroes.'

'Oh, stop being so modest,' Sadie said, smiling at him with such warmth and pride that Lucy looked vaguely surprised to see it.

'I have missed a lot since I last came over,' she said. 'I must try to visit more often.'

'Oh, you must,' Sadie said. 'Have you seen Mum and Dad and Gammy yet?'

'Not yet – Kat picked me up from the airport and we came straight here. In fact, I'd better go and find them. Catch you later.'

'Yes!'

Sadie turned to Luke as her sister went off to find the rest of the clan. By now, the beach was filling up with more locals and a few curious tourists too, keen to join the fun. Little fires were dotted along the sand where some families had decided to cook their own food rather than buy from the official barbeque. At the far end of the beach, close to the shelter of the cliffs, the fireworks were getting last-minute safety checks.

'I'm just too excited,' Sadie said. 'It feels like forever since Lucy was here. I mean she came to Gampy's funeral but that was horrible and she literally just went to the church, spent a couple of days at home with us and then flew back so it wasn't really a visit at all. I wonder how long she's staying – I must ask.'

Luke took her face in his hands and gave her a tender kiss. As he broke away she smiled up at him.

'What was that for?'

'You know, when I dreamt of that perfect life here, all those months ago when it felt as if I'd never be happy again, I never imagined that it would be this perfect. I never imagined anything could be this perfect. And I never imagined a woman could be as perfect as you.'

'Oh, I'm not perfect.'

'Well no…' he said, giving a solemn nod. 'But you're as near as anyone can be.'

'I…'

For once, Sadie was lost for words. Nobody, not even Declan, had ever told her she was perfect. She wasn't, but she'd soak it up anyway and enjoy the illusion of being perfect, for a few hours at least.

'Your family are coming back over,' Luke said, staring out across the beach. Now he looked faintly alarmed. 'All of them, en masse like a huge army. Do you think they saw me kissing you and are pissed off?'

Sadie giggled. 'They're just coming to talk to us.'

'So I shouldn't be running at this point?'

'Don't you dare!'

'Hello, darlin',' April said to Sadie. She glanced up at Luke. 'Hello. I don't think we've met before – I'm April, Sadie's grandma.'

They had met before, several times now, but Sadie just smiled and Luke dipped his head in acknowledgement. Graham had taken his mother to see the family GP, who had suggested that April was displaying the early signs of dementia and had ordered hospital tests. They were still waiting for an appointment date, but they were working with the provisional diagnosis and everyone was altering their behaviour around April accordingly. It wasn't what they'd wanted to hear, but in some ways they'd all been expecting something along those lines. At least now they could make some sense of what was happening and deal with it. Graham and Henny were already making plans to care for her and, when the time came, everyone would do their bit – even Luke had told Sadie he would give help and support in any way he could. Sadie had offered him a teary smile in return and tried to make light of the moment by telling him that maybe he was a keeper after all, but they both knew that his words had meant so much more to her.

'I'm Luke.'

'That's a good strong name,' April said.

'Isn't it?' Sadie replied.

'Sadie…' Lucy began. 'Do you have a moment? We need to talk to you…' She glanced at Luke, as if uncertain that what they had to say ought to be said in front of him.

'I can… I'll go and get a burger,' he said.

Sadie was about to tell him to stay where he was, that anything they wanted to talk about could be discussed with him there, but he was gone so fast, striding across the beach, that she never got the chance. She turned back to her sister. 'Sounds serious.'

'Not really. Well, a little, but I hope good as well.'

'There's a reason we asked Lucy to come over,' Henny said. 'It's wonderful to have her visit, of course, but we need her to come and sign something.'

'Actually, she volunteered to come and sign it,' Ewan said. 'And I'm going to sign it too.'

Sadie frowned. 'I don't understand.'

'We have a buyer for the waffle house,' Henny said.

Sadie's face fell. 'Oh.'

Why would they tell her this now? What kind of time was this to give her such horrible, disappointing news when they could see how happy she'd been? And what did that have to do with Ewan and Lucy anyway? Surely the only person who mattered was Gammy?

'I don't like them one bit,' April said. 'Don't care for their business plans at all.'

'I suppose you could refuse to sell it and wait for another buyer,' Sadie said. 'One who has a business plan you're keener on…'

'I could,' April said. 'But I'm not going to.'

'Aren't you?'

'No. I wronged you, darlin'. And I want to make amends. I was all set to cut you out of my will and then your brother… well, he told me what you did, and that you did it out of love for me… Well I'm an old lady now, and I guess I just couldn't get that into my head, and I thought I could do all the things I used to be able to, but the last couple of weeks have shown me that I was fooling myself.'

'Oh, Gammy, I—'

'So I'm signing the waffle house over to you three kids.'

Sadie stared at her. And then she stared at Ewan and Lucy in turn. 'We're going to own the waffle house?'

'*You're* going to own it,' Ewan said. 'I told you I'd give you my share.'

'And I'm going to sign over mine,' Lucy said.

'But…' Sadie wondered if she ought to pinch herself. If this was a dream it was a lovely one, but it was going to be a very disappointing one to wake from. She looked back at Lucy. 'Why would you do that?'

'What you've got to ask yourself is *what* would I do with a third of a seaside waffle house?'

'I don't know… sell it.'

'Who's gonna buy a third of a waffle house?' Lucy shook her head with a fond smile. 'I have the career I want. Ewan has his but you… you were always the one who loved that old place more than anyone. Grandma wants it to stay in the family, and you're the only one who ever shared that vision with her. It's only right now that it comes to you and that you be the one to serve those legendary waffles to a whole new generation.'

'I don't have to buy anyone out?'

'No.'

'And I can run it however I like?'

'You might want to take some advice from your grandma from time to time,' Graham said.

'But I can get staff… Oh my God, I'll be able to afford staff now!'

'You'll have to get someone, I expect,' Ewan said.

'This is…' Sadie was breathless, speechless. 'This is…'

'Good?' Ewan said.

'Exciting?' Graham offered.

'Bloody terrifying!' Sadie cried. 'Absolutely bloody terrifying!'

At that very moment, the rockets started to go off and everyone jumped. They lit the sky with showers of gold and crimson sparks that set off a round of applause from the crowds.

'Blimey,' Graham said, 'that caught us all off guard!'

Everyone laughed, and then Sadie started to laugh, which soon turned into crying. But it was good crying, happy crying, the tears of someone who had just witnessed the clouds that had been obscuring the sky of her future moving away to reveal it. It was iris blue, bright and warm, full of promise. And it might just have been the most beautiful thing she'd ever seen.

A Letter from Tilly

I want to say a huge thank you for choosing to read *The Waffle House on the Pier*. If you enjoyed it and want to keep up-to-date with all my latest releases, just sign up at the following link. Your email address will never be shared and you can unsubscribe at any time.

www.bookouture.com/tilly-tennant

I'm so excited to share *The Waffle House on the Pier* with you. I've loved immersing myself in Sadie's world and loved every minute of working on it. I truly have the best job in the world, and I've been so proud to share every new book with my wonderful readers.

I hope you loved *The Waffle House on the Pier* just as much as I do, and if so I would be very grateful if you could write a review. I'd love to hear what you think, and it makes such a difference helping new readers to discover one of my books for the first time.

I love hearing from my readers – you can get in touch on my Facebook page, through Twitter, Goodreads or my website.

Thanks,
Tilly

tillytennant

@TillyTenWriter

www.tillytennant.com

Acknowledgements

The list of people who have offered help and encouragement on my writing journey so far must be truly endless, and it would take a novel in itself to mention them all. However, my heartfelt gratitude goes out to each and every one of you, whose involvement, whether small or large, has been invaluable and appreciated more than I can say.

There are a few people that I must mention. Obviously, my family – the people who put up with my whining and self-doubt on a daily basis are top of the list. My mum and, posthumously, my dad, who brought me up to believe that anything is possible if you want it enough, no matter how crazy or unlikely it seems. My ex-colleagues at the Royal Stoke University Hospital, who let me lead a double life for far longer than is acceptable and have given me so many ideas for future books! The lecturers at Staffordshire University English and Creative Writing Department, who saw a talent worth nurturing in me and continue to support me still, long after they finished getting paid for it. They are not only tutors but friends as well. I have to thank the team at Bookouture for their continued support, patience, and amazing publishing flair, particularly Lydia Vassar-Smith – my incredible and patient editor – Kim Nash, Noelle Holten, Peta Nightingale, Leodora Darlington, Alexandra Holmes and Jessie Botterill – collectively known as Team Tilly! Their belief, able assistance and encouragement mean the world to me. I truly believe I have the best team an author could ask for and I could not continue to do the job I love without them.

My friend, Kath Hickton, always gets a shout-out for putting up with me since primary school. Louise Coquio also gets an honourable mention for getting me through university and suffering me ever since, likewise her lovely family. And thanks go to Storm Constantine for giving me my first break in publishing. I also have to thank Mel Sherratt and Holly Martin, fellow writers and amazing friends who have both been incredibly supportive over the years. Thanks also to Tracy Bloom, Emma Davies, Jack Croxall, Clare Davidson, Jaimie Admans, Steph Lawrence and Kerry Ann Parsons for their unfailing support. My Bookouture colleagues are all incredible, of course, vocal and generous in their cheerleading of fellow authors – life would be a lot duller without the gang! I have to thank all the brilliant and dedicated book bloggers (there are so many of you but you know who you are!) and readers, and anyone else who has championed my work, reviewed it, shared it, or simply told me that they liked it. Every one of those actions is priceless and you are all very special people. Some of you I am even proud to call friends now.

Last but not least, I'd like to give a special mention to my lovely agent, Madeleine Milburn, who always has time to listen to my gripes and does so with a smile on her face.

Printed in Poland
by Amazon Fulfillment
Poland Sp. z o.o., Wrocław

64133284R00176